Rum and Runestones

EDITED BY VALERIE GRISWOLD-FORD

Dragon
Moon

WWW.DRAGONMOONPRESS.COM

Rum and Runestones

ISBN 978-1-897492-07-9

Printed and bound in Canada

www.dragonmoonpress.com

Rum and Runestones

Introduction

VAL GRISWOLD-FORD

If sailor tales to sailor tunes, Storm and adventure, heat and cold, If schooners, islands, and maroons, And buccaneers, and buried gold, And all the old romance, retold Exactly in the ancient way, Can please, as me they pleased of old, The wiser youngsters of today:

—So be it, and fall on! If not, If studious youth no longer crave, His ancient appetites forgot, Kingston, or Ballantyne the brave, Or Cooper of the wood and wave: So be it, also! And may I And all my pirates share the grave Where these and their creations lie!
~Robert Louis Stevenson, "Treasure Island"

Pirate. The very word conjures up a picture, a fragrance, a spell: the rogue, cutlass and pistol in hand, standing on the deck of a three-masted ship, the tropical sun setting behind the sails as the scents of rum and black powder float on the warm breeze. It's a word whispered, half in terror, half in delight.

Pirate.

I was five when I decided my life's vocation was to be a pirate. Sadly, I was born about two hundred years too late, and I haven't found the time machine yet to take me back to a time when my lust for the Jolly Roger could be satisfied, so I've had to look for other outlets for my obsession. This book is one of them.

The thirteen authors in this anthology were given a single challenge at RavenCon in 2009: to write a short story featuring pirates and magic. That was the only restriction. What they came up with was a collection of short stories that range from the eerie to the humorous while sailing the seas of the past, present and future. Their ships docked on fantastic shores, carrying exotic cargo in their holds that they defended with cutlass, flintlock and sharpened wit. A more motley crew of tales I've yet to find.

Within these pages, you'll travel to Neverland, back in time and across the seas to far Eastern lands. You'll battle dragons, ghosts and your own fears. You'll learn to sing the chanties like a pirate, and learn to sail any sea. I only hope that you have as much fun reading this anthology as we have had putting it together for you.

I want to give special thanks to Gail Martin, Misty Massey, BA Collins, MJ Blehart, Tera Fulbright, Laurel Anne Hill, Davey Beauchamp, Danny Birt, Jim Stratton, Michael Ventrella, Stuart Jaffe and Danielle Ackley-McPhail for their amazing stories, and for rising to the challenge, and to Bryan Prindiville for the art gracing the first page. It's been an honor sailing with you.

Now, mateys, pour yourselves a mug of grog, or rum, or whathaveyou, and enjoy.

Table of Contents

Steer a Pale Course

By Gail Z. Martin

"Bring in those nets. Let's head for home." I put my back into hauling in the nets on my side of the boat. They were full of fish, but not so full as yesterday. Over the horizon, the sun was just coming up.

"Easy for you to say, Dante. You've got the skinny nets on your side." Coltt grunted as he and Nesh leaned into bringing their net into the boat. Lucky for me they're taller, with long arms. I probably would have gone over the side trying to haul in a net as full as theirs.

We should have been out to sea with the other men, and any other year since I'd been ten years old, we would have been. The rest of the men from the village had gone a day out on the water, where the big catches are this time of year. They wouldn't be back for another couple of days, salting the fish as they caught them to keep the catch from rotting. But this year, mother wasn't feeling well, and she normally heads up harvest, her and Nady, Coltt and Nesh's mother. But Nady died over the winter, and mother said that she needed our help this harvest. So at night, Coltt and Nesh and I went out on our boat just far enough to catch what we could, but close in enough to be back just after sunrise.

"Look, this one's sweet on you, Nesh!" Coltt held up a big fish whose mouth was opening and closing. "Just like Letta!" He threw the fish at Nesh, who caught it and leaned back after him, holding the fish's flopping tail to smack his brother across the face.

"And that's just what Letta would do if she heard you call her a fish." Nesh laughed, dropping the fish into the huge basket. Coltt and Nesh were cut from the same cloth. The Skinner brothers took after their mother. Tall and thin, with long, strong arms and a shock of straw-blond hair, they were freckled with the sun and still pink in the face from the summer just past.

Me, I was as dark as they were light. Their hair was a mop of yellow curls that looked like a bird's nest after a windstorm. My hair fell lank into my eyes, even more limp than usual from the salt wind. I'd cut it short at the beginning of the summer, and it wasn't quite long enough yet to catch back in a queue. Nesh and Coltt were skinny, but even at eighteen I already had my father's build: sturdy and strong, though I was slim-built. I wasn't as tall as the Skinners either, and they'd had more than enough fun at my expense over the years tossing a ball or my lunch or my hat over my head just out of reach. Still, they were the closest thing I had to brothers, what with three sisters back home. And if I had to be left behind when the other men went out to sea, having them with me made it bearable.

"Let's head back," I said, turning the sails for home. "The sooner we get the harvest in, the quicker we can get back out here and salvage some dignity with a decent catch before the rest of the boats come back."

Coltt and Nesh kept up their joking until the boat rocked so badly we nearly lost some fish over the side. As usual, I handled the rudder while the Skinner boys kept the sails. The wind was with us, and the morning breeze was clean. Despite the prospect of harvesting vegetables for the rest of the day, my spirits were high. Everyone in our village has at least a touch of sea magic. Mine was more than a touch, by a good bit. I could listen to the wind like it was telling me a story. The stars, too. Even as a child, I never got lost. Father said I could navigate on a starless sea, and he was right. Coltt and Nesh could barely find their way home from the well at the end of the village, but they could smell where the fish were hiding.

Good thing, too, because fish kept our little village alive and earned most of the coin to be had. Mother and the women raised some vegetables and a few scrawny hens, goats and rabbits. We did some trade with the boats and merchants who passed by our inlet. Like every village, Netters Cove had a weaver, a potter, and a blacksmith, a dyer and a hedge witch who gave cures and birthed babies and said the High Words over the bodies when some poor blokes drowned. It was enough to trade for us what we couldn't build or grow, but not so much that the pirates who sailed the waters just beyond the shoals had any reason to bother us.

"Look there." Coltt pointed as we sailed into the inlet. A strange boat was anchored just beyond the shoals, and two rowboats I didn't recognize were pulled up on shore.

"Not the usual season for traders," I mused. But a little extra coin sure wouldn't hurt.

Just then I saw a figure burst from the trees at the side of the beach. It was my little sister, Jana, and she was jumping up and down and waving her arms. We were still pretty far out, and I smiled at her enthusiasm. She always missed me when I spent the night at sea.

It wasn't until we were too close in to turn around easily that I realized something.

Jana wasn't greeting us. She was warning us away.

"Something's wrong." I had barely gotten the words

out of my mouth before another figure ran from the trees, toward Jana. It was a man I didn't recognize, and he grabbed her by the arms, dragging her backwards. To make his point, he held up a cutlass and then held it to her throat.

"Dante—" Coltt's voice was low, like a growl.

"I see."

"What do you think—"

"I think we'll find out more than we want to know once we land the boat."

We brought the boat ashore, but there seemed to be no one else around except Jana and the man with the cutlass. He watched us as we dragged the boat up, making sure he turned to face us as we moved, keeping Jana and the cutlass in between us. He was dirty and unshaven, and even at a distance, he stank. His cloths were torn and stained, looking like mismatched pieces he'd stolen off a clothesline.

Jana's eyes were wide with fear. Knowing Jana, she was likely to either bite the man or kick him in the shins, and that was likely to make things worse.

"Let her go." I was surprised how steady my voice was, but I was more angry than scared. "I'll be your hostage. Let her go."

The man with the cutlass just laughed. "We're going to the big building. You three go first."

I could feel how angry Coltt and Nesh were without needing to look at them. My worst fears were confirmed when we reached the lodge, a building large enough for our whole village of about fifty people to gather. We used it for holidays or smoking meat or important meetings. Now, all of the women, children and the men too old to go out on the boats were sitting in silence on the floor. I saw my mother sitting with my other two sisters in the front row. She looked up at me, scared and sick—and defiant. Letta, Nesh's girlfriend, sat with his younger brother on her lap, holding him close to her and patting his head. They both looked close to panic. Six men who looked as worse for the wear as the man who held Jana were in the building. They had muskets. We were out of luck.

I had a fishing knife in a scabbard on my right leg, underneath my trousers. Coltt and Nesh probably did, too. I had a small, curved knife on my belt, good for gutting fish and not much else. In my pockets, I had some dirty twine and a few small iron balls we used to help weight the nets. Nothing that would counter six muskets and a guy who looked like he knew how to use that cutlass.

I knew Coltt and Nesh were waiting for me to make the first move. It's been that way since we were kids. My heart was pounding, but I took a step forward, careful to keep my hands away from my sides. "What do you want from us?"

The tallest of the men stepped forward. He stood a head above even the Skinner boys, but his neck craned forward. Dressed in black, missing several of his teeth, with a ripped and dirty cloth wrapped around greasy blond hair, he reminded me of a buzzard. He smiled, showing his rotted teeth. "We've been waiting for ya," he said, and his smile wasn't pleasant. "They said you'd be home after dawn."

"What are ya waitin' for, Jammer?" A short, wiry man waved his musket toward the captives, and the women shrank back, wrapping their bodies around their children. "Just shoot the lot of them exceptin' the boys."

Jammer took on a crafty look, and I noticed that one of his dark eyes turned out to the right, where an old scar ran along the brow. "I don't think that's necessary—yet." Jammer stared at me. "Of course, it depends on what the boys say to my business deal."

"If you need goats and rabbits, take them," I said, knowing that giving up our livestock would mean a hungry winter. "We've got no coin."

Jammer's eyes narrowed. "I don't want your poxy goats. I want someone to go into the barrows and bring out something for me. Someone with magic."

"No one goes into the barrows."

Jammer leered and waved his musket toward the hostages. "Then I guess it's time to start killing until we find someone with the guts to try." He pulled back the hammer with his thumb.

"I'll go." My voice sounded too deep, since I was trying not to let it waver. To keep from squeaking, my throat tightened, making it sound like the words came all the way from my toes. I figured I couldn't hide that I was shaking, but I hoped I looked less scared than Coltt and Nesh, although to give them credit, they were still at my back.

Jammer smiled his unpleasant smile. "That's a good boy. There's a very special necklace buried down there. I want you to bring it to me."

"And then you'll leave? Without harming anyone?"

Jammer seemed to find my bargaining amusing. "Sure, boy. I'll leave. And I won't kill anyone if you do as I say."

I didn't trust him. But I'd bought us time, and maybe the men would come back and save us. Maybe there'd be a way to warn them. If all the pirates wanted was a necklace, then why would the dead care? They weren't using it. But Jammer wasn't asking me to go to the cliffs where we'd buried our dead for generations. He was asking us to go into the barrows. We didn't know who or what made the barrows. Maybe they were graves, maybe something else. The entrances had been walled up long ago, but the stories remained. Men had gone in, looking for treasure. No one came out.

We left the barrows alone most of the time, except in the Dead Moon, when we brought offerings and left them by the walled-up entrance. The hedge witch took a goat and sacrificed it, letting the blood run down into the barrow. He left the carcass there and said the Old Words, something he called a binding spell. Next morning, the carcass was gone. I swallowed hard. If whatever lived in the barrows liked goat blood, maybe it would like Coltt, Nesh and me even better.

"Tell me about this necklace."

They didn't send someone with us to the barrows. They didn't have to. We knew what would happen if we didn't come back with the necklace. The look in my mother's eyes bound me more to see it through than my word to Jammer. I didn't doubt Jammer would kill them if we failed or ran off.

"We could light a big fire and warn the men." Coltt had obviously been giving some thought to our options.

"One of us could run for the next village," Nesh offered.

I shook my head. "If we light a fire, Jammer will see it. We'd have to get the whole way to the other side of the cliffs to hide it, and if we do that, the men won't know it's for them. And it's a day's walk to the next village. Jammer said to be back by dawn. Even if one of us got there, he couldn't get back in time with a mob." I'd thought of the same things on the hike to the barrows. From the looks on their faces, Coltt and Nesh had reasoned through it, too. We had no choice but to go on.

For autumn, it was a hot day. We were all sweating by the time we reached the barrows. I stopped and took a deep breath. The barrows were about a candlemark's hard hike directly inland from the village. There were three of them, and they might have been mistaken for hills if the rest of the land weren't so flat. I'd heard about the barrows since I was a kid. The old women said that the barrow wights ate children who wandered away from the village. At first, I thought it was just a tale to keep the children from running off. Then I noticed that even the hunters made a wide circle around the barrows. I'd gone out once with my father to look for deer and I'd asked why we couldn't just climb the "hills" for a better view. He'd gone gray in the face and told me they were an evil place and to stay clear.

Now we were going into them.

Jammer let us take equipment to unseal the barrows. Coltt and I had picks and Nesh carried two shovels. The pirates seemed pretty confident we couldn't use them for weapons. Hell, they hadn't even cared about taking our knives. After all, they had muskets. I had the awful feeling that whatever was in those barrows wouldn't be scared of either knives or muskets. Nesh also had a bag of reeds and a flint and steel for torches. Jammer had thrown us some dried meat and cheese with a laugh that told me our meals were numbered.

"Can you feel it?"

"Feel what?" Coltt asked. Then he closed his eyes for a moment, and so did Nesh. I could see the change in their expression. My magic felt jangly, like warning bells in my mind. It was the same feeling I got when there was a bad storm coming at sea, long before we saw the waves. That jangle had saved us many a time out on the ocean, warning us to head home before the squall hit. Only now, we couldn't head home. We were heading straight into the storm.

Then I heard it. It was faint, like a voice calling from a distance. I pictured the necklace Jammer had drawn with a stick in the dirt floor of the lodge. The more clearly I pictured it, the louder the voice called to me, directing me to its barrow. I didn't like the voice, but I'd heard it before. I'd heard it in my dreams, bad dreams where a voice tried to call me out into the night, or onto the dark water. It was the kind of voice you knew in your bones only wanted you for your meat. I shuddered.

"Let's do this."

Coltt and I set to with the picks, while Nesh cleared away the rock from the entrance. We took turns with the shovel. It was hard work, and it wasn't until the sun was overhead that we broke through. Whoever had blocked that entrance wanted it to stay blocked. I wondered again what was down there, but I really didn't want to know. I was afraid I'd find out anyhow.

Cold air rushed toward us when Coltt's pick broke through. It should have felt good in the autumn heat, but it smelled like dead things. I saw fear in their eyes as I lit my torch, and I was pretty sure they saw the same in mine. We picked up our picks and shovels and headed in. Maybe we'd need them to dig out another blocked area. Or maybe it just felt good to have something heavy to swing at whatever lived in the darkness. I went first.

"How do we know where the damned necklace is?" Coltt whispered. Everyone down here was supposed to be dead, but I knew why he was whispering. It felt like we were being watched.

"It's calling. Can you hear it?" I could make out their faces by torchlight enough to see that they didn't hear the voice. Damn. I didn't like that it was only calling to me, not one little bit.

I ignored the voice in my head that was screaming common sense and followed the other voice, the hungry one. Inside the barrows, there were tunnels leading in every direction. There were carvings in the walls, too, and just at the edge of the torchlight, I saw statues and slabs that might have been coffins. I didn't look too hard. I was afraid something might be looking back. Whatever else was down here, it could stay. All we wanted was the necklace, and from the way it called me, I'd have said it wanted us to take it.

"No rats. No spiders." Nesh whispered, and I wasn't sure it was to himself or to the rest of us. But I knew what he meant. We'd gone caving in the cliffs by the sea all our lives. Part of the fun was discovering gross stuff, like bat poop and creepy crawlies. But not here. Things might exist here, but nothing lived. I was now sure of that. We saw nothing.

I don't know how long we walked. Without the sun, time meant nothing. The voice guided us, showing me which of the turns to take, which tunnel to follow. It kept getting louder and I followed it, even though inside, I wanted to run. Running seemed like a sane idea. Nesh carefully marked each turn by chipping an arrow into the wall. Just in case the necklace lured us in and didn't want us to get out. It occurred to me that maybe the necklace and Jammer had different agendas. Why Jammer wanted the necklace, I didn't know. Why the necklace wanted to be found, I wasn't sure, but the suspicions I had weren't good. I was glad Nesh marked the trail.

"There it is."

"Are you sure?" Coltt didn't move closer, but he leaned forward, peering through the shadows. The necklace lay beside a small box next to what was probably once a body. It was wrapped in a shroud but both the bones and the cloth were brittle with age. The necklace wasn't around the corpse's neck. It was clasped in its bony hand. I got a glimpse of gold and white, but I didn't have time to look closely.

"I'm sure." My sanity fought every step I took toward the necklace. My will made me keep moving. The necklace was screaming at me, screaming to pick it up. Something in me was very sure there was a good reason the necklace had been sealed in here. I didn't think it was a good idea to remove it. Then, when I got closer, the screaming was so loud I couldn't think at all. I tore it out of the skeleton's hand. I didn't care if every barrow wight in the place came after us, I just wanted that voice to shut the hell up.

I held the necklace in my hand and there was silence.

Beautiful silence. On instinct, I grabbed the box that was next to the necklace. Damn, it was heavy, like it was made from lead. Something told me to take it, too, that voice of common sense I'd ignored since we headed into the cave. The necklace didn't like it, but this time, I ignored the necklace. I took the box.

Suddenly, images flooded into my mind, pictures that were so crisp and clear it was as if someone had opened a window in front of me, although we were deep in the cave. Sunlight. Ocean. A path through the forest. The urge to run back along the tunnels for the open air was so strong I was shaking with the effort to fight it. "We've got to go," I said, the strain clear in my voice. "Now."

Whether they guessed that the necklace was pushing me or whether they just wanted out, I don't know, but Coltt and Nesh found the energy to walk back a lot faster than we walked in. I didn't trust the necklace. I checked our path at every turn, but each time, I saw Nesh's marks. I couldn't get out fast enough. Holding the necklace seemed to open up a whole new level of senses for me, something I'd never felt before in the magic. I could feel things moving in the distance, things that were cold and long dead. Some were angry, and for some, the hatred was so intense I cringed. Some were hungry. There were a lot of them, and I didn't want to meet them. I couldn't tell whether they liked me taking the necklace or not. I didn't want to find out. Without saying a word, we ran.

Jammer met us on the path to the village. He'd been waiting for us, even though we were back before dawn. "Did you get it?"

"Yes."

"Show me."

I tightened my hand around the necklace in my pocket. "We had a deal. I give you the necklace and you leave.

You promised you wouldn't kill anyone."

"Give me the necklace. I won't kill anyone."

I knew Coltt and Nesh were watching me. Two more men came out of the trees to stand beside Jammer, as if we might jump him and run for it. I pulled the necklace out of my pocket and opened my hand. The moonlight caught it and it glowed. For the first time, I got a good look at it with my eyes, but I'd seen it clearly in my mind. It had a wide band of gold made from hinged squares. In the center was a huge, white oval stone that seemed to pulse and swirl. It looked alive.

Jammer laughed and took it from me. He took the box, too. I thought the necklace might stick to my hand or refuse to let me give it away, but Jammer took it like it wasn't some kind of cursed thing. Maybe it liked him. "Good job," he said, with a smile I didn't like at all.

We walked back toward the village in silence. Jammer was in front of us, with Coltt, Nesh and me in the middle and the two men following behind. The moon was full and high that night. But even before I saw, I knew. It was too quiet. The magic was gone from the village. Magic only leaves for one reason. It leaves when you die.

Bodies littered the beach. We hadn't heard the musket fire because we'd been deep in the barrows. Or maybe, the necklace didn't want us to hear. Mother lay dead next to my sisters, face down in the bloody sand, a chunk out of her skull visible where the musket had blown away her ear. Letta lay next to her, face up, only they'd shot her in the face and from the nose down there wasn't anything left.

"You bastards!" Nesh launched himself at Jammer.

An explosion rocked the night. The fire from the pirate's musket flashed right by my shoulder. The ball caught Nesh in the back, tore a hole through his ribs big enough to shove an arm through. He staggered forward and collapsed in the sand. The two men behind us grabbed Coltt and me by the arms before we could move.

"You gave your word you wouldn't kill anyone!"

Jammer gave me that smile again. "I said *I* wouldn't kill anyone. *I* didn't. My men did." He clucked his tongue. "If you're going to bargain with pirates, you need to be more specific."

I didn't have to look at Coltt to know what he was thinking. We both lurched forward, ready to rip Jammer apart, ready for a musket ball to tear through us the way it did through Nesh.

My head seemed to explode as the man behind me brought the butt of his gun down on my skull. I could feel the blood rushing through my ears as the moonlight turned to darkness.

"Take them," I heard Jammer say from a far distance. "They'll be useful." Then, I didn't hear anything else at all.

"Dante?"

I heard Coltt's voice but it was faint. Must have been imagining it.

"Dante?"

Louder now, close to my ear. My head was pounding and I was afraid to open my eyes. I groaned. My hands pushed down against wood. Wood? As my senses returned, I felt rocking. I knew that feeling. We were on a boat. We were Jammer's prisoners.

"Where are we?" I tried to sit and Coltt grabbed my arm, pulling me up. It was a dumb question. I knew. We were on Jammer's ship.

"They must have bashed you harder than they got me," he whispered. "I thought they'd killed you. I woke up in the dinghy. We're out to sea by now."

I could feel the magic. It was always stronger near water. I listened for the wind although I couldn't see the stars. "We're headed south. Towards Chasston."

"Figures."

Chasston was down the coast from Netter's Cove. The whole coastline was a haven for smugglers and pirates, the bane of the king's navy. Chasston was the main port, and no matter how many of the king's ships were in port or how many soldiers were in town, it didn't seem to bother the smugglers. Father said the smugglers and pirates paid the soldiers better than the king, so they looked the other way. Might be. Of course, Jammer might not stop at Chasston. He had hot cargo. He might meet his buyer somewhere else, someplace a little quieter.

"Dante, why did they bring us? Why didn't they just kill us, like—" He didn't say it. He didn't have to. Like Nesh. Like everyone else.

"Because of the magic." It hurt to talk. It hurt to think. "We were too good at finding the necklace. There must be more things like that, and Jammer figures we can retrieve them for him. He'll keep us as long as there's a use for us." And then...we'd join the rest.

Coltt helped me bind up the gash on the back of my head. He had a bruise on his temple, but otherwise, he seemed in pretty good shape.

"I can't hear it."

"Hear what?"

"The necklace."

Coltt gave me a funny, sideways glance, but I figured he knew what I meant. Actually, what I said wasn't exactly true. If I listened hard, I could hear something, muffled and far away. And then I knew. Jammer must have put the necklace in the lead box. And the necklace didn't like it.

I looked around as soon as I could move without wanting to pass out or throw up. My head seemed to pound in time with the swell of the waves. But I knew how the magic worked. The longer I was at sea, the stronger the magic got. Not that it would do us much good. We weren't likely to get lost. We were locked in an iron cage.

I started to get up and thought better of it. "Don't

bother," Coltt said. "I had time before you came around. The lock is solid. No other welds or joints. Bars are tight. Tried to pick the lock with my knife but I couldn't."

"They left our knives?"

Coltt nodded. "Guess they were too busy to pat us down. Or they don't care. Maybe they figured we weren't likely to kill each other." Or ourselves, I added silently. I wasn't letting myself think too hard about what I'd seen in the village. There'd be time enough for that.

"They say anything else?"

"Jammer said they were due for 'the meeting' by midnight tonight. Whoever hired them didn't give them much time. Wonder who it is and what they want."

I wondered if anyone had asked the necklace what it wanted, but I didn't say anything. That sounded crazy even to me.

I could see the angle of the sun change from the light through the portals. We sailed all day. No one fed us. Maybe Jammer didn't mean to keep us for too long, after all.

The sun went lower and I slept.

In my dreams, the sea turned wild and the sky turned dark. Lightning struck on the horizon, and I could smell the way it charged the air. My dreams changed from the stormy sea to the massacre at Netters Cove. I saw the bodies of the people I'd grown up with, my mother, my sisters...all of them gone. In my dream, I fell to my knees on the shore and wept as grief and anger washed over me, as strong as the pounding waves.

What do you want?

I looked up from the bloody sands. "I want revenge."

What do you want?

"I want Jammer dead. I want them all dead. I want to kill the men who did this."

What do you want?

My voice tore from a throat raw from weeping. "I want to avenge them. I want blood."

Then blood you shall have.

Coltt's hoarse scream woke me. Our iron cage was sliding across the hold as the ship tossed like a cork. I didn't have time to brace myself before the cage slammed into a wall of crates and I hit the bars on the other side hard enough to make my teeth rattle. The cage thrummed as the shock vibrated through the iron. It felt as if all of my insides were shaking.

The cage door swung open.

Coltt and I exchanged glances, and went for the knives in our leg sheaths. We stumbled from the cage as the ship pitched hard to port, scrambling to stay out of the way of the cargo, which had begun to shift. Just then, we heard footsteps on the stairs from the deck. We hid behind the most stable thing we could find, the forward guns.

"Son of a bitch!" The first man to the bottom saw the empty cage. He was ugly even by raider standards, with a poxy face and one hollow eye socket he didn't bother to cover with a patch.

The second man's curse was more creative, but anatomically implausible. "They didn't go far." By comparison, he was the better looking of the two, although whatever fight had flattened his nose had also left a deep crease up his forehead.

"They'd better go nowhere, or Jammer will skin both of us."

We held our breaths as the two men began to search the hold. Around us, the wooden ship creaked and moaned, rushing forward as it rose with the waves and then dropping, freefall. I eyed the hold filled with barrels, crates and logs warily.

"I think I see something!" One-eye headed straight for us. I gripped my knife, resolved to go down fighting.

The ship pitched starboard hard enough that I thought it might rip apart. Coltt and I barely kept a grip on the heavy gun that strained against its chains. One-eye and

Flatnose weren't as lucky. They went tumbling. A crack like gunfire echoed in the hold. I winced, expecting musket fire. The ropes on the timber broke, and the logs surged forward, propelled by the violence of the sea. Barrels and wooden crates tore loose from the ropes that secured them, crashing into the center of the hold. Flatnose and One-eye screamed as the logs rolled over them, and their blood ran like wine from a press across the filthy hold floor. When the screaming stopped, the hold was silent, quiet in a moment's lull.

Coltt's face was ashen. I pried his hand from the gun and motioned toward the stairs as the ship began to rock once more. Carefully, we crept to the top of the stairs, holding on as the ship began to pitch once more.

Waves twice the height of a man pounded the ship's deck. Coltt and I barely kept our footing as the ship seemed to dive nose first down a steep wave. Behind us, we could hear the bloody cargo scrape across the hold as it shifted. A massive wave caught the ship from starboard, and a man screamed. Coltt grabbed my arm and pointed skyward, toward the top of the mast where the lookout had been thrown from his perch, falling to land on the deck with a sickening thud, only to be washed overboard as more waves followed the first, sweeping two of his fellow pirates with him.

Two dead down below. Three washed overboard. I'd only counted seven of them.

What do you want? I could hear the necklace, louder now. *Take what you want. Take your due.*

Rage clouded my vision. All I could see were the bodies of my family, my neighbors, left on the beach to rot. I could smell their blood above the musket smoke, could taste blood in my mouth.

Blood for blood.

I knew Coltt couldn't hear the necklace, but I saw a fury in his eyes I'd never seen before. I could guess his thoughts, or maybe the necklace told me. *They killed Nesh. Killed Letta. Killed them all. Kill them all.*

"Jammer's mine." I barely recognized my voice. It sounded more like a growl. Coltt nodded. After all, it had been Jammer's lieutenant who murdered Nesh. It was time to prove two fishermen could hunt.

I couldn't see Jammer, but I could hear him cursing even above the roar of the wind. I was betting he was at the wheel. The lieutenant had dragged himself forward to drop the sails and blunt the power of the wind.

We had a moment's reprieve between waves. Coltt and I sprang from our hiding place. Coltt was on the lieutenant before he ever saw him coming. Coltt tackled the man from behind with a cry, and I saw a streak of silver as he drew his blade across the man's throat as neatly as he'd learned to do hunting wild boar. He dropped the man's hair and spun the lieutenant around, sinking his knife hilt-deep into the man's chest for good measure, then grabbed for the rigging and watched the next wave wash the dying man into the sea.

I knew Jammer didn't dare leave the wheel, although his curses made it clear he'd seen Coltt. I'd been unconscious when they'd brought me aboard, but I recognized the type of ship, knew where to find the wheel. The storm kept pounding us, soaking me to the bone. Twice, I almost lost my grip as the ship tossed and pitched.

Take what belongs to you. Take what you want.

The necklace was screaming in my mind, or maybe I was screaming. I lurched up the last two steps to face Jammer. He stood with one hand on the wheel and one on his musket. As I cleared the last step, he pulled the trigger, musket leveled at my heart.

Nothing happened. Wet powder's a bitch.

Before he could draw his cutlass, I was on him, even as I spotted Coltt climbing his way up to help. But Jammer was mine, all mine. I think he meant to run, but just then, the ship dropped beneath us as we ran down a wave, and Jammer fell against the wheel. His right arm snapped as the wheel spun against it, out of control. He was pinned, with no way to draw his cutlass, like a jaundiced fish.

I've been killing fish all my life.

My knife rammed into his chest just below the ribs, and I let the momentum and the ship's movement force the blade all the way down. Guts spilled in a steaming mass to the deck, just like a fish. Jammer's mouth opened and closed soundlessly and his whole body started to quiver until he gave one final flop against the knife, and hung dead from the wheel.

I tore him loose to steer, and I didn't look back. I think Coltt threw him overboard, or maybe the next wave took him. The ship wasn't built for two men to sail, but Coltt and I had been on the sea since we could walk. It took all my strength to hold the wheel against the storm, but I knew that the worst was past. Whether my magic had called the storm or whether it had just fed its intensity, now that Jammer and the lieutenant were dead, all the fight seemed to go out of the wind, and out of me. I was shaking so badly I think my knees would have buckled if I hadn't been holding the wheel, and for someone who never was seasick a day in his life, I wanted to retch.

Little by little, the storm lost its fury and the sky turned from pewter gray to twilight blue. As the clouds parted, I could see the stars. I knew where we were.

Coltt trimmed the sails and climbed back up to where I stood at the wheel.

"We can't go home." He said it flat, without emotion. But I saw his eyes. "The men'll be back. We've got no proof of our story, only bodies."

"We've got the ship." But I knew what Coltt meant. If we went back, the murders would dog us the rest of our lives, and the men would look at us with questions in their eyes forever.

"Now what?"

I shrugged. "We head for Chasston. It's thick with pirates, smugglers and thieves."

"What if Jammer's friends come after us?"

A bitter smile crossed my face. "Doubt he had many. We know how to fish, so we won't starve. We know how to sail. We'll go to Chasston, find someone who needs a fast ship."

"And be pirates, like Jammer?"

My nerves were shot. I wheeled on Coltt. "We can smuggle whiskey and broad leaf. Father said the king's entire navy hasn't been able to plug up all the coves and inlets, no matter how many ships they send. We know the coastline. Way I figure it, cheatin' the king out of his taxes doesn't hurt anyone, and whiskey and broad leaf give a good bit of satisfaction to our fellow man. Makes it almost charitable."

"We stole a ship and killed the crew to do it. That'll earn us a noose."

"If they catch us."

I put in for the night in a hidden inlet up the coast from Chasston. Exhausted, hungry and soaked to the skin, I crawled down onto the lower deck and went looking for Jammer's quarters. Coltt had slept some while I steered us; he took night watch.

Everything in Jammer's cabin had been tossed around by the storm. Doors were open, drawers were spilled out and most things lay in a heap on the floor. Near the heavy wooden captain's desk, I found it. The necklace lay near the empty lead box.

I can make you rich.

Dead tired, I knew I had one more task before I could sleep. I used my magic to shield my thoughts as I approached the necklace, keeping my face blank. Its voice was sultry, like the whores we'd find in Chasston, full of promises, lies and clap. I sprang at it, shoving it into the box and slamming the lid closed even as I heard it shriek at me like a cheated tinker. I found a length of rope and wrapped it around the box, sealing the lid closed and then I tied it to the sturdy leg of the desk, to keep it from "accidentally" opening. The storm had washed Jammer's blood from my hands, but I knew what I'd done and how I'd done it.

Coltt was right. We'd done murder. Stolen a ship. Jammer's "friends" might want us dead, and his enemies might want the ship. The king's men wouldn't care. They'd hang the lot of us. But not tonight. Every bone in my body ached as I crawled into a dead man's bed and for once, I slept without dreaming.

The next morning, the sky was bright and clear. I woke just after dawn, and went looking for Coltt. Found him dangling from a rope off the bow of the ship, and for a moment, I thought he'd saved the king the trouble and hanged himself. Then Coltt hoisted himself over the rail, and I saw the make-shift rigging he'd made.

"Can't paint the whole boat, but I struck Jammer's flag and scraped off the name on the hull," Coltt said in a matter-of-fact tone. I knew that meant he'd struggled with our outlaw status all night and come to terms with it. He wasn't much for talking about things like that. "Went down in the hold and found some black paint. Should do until we get to Chasston, or wherever."

I peered over the edge. "Vengeance" had been painted over a scraped-bare spot on the hull. Probably not original, but Coltt had summed it up.

I turned to find him seated on the deck, looking at me, or maybe past me at the sky.

"What now?"

I dropped to the deck beside him. I didn't look at him; I looked at the clouds. Looking at Coltt would make me think of Mother and Jana and Nesh and I wasn't ready to mourn them, not yet. So I looked at the clouds instead. "Father had an uncle in Chasston. Took me down to meet him once, a long while ago. Cagy old man. Father said he ran a curio shop. Said that meant he bought and sold old and unusual things, no questions asked. According to father, Uncle Evann had a foot on both sides of the line when it came to the law, honest enough to not make trouble with the king's men, dodgy enough to not care about where his treasures came from."

"You think he'd help us?"

I shrugged. "If he doesn't, we find a tavern to set up shop and look for someone who needs cargo run cheap. It's worth a try." I was quiet for a moment. "I'm going to take the necklace," I said quietly, as if I was afraid it would hear me, lead box or not. "I don't want the damn thing around, and I don't want blood money for selling it. I just want rid of it."

"Can't blame you." Coltt might not have heard the necklace talking to him, but he was good about taking me at my word. I was glad, because I had enough trouble shutting out the memory of how the necklace had fed my blood lust. I'd killed Jammer without remorse, and I didn't like knowing that I could do such a thing, even if he deserved it. If I got rid of the necklace, maybe I'd never feel that way again. Ever.

By night, we'd hiked into Chasston. We'd looted the dead pirates' quarters for some coin, enough to buy dinner and some ale. We were unshaven and smelling of salt water, but the whores in the narrow Chasston streets came on to us anyhow. I gripped the box under my arm a little tighter and kept on going, weaving my way through the crowded alleys and ginnels, to a small shop a few streets back from the docks.

"Trifles and Folly" was the name of the shop. A bell rang as we pushed the door open. Inside, it smelled of old wood and whiskey, and a musty smell that reminded me of the barrows. Things of every description were piled on shelves, spilling onto tables and into stacks on the worn wooden floor. Sextants and spyglasses and armillaries, enough to navigate a navy, filled one corner. Carved ivory tusks and wooden masks with staring eyes and sharp, bone teeth glared down from high shelves. Boxes inlaid with gold and jade were stacked next to larger boxes of teak and mahogany in every size and shape. There was magic here; I could feel it. I looked around the shadowy interior and knew that, like my necklace, many of the "trifles and follies" in this store were not what they seemed.

"Looking for something?" The voice startled me. The words were neutral, but there was an undercurrent of something sharp as steel beneath them. I turned to find a bent old man with white hair and a long, high-necked frock coat staring at me with cold blue eyes that seemed to see straight through me.

"Uncle Evann?" My voice came out like a croak. So much for being a big, tough pirate.

The old man frowned, and stepped closer. He reached out and grabbed my chin, turning my head to see my profile. His grip was tight and his yellowed nails dug into my flesh. And then, when I thought he might draw blood, he released me. And laughed.

"You'd be Dante, wouldn't you? Eric's son."

I swallowed hard and nodded. "Yes, sir. And this is my friend, Coltt."

Evann looked from me to Coltt and back again. "You're a long way from home."

I stretched out my magic, looking for a clue as to whether or not I could trust Evann. I could sense the necklace, shrieking its fury at being restrained, muted in its box. It wasn't the only voice I heard coming from objects that shouldn't have a voice at all. The voices were muffled, like a conversation in another room, just beyond my ability to make out what they were saying. But there was magic here, and I was pretty sure Evann could hear those voices, too. We were already in this up to our necks. I decided to trust him.

"There's been a problem." I glanced at Coltt. "Is there somewhere we could talk? Somewhere a little more private?"

Evann looked at me in silence for a moment as if trying to make his own decision about whether to trust me or not. Finally, he gave a jerk of his head toward the rear of the store. "Come on. Just about to close up when you came in."

He locked the door and motioned for us to follow him. Behind the shop was a one-room apartment that held a bed, small stove and a table. Evann took a kettle from the back of the stove and stoked the fire, saying nothing until he'd poured us all hot tea. We sat around the table, and Coltt and I stared into our cups until I got the nerve up to spill out our story. I told him everything, even about how I could hear the necklace, even about how it called to me the night of the storm. I'd set the box on the table between us, bound with rope and wrapped in rags. The necklace was silent, and if I could read its mood at all, it was nervous.

Evann listened without a word as I told the whole, painful story. He said nothing as my cheeks flamed when I told about killing Jammer and the lieutenant, even though my heart was hammering in my chest. I half expected Evann to jump from his chair and call for the soldiers, but Evann didn't move at all. Finally, I was out of words. Coltt hadn't said anything. I stared into my cup as if I could read the future from the bits of leaf scattered in the bottom.

"You brought the necklace." It wasn't a question. I nodded toward the rag-wrapped lump and moved to open it, but Evann grabbed my wrist.

"Leave it be." He took a long drought of his tea and set down the cup. "I'm glad you thought to come here. There's someone I want you to meet."

I saw the same alarm in Coltt's eyes that flooded through my system. Damn, Evann was going to give us up to the soldiers.

A slight smile softened Evann's features. "No, I'm not going to call the guards. I have a...business associate... who will want to hear your story. You can trust him. Leave nothing out. Tell him just what you've told me. If there's more to say about the barrow, he'll want to know that, too. I wager he'll know what to do about that necklace." He rose and took down a loaf of bread, some hard cheese and a length of dried sausage and put them on the table. This time, he filled our mugs with mulled cider and rum. "Eat."

"Won't we interrupt your...associate's...dinner?" I asked, losing no time grabbing a hunk of bread.

Evann's smile was unreadable. "I hope not."

Coltt and I ate in record time, thanking Evann for our first real meal in two days through stuffed mouths. When we were done, we followed Evann out the back of his flat into the alley. It stank of urine and horse dung. Clotheslines heavy with damp shirts and sodden pants hung from side to side from the tenements above. Evann wound through the narrow, slippery ginnels, up the hill from the port. Gradually, tenements gave way to wide cobblestone streets and villas. I glanced nervously at Coltt.

"We're not dressed to be seen anywhere decent."

Evann chuckled. "Sorren won't mind."

We stopped at an iron gate set into a high stone wall. Evann said a word to the man who waited in the shadows on the other side, and we were admitted. Coltt and I exchanged wary glances, but we said nothing. We walked back a long carriage road through tall trees hung with moss. I was sweating hard enough that my shirt stuck to my back by the time we reached the large, stately home. Whoever Sorren was, he had money. I glanced at the wrought iron railings, the tall columns and the large windows hung with heavy draperies. It was an old home, and my magic told me the ghosts of former inhabitants liked it well enough to stick around.

A servant opened the door and smiled at Evann. "Good to see you again, Mr. Evann. Mr. Sorren is always happy to see you."

With a nod of thanks, we moved into the large entrance hall. Candles illuminated the foyer, but of the rooms that opened off of the entrance way, all but one were dark. Evann motioned for us to follow him down a long hall hung with portraits and artwork from distant ports. I wondered whether Sorren was a sea captain or someone with connections to royal trade. As we neared the end of the hallway, my magic made me edgy. I recognized the feeling immediately. It was the same edginess I felt down in the barrow, when I knew that long-dead things lurked in the shadows. I passed a darkened room and repressed a shiver.

Evann knocked at a door at the end of the hallway. A muffled voice gave permission to enter, and Evann opened the door, leading the way. Sorren was seated in a wing chair next to the large fireplace. He stood to greet us and embraced Evann warmly. I sized him up. He was a tall, spare-built man with blue-gray eyes. His frock coat was understated, but obviously expensive, in cut and cloth. Even by candlelight, he had an ashen pallor. I glanced around the room. Leather-bound books lined shelf upon shelf floor to ceiling. A desk with a globe and an armillary stood on one side. Heavy damask draperies were pulled across all the windows. Beside where Sorren sat, an open book and a goblet of red wine sat on a side table.

"I've got two lads here with a story I think you'll want to hear," Evann said by way of introduction as Sorren gestured for us to sit. His eyes seemed to follow me, and I could have sworn they saw down to my bones. My magic made me jumpy, a jangled feeling that usually warned of an impending storm. "They've brought you a gift."

At Evann's nod, I held out the cloth-wrapped box. Sorren reached toward it, then drew back. A look of concern mingled with heightened interest flashed in those gray eyes. "He brought you this?" he asked sharply, with a glance toward Evann, who nodded. Sorren looked back at me, and his gaze seemed to capture my full attention. "He has magic," Sorren said finally, breaking the gaze. "Strong magic."

"Let him tell you his story."

At Evann's prompt, I told our story one more time—the last time, I hoped. Once again, Coltt remained silent, and I could tell Sorren made him extremely uncomfortable. Maybe it was Sorren's wealth, maybe it was hearing the story again, which felt like salt in a bleeding wound. But I was betting that Coltt's own magic felt as jangly as mine.

Sorren watched me with eyes the color of a coming storm. His intensity spooked me, but I kept on until the bloody end of the tale. When I was finished, Sorren leaned forward.

"You both went into the barrow," he said. We nodded.

"You used your magic to find the necklace, and it talked to you."

"Actually, it talked to Dante. I didn't hear it," Coltt said quietly.

I was surprised that none of this alarmed Sorren or seemed strange to him. Finally, he sat back and picked up his goblet, swirling the red liquid as he thought.

"So tell me, Dante, what will you and your friend do now?" Sorren asked quietly.

I took a deep breath. "Not rightly sure yet, sir. We can't go home. I guess from the king's perspective, we're outlaws. We have Jammer's boat. We thought we might run some whiskey and broad leaf, other cargo. And fish. It's all we know."

Sorren took a sip of the red liquid. "Did Evann tell you why your necklace would interest me?"

"No, sir."

Sorren looked toward the fireplace, although no fire burned there. "What you sensed in the barrow was real. What's sealed in there is more than just ancestors, or the ancient dead. Long ago, powerful mages fought a great battle. One side conjured...things...that should never have walked abroad. They were defeated, and what they conjured was entombed in the barrows. All that survives of those times are legends, stories that have been watered down to tell how the mounds were used for rituals." He shook his head. "Rituals. Every generation, mages must reinforce the wardings to keep what's buried inside. The magic is old and complicated. Some of the mages use anchor items—artifacts--to store power, or the spirits of familiars, in order to work their spells. So did the mages who created the...things.

"The wardings are growing weaker. It's time for them to be renewed. And there are some who would raise the barrow wights for their own purposes. And so...collectors from both sides seek the artifacts that have been stolen, lost or misplaced. Some of these collectors hire men like Jammer. Others use men like Evann to watch what unwitting travelers bring back with them and funnel those special purchases to buyers like me."

"Which side are you on?" My voice sounded sharp because my heart was in my throat.

"I want to keep what's buried in its place." He smiled then, and I saw the tips of fangs.

Sorren is a vampire. Shit. What's down in the barrows scares him. Damn, damn, damn.

"I'd like to make you and your friend a business proposition," Sorren said. "I'm prepared to outfit a ship for you and hire a crew. But finding two mages I can trust...that's the hard part." He leaned forward. "Your village isn't the only one men like Jammer have visited. It always ends the same way. I want to find those artifacts before the other side finds them. Things like your necklace. I think you have an idea of just how dangerous they are."

I nodded, my head spinning. "You're looking for pirates."

Sorren laughed again, a deep, rich sound. Again, I glimpsed his fangs. "I prefer the term privateer. Help me locate the anchor items. Along the way, you'll have plenty of opportunity to rid the world of men like Jammer. I know it won't bring your family back, but it could keep many, many more people from dying."

"Why do you care? You're already dead." My fear made me bold, or maybe stupid.

Sorren smiled broadly, genuinely amused. His long eye teeth were now completely visible, and I felt Coltt shudder. "Let's just say that in this, undead and mortals share a common cause. What do you say, Dante?"

I glanced at Coltt. He shrugged. We'd been together long enough, I knew to take that as a yes. "We're in."

"Good." Sorren turned to Uncle Evann. "Daniel will see you to rooms. It's best you stay here tonight. If the boys came in with Jammer's boat, some of his friends may be looking for his cargo."

No one asked what we thought about staying the night in a vampire's mansion. But given the choice of a rather civil vampire or more of Jammer's friends, it looked like a good idea. Upstairs, we were shown to comfortable rooms, one for each of us. I drew the heavy drapes apart and opened the window to walk out on the balcony. From here, I could see the moon on the ocean. Its light cast a pale course for beyond the horizon. A ship. A crew. In two short days, I'd gone from fisherman to smuggler.

Aw, hell. Screw that.

I'm a pirate.

Cursed Luck!

By BA Collins

It was a warm Saturday after a huge storm. The public beach sandwiched in between the miles of private beach at Manomet Cliffs was busy with pale-skinned New Englanders trying to make up for the sunless days of the past winter. Luckily, the private beach was far enough from the public areas that I could ignore the tourists. I sat under my beach umbrella below my husband's family cottage, and tried to enjoy the day. I heard lots of traffic up on the road, only slightly muffled by the trees crowded around the old cottages. A bunch of motorcycles roared over the car noises.

A gaggle of people in leathers came down the sand, loud and cheerful sounding. I thought about picking up and moving when they headed straight for the open area of beach below me, on the private side. I wasn't about to go tell them they were trespassing. No one had yet colonized the damp area where the tide was receding. Calling it sand was a stretch. The storm had ripped away tons of sand. What was left was mostly rocks and seaweed. They were welcome to it.

Before they took their jackets and vests off, I saw they

weren't casual bikers. All the guys had gang colors on. I didn't catch the club name, but there was a devil fish with wheels in the middle. Scruffy, scraggly guys, the lot of them. Some of the women with them were amazingly gorgeous. Tall, blond, chesty. Why the hell were they dating these scraggly bearded outlaws? The rest of the women ran the gamut from grandmas to scary harsh chicks I'd hate to mess with. They had coolers and chairs and towels. Even picnic baskets. They obviously planned on staying for the day.

As I thought seriously about leaving, I saw a couple of guys drifting my way. I tried for invisible. *I'm not the porn model you're looking for,* I thought. *Five foot two, B-cup and a big ass is not in your damn universe!* I thought about going up to the house, but then they'd know I lived right up there in sight of the beach.

Invisibility didn't work. I kept my face turned down towards my book, but I could see them working slowly closer to me. I folded my hands so my wedding ring was more visible.

"Hey, babe, where's yer old man?" one of them asked, right in front of me. He was the better looking one. Tall, dirty blond hair in a ponytail. He still had a vest on, and swim trunks. Made it easier to see the muscles and golden body hair. He was tattooed, but the designs faded into the background with all those muscles.

In Dallas, banging his secretary. I almost said it out loud. Jerry made no bones about his crush on his secretary. It hurt my feelings, but he only seemed to date her on business trips. She had a boyfriend, and visibly didn't take Jerry very seriously. "He'll be getting here soon," I tried. *He'd never come down here. He'd dial 911 as he ran away.*

The other guy laughed. He had a vicious face, marked by a big scar over one cheek that twisted his expression into a snarl. He was shorter than the blond guy,

Mediterranean in complexion. "Sure, that's why you got that big smut book to read, and a backup." He looked down into my beach bag.

Damn historical romances. Smutty or not, they always have a half-naked woman on the cover. The one I'd been reading featured a lady wearing not much more than a bodice and a ripped skirt being mauled by a guy in Hollywood pirate clothes.

"Look, I'm married. Not interested, sorry," I said, as calmly as I could manage.

"That's why you were watching us, I bet." Blondie dropped down on one knee to get a look under my hat. He did have a cute grin. I could just see the dimple on his cheek under his beard.

"Nothing personal." I dropped my book in my bag with a fake casual sigh. I had a gardener and a butler up in that fucking mansion pretending to be a beach cottage. Where the hell were they? I managed to get my cell phone in hand and clicked it on. Jerry had insisted I get one with a panic button on it. It would beep right to the house phone. I'd forgotten about the cheerful little chirp it made when it turned on.

Blondie caught my hand and pried the cell phone out of my grip. "Nice phone." He glared at me.

"Okay, never mind. Just let me go! I'm not interested!" I struggled to get loose. Shit. I could have used some help, like right then! The public beach had emptied after the bikers arrived. I was too far from the road for anyone up there to hear me scream. Where the hell were Tony and Raoul?

"Sit back down, chickie. Relax." Blondie pushed me down into my beach chair, stuffing my cell phone into a vest pocket.

"I suppose sharing's out of the question?" the scarred guy asked.

"Beat it, Joey." Blondie gestured at him to make him leave.

Joey chuckled and moseyed off.

I will not cry or panic. I'll figure this out. I told myself.

"I'm Jack." Blondie sat down on my towel and held out a hand.

I didn't return the favor. I wasn't going to give him the least bit of encouragement.

"Let's be polite." He picked up my right hand and squeezed it. "You look like a bored rich chick looking for a guy to cheat with. Bet your old man is out banging some brainless hottie right now."

"How the fuck could you know that?" I snapped. Shit. That shouldn't have been out loud.

"You're cute. You look like the girl next door. Married, right outta college and your old man's got wads of dough." He picked up my left hand. "There's two carats of diamonds in those rings. He's a rich idiot."

I winced. "Do you read palms, too?"

He gave me that cute grin again. "How's that marrying a rich guy thing going, babe?"

I don't know why I talked to him. He seemed to have grabbed me to keep me from getting away so he could talk. Not so he could mash me down into the sand and rape me. Maybe it was his bright blue eyes. Maybe he was the first to talk about marrying for money without a sneer. "He's okay. Good looking. Only cheats on me when he's away."

"Doesn't rock your boat, though?" One eyebrow went up.

"He's good. Fun when he's around." His family was getting tedious. They wanted grandkids. Like, now.

He chuckled. "Ain't what I meant. You ain't in love. He didn't make you crazy for him."

I blushed. "No. And you will?"

He was leaning close enough to run a finger over my hot cheeks. "Only one way to find out."

My lips felt awfully dry. I wet them, as his fingers

brushed over them too, then down my neck onto my chest. I had a cover-up over my bikini, but it was open in the front. He traced the curve of the bikini very slowly. His face got closer, eyes watching me so hard, like I might disappear if he blinked.

I wasn't ducking. Maybe Jerry was going to get cheated on. He pushed my hat off and set my sunglasses up on top of my head. "Brown eyed girl." He smiled as he started to kiss. His beard and mustache were soft and tickled my cheeks. Jack leaned closer, his hand going up under my bikini and onto my breasts. My nipples were tight as hell when he reached them. I put my arms up on his shoulders.

This is dumb. I'd been terrified and hoping to be rescued a minute ago. I shouldn't be interested in him after he grabbed me! I was not some dumb bimbo in a costume pirate romance!

His other arm went around me hard. He half picked me up, and tossed the beach chair aside. He set me back down on the towel. I gaped my lips open in surprise. He pushed his tongue right in my mouth and kissed harder.

Oh hell. I kissed him back. That got me pushed back onto the beach towel with him on top of me, both hands on my tits, my bikini pushed down and out of the way. His vest had studs on it that dug into my skin, but I barely noticed that over the tingling of my breasts.

One hand drifted down my stomach and into my bikini bottom. Gentle fingers ran over my mound and found moist pussy. I squeaked in surprise. "Oh, you hot little bitch," he whispered.

His fingers explored while he kissed me again. I moaned into his mouth when a big finger started rubbing my clit. I forgot to think, and nearly to breathe as he fingered me slowly.

"Hey, Jack! Quit messing with the broad. Come look at this!" somebody shouted.

Jack's fingers moved away. He rolled over to look. "What?"

"You gotta see this! Bones and a fucking treasure chest."

"You're shitting me." Jack sat up.

A big, heavy set guy waved what looked very much like a human leg bone in one hand. "No."

"Son of a bitch." Jack looked at me. "Hold that thought." He got up and went that way. As he walked away, I got a good look at his colors. The Devil Fish?

"Hold that thought?" I snapped. My body was aching and he was just running off? As soon as he turned his back, I was on my feet. I grabbed my bag and ran for the road. I didn't stop when I heard shouting behind me. They wouldn't know I lived right there if I went to the road and then out of sight back to my house.

I walked the half mile home the roundabout way through woods and stomped around my empty house. He grabbed me, seduced me and then walked off! Wait. Where were Tony and Raoul? Or that useless little bitch Diane, my alleged maid? I went towards the back of the house. They had the door shut, but it didn't take a genius to figure out what all that giggling and bouncing spring noise meant. A threesome? Great. *Good thing I didn't actually need rescuing, you idiots.* I thought about yelling or pounding on the door, but no. I would just tell Jerry to fire them later. I had kinda needed a rescue five minutes ago, and they were too busy in the back room to even notice.

So what were the bikers doing? I glanced out at the beach and it was deserted. Son of a bitch... They'd done some digging and were gone. After a while, I walked down to get my beach stuff. Should I look to see what they'd done?

The pebbly sand down there had been below at least four feet of beach sand before last night. I took a few steps and smelled something rotten. They'd said something about bones. A treasure chest? No way. But there was a big hole down there. I ignored the rotten smell and picked my way across the rocks. There were lots of footprints, from bare feet and flip flops and some heeled boots. A broken shovel lay next to the hole. Hey! That was our shovel! One of those assholes had snuck up to the shed below the house and stolen it. It was thoroughly broken. I looked into the hole. A few rotted bits of wood lay in the bottom. They'd found a wooden chest.

Something scraped near me. I looked up, to find that the beach had gone foggy while I was distracted. Another scrape. I backed up. It could be a boat on rocks just off shore. The tide was very low. You couldn't bring anything in here bigger than a row boat. Someone cursed in muffled tones.

I took a few more steps away. The fog was getting thicker. Something splashed. Then something else. People getting out of a boat? Not heavy enough. Slosh-slosh. Something was walking my way. I didn't want to see them. I turned around and ran. I didn't even know why, but I didn't slow down until I got up to the house and slammed and locked the door. I couldn't see the beach through the fog. A few noises echoed up. Crashes, splashing and crunches. One angry shout I couldn't understand. Then more splashing and the noises of a row boat with multiple oars going offshore. I couldn't imagine what could have come up through the rocks at low tide like that. I pulled the blinds down and turned up the TV and tried not to think about it for the rest of the afternoon.

The threesome eventually broke up and they slowly came around, red faced as soon as they noticed I'd been in the house for a while. I ignored them as much as I could. Finally I turned around and looked at Diane, who was puttering in the kitchen. "Look, why don't you three take a couple days off and get it out of your system?"

She blushed nearly as pink as her painted fingernails. "Jeez, Dana, I'm so sorry. We, uh, thought you'd be out all afternoon."

"No. There were some annoying bikers on the beach. I came in to get away. After one of them bothered me." I turned to Raoul.

He flushed dark red under his tan.

"I don't really care what you do in your time off. When you're supposed to be keeping an eye on things isn't the time to fuck around." I never spoke to the guys like that. They both looked pretty startled.

"I had the phone on me." Tony protested. "I'd have come out if you beeped."

"He swiped my phone, so I couldn't."

Raoul winced. "Oh, fuck, Mrs. C, they didn't...?"

"No. Somebody distracted him and I got away. All by myself," I snapped.

"Mr. C. would have a heart attack if we took off." Tony shook his head.

"It's my fault. I jumped them," Diane admitted with a grimace. "I guess I'm done here?"

"Just take a couple of days off. Then, um, stick to time off?" I relented a little. She had a kid and needed the job. I shouldn't have been nice. She was a horrible cook. She'd spent more on silicone boobs than on cooking school or learning to clean.

"Uh...she's here so Mr. C doesn't worry about us," Tony protested.

I resisted an urge to throw things at him. "Oh, so she selflessly jumped you to save me?"

"Don't dig it deeper, man." Raoul waved him off. "I'll call my mom to come cook here. She'll keep us honest."

"That sounds good," I agreed and let Diane escape. His mother was an Italian old lady in a black dress who could keep the devil minding his manners.

The next morning I turned on the TV and dropped my coffee cup. Jack's picture flashed up on channel five news. "Known outlaw biker gang Devil Fish members last night had an altercation with other bar patrons at the Salty Dog. They are also alleged to have had an altercation with police officers summoned to the scene." Must have been a good fight if the Salty Dog owner called the cops. His Hell Knight bouncers should have been good enough to scare anyone, or put them down if there was trouble. Apparently Jack's club was based in Hampton, and had a big long history of being in trouble with the police. They'd disappeared after the fight.

The news went on. No mention of bones or treasure chests.

Mrs. Bendenelli snorted as she washed the kitchen. She'd agreed with me about Diane's skills. "Those Devil Fish, they're bad boys!"

The very next news item flabbergasted me. "The tall ship SS Victory, just docked in Portsmouth during a training voyage, has disappeared from its dock. It apparently sailed out in the middle of the night. The harbor master was found unconscious on the dock at six A.M. by returning members of the crew who had been on shore leave."

The camera cut to a short, Oriental-looking man in a white jacket with an SS Victory logo on the chest. He was furious, angry enough to be losing his command of English. "My ship has been stolen! The Coast Guard must find it!" He went on, but the sound cut out. He was swearing, clearly.

"The Coast Guard is hot in pursuit of the valuable SS Victory." The announcer gave a few details of the stolen ship.

Nobody steals tall ships, do they? You have to know what the hell you're doing to run one. Jerry and I had been married on one, and then taken a really fun cruise. I'd learned to climb rigging and haul sails in, and he'd spent his time getting plastered on the deck.

"Several crew members are missing. The third mate was found with the harbor master, unharmed but knocked out cold."

"Pirates? In this day and age?" Mrs. Bendenelli had stopped cleaning to watch the TV with me.

Good grief, and they'd kidnapped a bunch of college kids. Women, of course. Oh lord. I shivered at their probable fate. Maybe I wouldn't be finishing that stupid pirate book, after all.

Days went by. The disappearance of the Victory was international news. The police weren't finding Jack and his gang, either. Tony had immediately had my cell phone disconnected and got me a new one. He and Raoul were keeping an eye out. No more mysterious fogs or bikers appeared around the house. The hole filled in with sand after a day or two.

Jerry came back from Dallas later that week in a sober mood. "Dana, we need to talk."

That didn't sound good. "Oh?"

"Well...you're a nice girl, and I'm fond of you. But we're not in love. I've finally found someone to love." He looked agonized.

"Personally, I think you've found a 42DD chest," I snapped.

"No, Pippi loves me," he said with a sappy smile.

"You idiot, she loves your money!"

"And you don't?" he asked wryly. "Dana, I'm a geek, not an idiot. You like me, but you married me for money."

Sometimes you just have to read the writing on the wall. "And you think Pippi's different?"

"Maybe," he said hopefully. "I want a divorce."

I simmered. "Fine. We didn't sign pre-nups. I own half of you, asshole."

"We'll see." He smiled. Not his usual sappy grin. This was his courtroom smile, the shark teeth showing. "I won't give you half, Dana, but I'll be generous."

I sagged. "Okay. Go away. I'll stay here at the beach house for the moment. I'll be getting a lawyer."

He nodded. Perfectly reasonable again now that he had his way. He collected his bags and drove off in his Mercedes coupe.

The next couple weeks went by in a haze. I got a good lawyer—from a firm that has always been rivals with Jerry's firm. I'd be a damn well off divorcee. He gave me the beach house. His mom's adjoining cottage went up for sale the next day. Tony and Raoul left, along with Raoul's mother. She had the grace to be embarrassed about the situation. They looked relieved to get out from under her thumb. That left me alone in the house with a high tech security system.

The Victory was sighted less than a hundred miles away. More than sighted, in fact. She'd come up alongside a freighter and pretended distress. Men boiled over the rails with military rifles and overpowered the crew. They stole an "undetermined" amount of cargo.

The papers loved it. They printed pictures of the Victory with a big caption underneath, "PIRATE?" That left me in giggles for half the morning.

That night wasn't funny. I half woke up as someone jammed a smelly cloth down over my face. I went back under without even a scream.

I woke up cold, tied up on a bumpy, noisy floor. I was blindfolded. It sounded and felt like I was on a bumpy, fast moving motor boat. I didn't move. What the hell was going on?

"Where do we dump her?" someone said, in a familiar voice.

"Out further. Weights on the body and she won't be washing back up on shore in a month." That was Raoul. The other voice was Tony.

"Oh no!" I moaned.

"Hey, she's awake." Footsteps.

"We could have some fun first," Tony suggested. "Make up for her sending that hottie Diane off."

"Please don't hurt me!" I begged. Rough hands picked me up. My nightie tore away in a split second. They were thugs after all. I never really bought the 'butler' and 'gardener' labels Jerry had hung on them when he hired them.

Raoul laughed and kissed me roughly. Five o'clock shadow, like sharpened sandpaper on my cheeks. I tried to bite him and got slapped hard. "None of that!"

I cried, but he ignored it. I got mauled and kissed and hands in my pussy. *I'm gonna get raped and murdered. And all by order of my asshole husband.* Guess I was getting too much money from the divorce. Oh please, someone save me! That was a joke. We were probably miles out to sea already.

"What's that?" Tony said. "Looks like a fucking sailing ship."

Raoul dropped me down on the deck. "Yeah. It is. Must be the one that got stolen. Those ballsy assholes. Every Coast Guard boat north of DC is looking for those fuckers. Here they are, five miles off the fucking Cape."

"With AKs as I heard it." Tony snorted.

"Turn east. They ain't gonna catch up to us. Those big ships can't do more than five or ten knots," Raoul ordered.

I felt the motorboat turn fairly hard. They were quiet and tense. At least they were ignoring me.

"No shit, they got seadoos. We're fucking screwed," Tony moaned. I heard more loud motors approaching.

"We got something to trade." Raoul gave me a push with a sneakered foot. "They're fucking pirates."

"Let's stop and ask to 'parlay,'" Tony laughed. They idled the motor. The other motors got closer.

"Hey, it's smart people!" Someone laughed loud enough to be heard over the motors.

"You assholes must be the pirates. Parlay?" Tony said loudly.

"What ya got for us?" A rough voice asked.

Raoul picked me up and dangled me half over the side. "This little bitch is doing her hubby for a couple million. He wants her gone. In return, you let us go."

"We could do that. Give her here." I got handed down into someone's arms. He held me upright and idled the seadoo backwards, probably away from the boat.

"Great. Good doing business with..." Raoul's voice was overrun by two sharp bursts of gunfire. He didn't even get a scream out. Just a horrible gurgle and a wet thud.

I shivered. I couldn't be upset that they'd killed the guys that were going to rape and murder me. But what the hell would happen now?

"Assholes. Ya don't parlay with marks," someone growled. "Joey, get that tub going again. We got us a new boat."

"And we got us a new broad."

"Take that blindfold off her."

"Hold still, lady." The blindfold slipped away. After the darkness of the blindfold, the moonlit night seemed quite bright.

I was surrounded by guys on seadoos. They were wearing vests and trunks, most with guns slung over their shoulders.

"Hey, chickie." The guy on a seadoo next to my captor's shook blond hair from his face. "Fancy meeting you here."

"Jack?" I gulped.

He grinned. I looked to see Joey, the scarred guy, dumping bodies over the side of the motorboat.

"You're the pirates?" I gaped.

"Give her here, Mike." Jack pulled closer. I got handed over like luggage again.

"This the little broad you made out with on the beach that day?"

"Yup. And there's nowhere to run on the ship." Jack smiled. He slipped a knife between my tied wrists. I relaxed gratefully. "Hang on!" He shifted me behind him and as soon as I grabbed his waist, the seadoo came to life with a roar and we zipped away.

The ship was moving across the water under sail. It was absolutely beautiful in the moonlight. As in the pictures I'd seen, the Victory had two masts and multiple jib sails, the foremast square rigged and the main mast fore and aft rigged. It was smaller than the ship I'd taken my honeymoon on.

People hung over the rails, looking down.

"Go on up, Dana." Jack backed the seadoo around so I could reach the rope ladder.

"I'm naked!" I protested. And how the hell did he know my name? Oh. He'd had my cell phone.

"Nobody mess with her," he shouted up.

"Oh, I feel so reassured." I managed to grab the rope ladder and climbed up. It wasn't fun. On deck, someone threw a blanket around me. It was a worried looking woman in a t-shirt and shorts. She didn't look like a biker chick. Her tee-shirt said something about "Woods Hole Oceanography"

Jack climbed up. "Thanks, Elaine." He smiled at the

dark haired woman.

I clutched the blanket around me. I was getting eyed by a half dozen men, mostly looking like bikers, and a few women. Two or three looked like bikers. The rest looked scared or tired. More seadoos came alongside the ship.

"Bring those seadoos aboard." Jack ordered. "I'm going below. Joe, you have the helm."

"Aye, sir." A younger biker saluted. He started shouting commands.

Jack's quarters were aft. They weren't a picturesque pirate cabin, more like a cramped stateroom on a modern ship. "Ain't too big, but it's private."

I kept the blanket tight around me. I was glad it was him, not one of Jerry's thugs, but he'd nearly molested me a month ago. *Oh, molested, right! You weren't exactly fighting him off!* "Thanks for saving me. They were going to kill me."

"Old man wanted a divorce?"

"Pippi got herself pregnant. Suddenly he was in love!" I snarled, tears in my eyes. "I thought it was all cool, he was being fair and reasonable...then I woke up getting kidnapped."

"So you ain't about to be killed. It's better." He hugged me. No sex, just a hard, comforting squeeze. "And this time, you aren't going to run off when I turn my back."

"Jack, don't go there. I almost got raped." I tried to squirm away.

"I know." He frowned. "I just don't want to turn around and have you gone again." He didn't let go. "I should have towed you along to look at the bones."

"Surely... you aren't going to keep me?" I gasped.

"I expect you'd be worth a bit of ransom." He grinned. "But only if ye want to go." His accent had shifted. He was from the North shore. When did he grow an English accent?

"You're nuts. The Coast Guard will catch up to you!" I gasped.

"Not so far." He sat down and pulled me into his lap. He buried his face in my hair and didn't move for a bit. "Thought about coming for you, but we've been a little busy." Back to his regular accent.

He is crazy. They all are. I kept still. *Pirates on a sailing ship? In the US? They get sighted by a Coast Guard cutter and it's all over!*

"Relax, I'm not going to do anything," he whispered. "Nobody gets raped on my goddamn ship."

"Jack. You're a biker. Not a pirate," I whispered back.

"Yeah...right. Don't be too sure of that." he said in unsteady tones.

I looked at him. Maybe it was the light, but for a moment I thought his blue eyes were overlain with brown, and his hair had become long and black. I shook my head and he was back to sun bleached blond hair. *That was freaky.* Very nearly unseen-boats-in-the-fog creepy.

"We'll find some clothes for you in the morning." He pushed me towards the bed. "Get some sleep. Don't run off." He gave me a big grin, dimple peeking through the beard at me.

I waited until he left, then crawled into the bunk. He surely hadn't left me with any weapons. I fell asleep a hell of a lot quicker than I thought I would.

I woke up crammed into a corner of the bunk. Someone bigger and heavier than me was snoring, sprawled across the majority of the available space. This cabin had a porthole. Grayish daylight was filtering in. The cabin was rocking more than it had been when I feel asleep.

It was Jack, blond hair half out of its ponytail and flopped over his face. I woke up a bit more and realized he wasn't wearing any more clothes than I was. "Hogging the bed, ain't I?" He stretched and turned on his side.

"You're crazy, you know." I found it hard to believe it wasn't a dream.

He didn't laugh. "I know. This is crazy shit. The Coast Guard can't find us. Damn if I know why." Jack ran his hand over my face lightly.

"This isn't an old wooden boat. It's steel hulled. It should show up on radar. It must have a repeater and a locater." I looked around again.

"They won't be finding us, wench, don't ye worry!" Jack said. Again that flash of someone else talking.

"Um…"

"Cut it out." Jack threw an arm over his face and lay back again. "I am in charge of my own fucking body, dickbrain. Leave me alone for a few minutes!"

He was going crazy. I was trapped on a ship with a nutcase.

"Don't be scared, Dana. Just this thing going on. I'll explain later." He took a deep breath and opened his eyes up. "Right now, I got something else in mind."

I was back against the bunk with nowhere to go. "Jack, what's going on?"

"I'll explain later. I've been wishing I hadn't let you go for weeks." Jack pulled me closer and kissed me.

I didn't dare fight back, but I wasn't in the mood. He caught that after a minute or two.

"Damn. Stupid fucker scared you off. If I could reach him, I'd…" his voice trailed off.

"Get the lights knocked out, ye street scum!" a far different voice continued. In the half light Jack's hair went dark again. His eyes darkened too, impossibly.

"Jack?" I shivered. Just that slightest smell of rot again. I wanted to run, but there was nowhere to go.

"Bill Bones, lassie." Those dark eyes bored into me. They might not take no for an answer.

I couldn't argue that ridiculous name. Even his eyebrows had gone dark. Was there a sword hung on the edge of the bunk? He hadn't been wearing one before. What the hell? Maybe I was the one going crazy. "People don't shift from blond to dark in the middle of a conversation." I touched his face. His beard had changed too, from a blond fringe and mustache to a dark fu manchu mustache and goatee. The goatee was real. So was the five o'clock shadow around it. I wasn't just losing my mind. He felt alive, at least. Warm.

"Not without a bit of magic in the air," Bill agreed and caught my hand in his gently.

I wanted to say magic didn't exist. I couldn't. He was impossible, and playing with my fingers. As I hesitated, he pulled my hand to his lips and kissed it. His lips were as hot as I remembered. I shouldn't have been any more interested than I'd been a moment ago. His eyes laughed at me as he sucked my fingers into his mouth. That should not have been so sexy. I gasped.

"Laddie doesn't know how to get a lady in the mood," Bill whispered and nibbled his way up my arm.

I whimpered at the sensations. A little painful as he nipped, and then kissed the spots he'd nibbled on, making tingles that spread all down my body. I couldn't get a word of sensible objection out. His dark hair spread over my breasts as he reached my shoulder and continued onto my throat. I tried to grab his face, only to have my hands gently pushed back and held against the pillows. It wasn't painful, but I wouldn't be getting away.

No wonder people romanticized pirates! I thought and wriggled to touch more of him.

He smiled as I moved and let one of my hands go so he could stroke down my body. I didn't fight it when his hand explored over my mound and into my pussy. He ate my moans with his lips. I pushed my hand between us to try to touch him.

"No hurry, lassie. Himself's just fine," he murmured and pushed two fingers into me slowly.

I felt that over my whole body, a wave of pleasure, moving with the boat's motion and then his own, in and out, fucking me with those two big fingers. It was crazy, going along with someone being possessed by a pirate. But crazy or not, my thought process had gone completely south. All I could think about was how he felt and what he was doing.

He began to rub my clit with his thumb as he fingered me. I yipped and thrashed in surprise and pleasure. "Now, may I fuck ye?" He continued what he was doing.

I should have said no. I should have done a lot of things. "Oh god, please!" I tried to push his fingers deeper.

That deep voice, so different from Jack's, chuckled. "With a will!" He shifted, pushing my legs apart with his. His body had more scars than I remembered on Jack, and only one or two tattoos. His penis was big and quivering, drops of precum smeared on it. "Four hundred years in a grave and I'm that ready to go!" he said and plunged it into me roughly.

I screamed, not from the pain as I stretched to accommodate his flesh, but from the momentary glimpse of a skull superimposed over his face. Then he was back to dark hair and eyes, holding himself over me and thrusting as if his life depended on it.

"Move, lassie, it takes two bodies to make fucking!" Bill commanded.

I gasped and began to rotate my hips a little.

"More." He jammed into me violently, his balls slapping into me. Even his crotch hair was dark and much thicker than Jack's.

I grabbed him by the forearms and slammed him back with my hips.

"Oh yes, I want you, I want to watch you scream, little girlie." He twisted easily out of my grasp and grabbed me instead, pinning my arms to my sides and holding my shoulders in a bruising grip. I didn't dare stop moving, but couldn't do much held so tight.

It hurt, but something inside felt good too. I moaned as it began to build. He buried his face in my shoulder and his hands loosened just a little, so I could clutch him.

"Come on, lassie, give me your pleasure!" Bill whispered into my ears, letting go with one hand to push a finger over my clit again.

I screamed into orgasm at the one extra touch, bucking under him and clutching him hard, digging my fingers into his sides.

"Lord above and below!" He rode it and spurted, pumping into me in shuddering gasps, groaning as he emptied himself out.

We lay together, my eyes closed as I remembered how to breathe again.

"That fucker," Jack groaned in his usual voice.

Back to blond and tattooed, Jack looked more annoyed than anything else. I searched for something to say. What do you say to someone who just fucked you while being possessed by a four hundred year old pirate? "I hope you got to feel that," I ventured.

"Oh yeah. Every bit, while he laughed at me for not having the skills to get you in the mood." Jack groaned. "Fucking Don Juan the pirate."

I wriggled under him, trying to get room to breathe.

"And of course he didn't use a goddamn condom." Jack pulled out of me. "I hope to fuck you're on the pill, babe."

"Implant." I hadn't even thought about it, which was scary.

"Having a knocked-up broad on the impossible fucking pirate ship would be the absolute end." Jack groaned. "I'm clean, as far as I know."

That wasn't reassuring. "Me too," I grumbled. I'd had tests done monthly after Jerry started cheating on me.

Someone knocked on the door.

"Yeah?" Jack turned around to look that way.

"Uh, Cap'n, there's things doing you need to see," someone said through the door.

Jack sighed. "The fucking captain on this ship has no privacy at all. He's probably been waiting for us to finish for five minutes. And if it was critical, he'd have interrupted." He got up.

I sat up. The sword at the headboard was still there. I pointed at it.

"That was in the hold, fuck it all." Jack put his jeans on and glared at it. "Oh all right, I'll wear it." He buckled it on a baldric over his back. "There's some clothes there for you, Dana."

I saw the pile and got up on wobbly legs to dress.

The daylight filtered down reluctantly through a thick fog. Despite that, the ship sailed briskly along. Modern ships had radar and charts and could navigate blind, but there wasn't any sign of that. Jack had been happy to hear that I had a bit of tall ship experience and had assigned me to Elaine.

Elaine promptly took me up to show me the ropes, quite literally. That took us a while. The ship I'd honeymooned on had been smaller and designed to be easier to work for tourists.

"This is nuts." I looked down at the seadoos and guys with guns on the deck.

"Tell me about it." Elaine stared down too. "At least... they haven't bothered anybody. Or killed anyone except some drug dealers and those guys who were, um, kidnapping you."

I didn't really want to think about Raoul and Tony, left in the water to get eaten by the fish. She must have seen my expression.

"Did the captain, um...?" Elaine winced.

"No. Well, yes. But it wasn't rape." I felt my face get hot. Her eyes widened. "He dragged Joey off me the first day."

Joey did seem like that kind of asshole. "I guess Jack has a few scruples. I'm not so sure about Bill," I muttered. "I meant the whole Jack turning into a dead pirate named 'Bill Bones' with long black hair thing, actually," I went on, working my way up the mast with her.

"Oh, that." Elaine grimaced. "They all turn different sometimes. Joey gets red hair and a brogue you could cut with a knife." Her voice changed just a little. "And answers to Sean."

No. She didn't have a crush on the alter ego of a guy who'd tried to rape her? That was just as crazy as the fact that he had a pirate possessing him.

"Any idea what the hell is going on?" I climbed into the crow's nest with her.

"They dug up some bones and a treasure chest on the beach. Then they started turning into pirates. They stole our ship! Somehow or other nobody can find us," she summarized. "They keep mentioning a curse, but not what, and I don't dare ask."

"A curse? Oh my god. No, that's ridiculous." I wanted it to go away.

Elaine shot me a disgusted look. "More ridiculous than what? Magical fog, outlaw bikers possessed by pirates or something else?"

I didn't have an answer for that.

Someone down on deck was bawling out orders.

"Cap'n wants the topgallants let out. He's setting a new course." Elaine listened.

"Where to?"

"East North East?" Elaine puzzled. "Nova Scotia?" We got busy hanging more sail, with some help from one of the other interns, a very quiet guy with a darkly tanned face named Roger.

"Did you hear?" Roger whispered loudly. "Sable Island!"

Elaine's eyes bugged out.

"What?" I wondered where that was.

"It's off Nova Scotia, just a little sandspit with shoals and hundreds of old wrecks around it," Elaine answered. "Lots of legends about ghost ships and treasure, too." She sounded more excited than worried.

"Going to Sable Island makes being kidnapped better?" I asked.

"Uh. Well...I'm a history dork. I guess it does." Elaine blushed.

"Look lively up there!" someone yelled. We stopped chatting and went back to work.

When we finally went back down on deck, I didn't recognize any of the bikers. They were all looking a lot different. Even their clothes had shifted. Jack had turned into Bill and was up on the poop deck, listening to a discussion I couldn't quite hear.

"Don't mess around when they look like that," Elaine hissed. "They act just like they look. Flog you for insubordination."

"Did they?" I gasped.

"I talked back and got five lashes." She nodded, not looking as upset as I'd have thought.

"Holy shit." I pressed my lips together.

"It's healed." She shrugged. "Just stay out of the way and busy."

We managed that without any problems. Tall ships are busy places. I still didn't understand why the lovely steel hull and modern oceanographic equipment hadn't given the ship away.

"We will surely sail out of this fog sometime." I grumbled.

Elaine shook her head. "Not so far. I think they're keeping it up—or something is."

"You mean you've been in the fog for a month?" I boggled at her.

She nodded. "Creepy. Once in a while it lets up, but only if there's something to attack. Like last night. They thought it was drug smugglers."

"But they're pirates. Isn't everything prey?" The mystery noises in the fog came back to me. Had that been the pirates? Or somebody else? These guys didn't use row boats. They had seadoos. Wait, that had been the same afternoon. They wouldn't have even had the tall ship then. It hadn't been the Devil Fish. I shivered, glad to follow Elaine down to the galley to eat. Dinner was stew made from dried meat and rehydrated veggies. Not my usual dinner.

A coarse laugh stopped Elaine dead as she opened her mouth to answer. Joey, the scarred biker came down the hatch behind her. "We should be so fucking lucky, chicky," he snorted to me.

I winced. Would I get punished because he was sneaking around listening in on conversations?

Elaine bit her lips and bent her head over her dinner. Joey slid onto the bench beside her, close enough to touch. He quirked a smile at her. Her cheeks slowly reddened.

"No. We can't just go jump any old ships," Joey growled. "Just ones with scum like us on them. Kidnappers, drug dealers, probably fucking pirates if we go that far." He rubbed his scar thoughtfully.

He was looking modern. Perhaps I could get away with a question. "But aren't you, um, sharing bodies with old time pirates?" I ventured. The room went quiet around us.

"That's a nice fucking way to put it." He sighed. "No, the stupid fuckers got themselves cursed. And us, because we messed with their bones."

"Yeah, but you deserve it, Joey." Blond Jack joined us. "I'm too fucking lily white for this gig."

Joey snorted. "Oh yeah?"

"I kept us out of all kinds of shit and you know it." Jack helped himself to stew and slid in next to me. "I like to fight and drink and party. Not hurt people who ain't volunteered or sell illegal shit."

Joey nodded. "Yeah, you're Dudley fucking Do-Right compared to me. This could be an awesome gig. Nobody can catch us, we could steal shit and sell it anywhere!"

Jack's eyes went brown. "And then, Sean, ye know what would happen," Bill said slowly.

"Och, aye. Tha turdheaded scum I live in wants a pile of loot to buy wine— pardon me, weed and hot wenches." Sean threw an arm around Elaine, who flinched but didn't duck away. "He's beginning to see that we got what we need right here. I ain't one to complain that half the damn crew got tits!"

Bill chuckled. "Got to find some better rags for them."

"On a boat? I'd look pretty silly swinging around upside down tangled in the lines by a dress," I sputtered.

Bill raised an eyebrow. "For dinner, lassie. Much as I like watching you scramble around half naked aloft, I'd like to see you in silk too."

I felt my own cheeks get warm. His expression told me I wouldn't be wearing those silks long. "M-may I ask a question?"

Bill nodded slowly.

"What would happen if you really turned pirate?" I asked.

"We'd go on back to Hell, or so I think. Good deeds to balance the ill we did so long ago," Bill answered.

"But when does it end, Cap'n?" Sean asked with a grimace.

Bill shook his head and shrugged his shoulders. "That I can't say."

"D'ye want to spend the night with me?" Bill asked softly later, nudging me into a corner by the pilot house. He was still dark haired and wearing breeches and hose, a wool jacket with turned up sleeves and gold braid.

"I don't know," I said honestly.

Those dark eyes searched my face for a long moment. "Ye liked what ye got this morning." He ran his hands over me slowly.

I nodded. "You scare me, though, Cap'n."

"Good. If that's all, I'll see you in me cabin later. I like the sleeping arrangement, even if we do nothing else." He dismissed me with a nod.

As it turned out, I fell asleep long before he came in. Nor did we have time in the morning. A storm blew up, and we were desperately busy keeping the boat afloat, caught in the wrong quarter of the storm to escape it. I don't think anybody slept for two or three days. The storm blew us straight on a course for Sable Island, though. Nobody said, but it couldn't be just coincidence. The Coast Guard even trailed us for a while, but couldn't get close enough to sight us. Thirty-foot waves will do that.

"Damme, it's the shoals of Sable," Bill said loudly, using a spy glass. The storm had finally calmed, leaving us in a weirdly lit afternoon. "And they've claimed a new toll."

A broken fishing ship hung over rocks a half mile away. Someone fired off a flare.

The modern people of the crew looked hopeful. You had to answer that.

"It's a good deed, Cap'n," Sean snorted, massive arms folded over his chest.

Elaine grinned up at him from beside me.

"Aye. This'll be interesting. Anchor us here and launch boats and those wee seahorses," Bill ordered.

The fishermen were glad to see us. Their radio equipment and locaters had gone away with the other half of the boat. They were mostly Norwegian. Only one of the six survivors, the second mate, spoke more than a few words of English.

"Pirates?" he asked Bill, eyeing his dark coat and breeches.

Bill nodded. "Of a sort. We'll set ye on shore at Sable in a day or two. They tell me there's help to be found there."

The fisherman nodded. "Coast Guard. They hunt you."

Bill chuckled. "Any objections if we salvage from yon wreck?"

"Insurance cover that." The fisherman shrugged.

We had fish for dinner. And lunch the next day, while Jack slowly sailed through the shoals, getting out onto a seadoo and hunting for something.

"What he look for?" Sven asked Elaine.

"Our ship," big redheaded Sean said.

"But it'll be nothing but splinters and rust by this time," Elaine said with a grimace.

"Mind your tongue, lass." Sean stroked her back gently.

Elaine shivered. I'd seen her back when she hosed herself off one morning. Whoever had whipped her had left red scars across her entire back. Was it him? She wasn't cringing. If I had to guess, she was more turned on. "S-sorry, sir." She ducked her head. He kissed one of her shoulders.

The noise of that one seadoo cut out suddenly. Jack whistled loudly and indicated he wanted the ship moved with gestures. "Get out those toys to look at the bottom of the ocean!" He leaped up on the deck, back to Bill Bones in an instant.

I managed to squeeze into the science cabin to see what the cameras on the bottom were looking at. Elaine was running the robot, which had been her project before the pirates stole the ship. The monitor showed lumps and things on the bottom, just barely not rocks, coated with barnacles and hundreds of years of silt. I honestly couldn't make out a thing, but Bill and Sean were clearly excited, directing Elaine, who was scarcely less enthusiastic.

"This wreck is so old it's not even on the charts!" she burbled.

"There it is!" Sean put his hand over hers, stopping the movement of the joystick she controlled the robot with.

"My bonnie lassie." Bill pulled me closer. "The figurehead. A little saucy wench like you."

Elaine carefully directed the robot to blow jets of water over the lump. It emerged as a roughly carved female figure with big tits hanging out of her dress, hands on carved hips.

"Bring it up," Bill directed.

Elaine bit her lip and slowly complied. Disturbing the wreck was an awful thing, archeologically.

Twenty minutes later, the delicate chunk of wood slowly swung up over the side of the ship and into a waiting bucket of seawater.

"Now what, Cap'n?" one of the pirates asked.

"Now we fix it on this bonny ship and the Saucy Wench will come back, just as we have!" Bill said in great satisfaction.

BOOM! The entire ship rocked in reaction to the explosion. Something very big had just shot over us.

"Lookout!" Bill howled, picking himself up.

The lookout was gone. Several of the interns shrieked out loud at the spatter of blood where she'd been carried away in pieces. Bill and Sean ran across the deck. I followed. Were we rescued?

No. That wasn't a Coast Guard ship a quarter mile away. Long and sleek and fast looking, like a yacht gone evil, with quite modern guns at the front, back and sides.

"We are hosed." Sean had turned back to Joey quite abruptly. "They'll blow us out of the water in thirty seconds.

Blond Jack shook his head. "Pirate dude has a plan." That dimple peeked out. "Look like bikers, guys. Now here's what we do..."

"This had best work." Elaine's face was pale under her sunburn. "Run up the distress signal!" she shouted to another intern.

I kept the gun she'd handed me trained on Jack and Joey, face down on the deck, looking quite helpless tied up. Well, if we looked scared, nobody would be surprised.

The other ship drifted closer. Somebody on a bullhorn asked what our distress was. They'd shot somebody right off our deck and they were asking what our distress was? How stupid did they think we were?

Elaine picked up her own bullhorn. "We were kidnapped! Our radio is dead!"

"Stand by." The other ship came alongside. Close up, it turned out to be quite the yacht, armaments and all, manned by a dozen very scary looking guys of several different ethnics. Were they real pirates? Drug smugglers? If they weren't bad, they wouldn't have spotted us, if Jack was right. They really must think we were idiots.

Lines lashed the two boats together so a gang plank could run between the vessels. A big guy with a very swarthy Latin face came aboard. "Eh, you don't do so bad for a bunch of chiquitas!" He grinned down at the guys tied up all over the boat. Even the fishermen were tied up. I wasn't sure they understood a thing, but they knew a big gun when they saw it.

"Uh, thanks. That shot you fired let us get the drop on them," I said, my face sweating and bright red.

"Haha." He walked over to Jack. "I know you. Jack the Devil Fish! My old man said you were trouble."

Jack looked up and swore. "Fuck off."

For his pains, the Hispanic guy kicked him hard in the side. More of the scary guys swarmed on board.

"You girls shouldn't be holding those guns. Chiquita, the safety is still on." He took my gun from my hands. It was also empty, which he'd find out in a moment.

"Hey!" I tried to grab it back.

He cracked me efficiently in the side of the head with the butt and I fell back, seeing stars and pretended to be knocked out cold, draped over Jack and Joey.

"Now, drop the guns, chiquitas. The situation is under control." The Hispanic guy gestured with the gun and the other interns obligingly put their empty guns down.

"Yeah, it is." Jack and Joey leaped up with yells, followed by every other guy. I got knocked aside into a bulkhead and stayed there. Most of the other girls had ducked too. Elaine had grabbed a brass belaying pin which was already bloody. The pirates were out again, using sword and fists, too close to the thugs for their guns to be a lot of use. Despite that, a lot of bullets were flying around. Elaine shrieked loudly and dropped her belaying pin to clutch a shoulder.

Oh shit. A thug was lining up on her. I fought the screaming pain in my head, grabbed her belaying pin and tried to send his skull for a line drive. He went flying. Some of his skull went different directions than the rest of him.

"Fuck!" Elaine grabbed the guy's gun with her good hand.

Bill the pirate was grappling with the head thug up on the poop deck. Someone was lining up on them from the other ship.

"Elaine!" I pointed.

"Oh yeah?" She glared. She pointed the gun in her hands, but it clicked on an empty magazine. A loud blast and smoke startled all of us, washing over the thug. He turned and looked, clutching his chest as if he'd been hit. Where had that come from? The smoke trailed down towards the water,

Bill shouted above us and the thug came crashing down onto the deck. "Where the fuck did that come from?"

I ran to the rail in time to see a long rowboat pulling away.

A grayish man with seventeenth century clothes, like the pirates wore when they appeared, glared up as even more faded men rowed.

Bill the pirate stared down in surprise. "Well, if it ain't the fucking mutineer. I knew I should have shot you dead."

The graying, semi-transparent man pointed at Bill and slashed a finger across his throat. The rowboat faded into the fog.

"Now why the Hell would that old bastard be saving my life?" Bill murmured, looking over the rail into empty water, where smoke still trailed and I could smell the sulfurous stink of black powder.

I gasped and gagged on the taste and smell of blood. "Who?"

"Mad Dog Mulligan. He was after me treasure when we ran aground here and the goddamn Brits caught up with us. Didn't know he was still about." Bill's face flashed to the skull for an instant.

I shivered in the warm air. He might just be a ghost if nobody had found his bones.

"Can't shoot a wraith. We'll be seeing him again," Bill snarled and turned away from the water to look the situation over.

"Well, Cap'n, or should I say Commodore?" Sean

asked a few minutes later, looking up from the deck of the thugs' ship.

"Just Cap'n. Don't give me airs. Better we take a ship from them than this peaceful—and unarmed—little teaching ship." Bill shook his head.

"All right!" Sean turned back into Joey. "This is my kinda boat!"

"That too, man," Blond Jack agreed. "A little easier to go into ports in. Shift your gear, guys!"

The bikers moved gear, while one of the Norwegian fishermen cleaned Elaine's shoulder wound out. I focused on helping them, trying not to see the stack of bodies—two of which were bikers—heaped behind me. Would Jack leave me behind?

"You folks should manage to get to the Coast Guard on Sable," Jack said a few minutes later, after most of his guys had already embarked onto their new ship. The figurehead had gone with them, carefully packed into its bucket of cold preservative seawater.

Roger nodded. He'd earned a set of black eyes and a bullet graze across one cheek. "We'll radio them when you get clear."

"Nobody will believe the story." Jack grinned.

"What story?" Roger shrugged. "We got kidnapped by a bunch of biker thugs and then they found a better boat. I have no fucking idea why the Coast Guard and Navy couldn't home in on us. Though maybe we better heave the locater over, come to think of it."

And that's how it would be. We were kidnapped and forced to sail around with crazy bikers, who would be gone in five minutes. Never to be seen again. I'd be able to get Jerry charged with attempted murder and probably get all the damn money. I found myself biting a lip, trying not to cry. *I'm not little Dana the rich girl any more. I've killed people and fucked a four-hundred-year-old pirate ghost.*

"The chest is shifted, Cap'n." One of the bikers saluted, looking like a biker but sounding like a pirate.

Jack turned to me. "Dana?"

"Yes?" I stood up.

He caught my hand in his very gently and pulled it up to kiss. I thought of that morning that seemed so long ago. He stayed blond. "Come with us? Be my bitch, my wench?"

That would mean also taking his orders. Being accountable to a captain who would order floggings. The alternative was going back to Boston and getting in a lot of court battles and then being bored and alone until I found a boy toy or another rich asshole to date. "Do you love me?"

"What the fuck do you think, babe?" He grabbed me and kissed me hard, right up off my feet, to applause and laughter.

"O-okay," I gasped when he let me breathe.

"I guess that's it, then." He kept his arm around me, looking over the people still on the Victory.

"We come too." Sven stepped forward. "Not so many fish in the ocean these days, but lots of pirates and criminals."

"We could use you." Jack raised his eyebrows. "Get your stuff. We'll need some fishnets someday, I guess! You too, Dana." He gave me a push.

"You're crazy," Elaine said below deck.

"Yes," I agreed. "What's that next to you?"

"My seabag and chest. I'm crazy too," She grumbled.

I went over the gang plank carefully. The sea was getting rougher. Fog was drifting back in across the boats. I heard oars and looked around. Was that a ship's boat down there in the fog? I glared down but it disappeared into the fog.

"What are you playing at?" Sean shouted over my shoulder.

"Catch!" Elaine yelled and threw him her seabag.

"Nay. Go back, wench." Sean shook his head, letting me by but blocking her way.

"I don't trust you idiots to take care of that artifact!" Elaine said with a big grin.

"Bitch, I'm too old for you. I could be your fucking father!" Joey stood there instead of Sean, his shoulders and back knotted up in tension. The scar on his face stood out blood red.

"Like I give a shit?" Elaine snapped and swarmed across to kiss him.

"Well, put it like that," Joey mumbled and backed up, taking her sea chest and letting her aboard.

Jack put his arm around me. "Don't give me that look. It ain't one of your fucking smut novels, babe. We ain't sailing off into happily ever after."

"Good. I tried that. It was boring!" I smiled and snuggled up to him. To my pirate.

"Dunno what we'll do, babe, but it won't be boring!"

Booty Haul

By Danny Birt

Sand was getting in unmentionable places as the naked wizard hoofed it back to his beach bungalow. According to his useless guard imp, Sasisu, he would be lucky if he had enough time to get there before the invaders did.

"And why did you not see fit to give me warning earlier?" the wizard panted as he ran.

"I gave you your warning the instant they set foot on your island, Master Reef," the imp replied, smirking. "If they had continued sailing by, why, they wouldn't have been invaders, would they?"

"A vessel sailing under the Jolly Roger making straight for the island didn't give you a hint as to their intentions?" Coral demanded.

"There's nothing in our Pact about guarding you from intentions, Master Reef," Sasisu pointed out. Letting his smile grow teeth, the imp asked, "Would you care to renegotiate?"

"No," Coral growled. Making deals with the underworld was always difficult, and any alteration made to a Pact could have disastrous consequences. Coral knew that he had a very good thing going with Sasisu, and he dared not disturb the status quo. It was just that, even when an imp liked you, they did all they could to bend every rule and make life harder. It was in their blood...or whatever they had in place of blood. Imps, by definition, misbehaved.

Coral heard the first "Arr!" at the same time as he came in sight of his palm branch-roofed dwelling. He poured on the speed. Ignoring his staircase, he hurtled onto the back porch, sailed through the door, and got behind the screens that he used to delineate his bedroom from the rest of the bungalow.

"Where the heck is my robe?" he muttered, throwing drawers and chests open with waves of his hands.

So single-minded was his search for what he did not see that what he really was seeing did not register in his mind until several seconds had passed. He stopped. *Why are my drawers full of seashells instead of clothes?*

He whirled. "Sasisu, did you do something with my clothes?"

"Yes," Sasisu answered.

"Where are they?" he demanded.

The imp shook a finger. "Ah, ah, ah. You've had your three questions answered for today, Master. I don't have to answer any more, according to the Pact."

"And I believe the consequences of stealing from your master are in our Pact, too!" Coral threatened.

"Why, Master Reef, I'm hurt!" Sasisu protested in his best defense attorney voice. "I didn't steal them, I relocated them for safekeeping! You're being invaded, after all."

"Put them back right now, Sasisu!"

The imp rolled his eyes and made a magical gesture with three fingers. The seashells disappeared and were replaced by clothes in a very rumpled state.

Coral snatched up a turquoise robe and put it on. "Go away. We'll talk about this later," Coral promised his imp quietly as the first of the invaders arrived through the door.

By the sound of them, there must have been about a dozen men in the bungalow. Coral had no idea how they all fit—it was a small, one-room home that Coral had never planned on sharing with anyone. He had moved here from England for the solitude as much as the tropical weather, but now the level of noise was so unbearable that Coral was having a hard time thinking of a spell he could use to eject the barbarians without blemishing his beautiful bungalow.

Just then, Coral heard one of them say something that in all his years of experience he never would have expected such a man to say:

"Put that back!"

Coral was so shocked that he popped his head around the screen.

The pirates looked at Coral.

Coral looked at the pirates.

After none of the pirates made the first move, the rest of Coral emerged from behind the screen. He spoke. "I do beg your pardon, gentlemen, but have I been operating under a misconstrued belief when I assumed that you were corsairs?"

The pirates exchanged glances. One of the men with a patch over his eye essayed a tentative, "Arr?"

"My apologies. What I meant to inquire was, are you buccaneers?"

Still no one answered.

The wizard sighed. "Be ye pirates?" he asked.

"Arr!" shouted the group proudly.

"I be Patch, of the Topsy-Turvy. Be ye the Wizard of the Eastern Caribbean?" asked the one with the patch.

"Arr. Er... Aye. I are. Am. Oh, ow!" Coral clutched at his head. Speaking like a pirate was bringing him entirely too close to spraining his tongue.

Patch looked at him, unconvinced. "Be ye sure?"

"Indubitably." Coral felt better.

The pentasyllabic word seemed to reassure Patch as well. "Aye, then. We've found 'im, lads!" he announced.

"Arr!" the lads rejoined in jubilation.

"Ah, jolly good fun," Coral said, clasping his hands together in front of himself in preparation for a spell. "So I am being pirated then, am I?"

"Nay," answered Patch. "Ye be summoned to parlay."

Coral held back on his spell. "Parlay? You mean parley?"

Once again the pirates fell silent. A hurried, whispered council was held, wherein it was decided that parley was a small, green vegetable sometimes sprinkled on top of fancy meals to make them look fancier and cost more. The council broke up.

"Nay," said a pirate with a functionless but nonetheless archetypal wooden leg strapped over his shoulder. "It means the Cap'n wants to have words with ye."

Diplomatically, Coral said only, "I see. And which one of you is the Captain?"

"Nay, the Cap'n be back on the ship!" Patch said. "Sent us to fetch ye."

"Ah. Very well, then. Lead on, gentles," Coral said.

Patch drew his cutlass and pointed it dramatically at the door. "Back to the ship, lads!"

"Arr!" they shouted excitedly.

"And put him back down! He's not booty!" Patch added to four overly-enthusiastic crewmembers.

Coral was expecting the unexpected by now, but he was still caught unawares when he was introduced to the leader of the men.

As first mate, Patch was the first crewman up the rope ladder, and therefore the first on the deck of the Topsy-Turvy. "We've brought back the wizard, Cap'n!" he announced.

A query was made that Coral could not hear.

"What's yer name?" Patch hissed down to Coral.

"Coral Reef," he answered as he climbed.

Patch made a face like Coral had just offered him a piece of chocolate-dipped catfish.

"With a mother named Moon Dancer and a father named Gentle Flower, what chance did I have at getting a normal name?" Coral asked in his own defense.

"Still, 'Coral Reef' isn't very piratical!"

"I'm not a pirate."

Patch gave a sardonic smile. "Right." He turned back around. "Cap'n, I present to you Carl the Reefer. Carl, I—well, hurry it up, man! Carl, I'm presentin' you to Cap'n Jackie of the Topsy-Turvy."

"Carl" had his hands on the ship's rail and was in the midst of hauling himself onto the deck when he heard the name. He paused with one leg over the railing, and turned around to find himself nose-to-nose—figuratively speaking—with a tremendous expanse of very smooth, very curvaceous, very "touch me and die" skin. This was the first bosom that Coral had laid eyes on in years, but it was ample enough to make up for lost time.

Captain Jackie rolled her eyes and sighed, making Coral want to thank her. "Help him over," she said to her crew.

Patch and another pirate got Coral's other leg over the railing and propped him up. They understood what Coral was going through. They had gone through it themselves shortly before signing on under Captain Jackie, as had every other member of the crew.

Surreptitiously, Patch trod on Coral's foot, making the poor man look over at him. His gaze cleared after a moment, and Coral nodded ever so slightly to Patch. That must be what a mouse feels like when a cobra is hypnotizing it with its stare.

"Wizard of the Eastern Caribbean," Captain Jackie said. "I thank you for placing your trust in me and my crew in order to come to this parley."

Coral raised an eyebrow at the correct pronunciation of the world. A drop-dead beautiful and educated woman? This is a dangerous pirate vessel indeed!

"Madam, I am at your service," Coral responded with a flourish.

"Glad to hear it. May I invite you into my cabin?" Captain Jackie waved a hand toward the stern hatch.

"But of course."

They walked toward the hatch. As he went below, Coral heard someone on deck mutter, "Lucky git."

The wizard found the captain's cabin bedecked like a boudoir. He couldn't fault it for gaudiness, though. It was tastefully and richly done—so richly, in fact, that there was real gold paneling on almost every surface that wasn't already mahogany, satin, or marble.

So Captain Jackie is trying to tell me that she and her crew are very successful, Coral thought. What does she want of me?

Captain Jackie held up a crystal decanter. "Guava juice?"

"Yes, thank you."

She poured, and walked over to the couch upon which Coral had seated himself. "I hope the boys weren't too rambunctious with you. Normally I don't let them out of my sight unless we're on a raid, but I figured that if a wizard couldn't handle himself with my crew, he'd be of little use to me anyway."

"Your crewmen are nothing if not enthusiastic," he said, letting her draw whatever conclusions she could. "Just the sort of crew a captain would need to get most any job done."

"Yes, I'm proud of my boys," Captain Jackie agreed. "We've been extremely successful since I took over the Double-Tee."

"Rraak! Teetees! Teetees!"

Captain Jackie hurled a cracker at the parrot in the far corner. "Quiet, you."

Coral turned and contemplated the parrot. "Beautiful bird. Lovely plumage."

"Thanks," she said. "It comes from the Norwegian fjords. I sort of inherited him."

"From your father or your mother?"

"From the Black Island Buccaneers," she corrected him. "They thought they could take me and my crew. They were wrong. The captain's parrot found his way into my room during the fight, and he's stayed with me ever since."

"Ah."

Captain Jackie drained her juice in one marvelous quaff and set the glass aside. "Wizard, I have a proposition for you."

The parrot made a noise that was remarkably like a snicker.

Coral ignored the parrot. "Propose away."

"Join my crew for one mission, and you may have

two times an equal share of the bounty when the task is completed. We will return you to your island, and we will see to it that no harm comes to you."

"Ah, my dear captain, I must refuse," Coral said sadly. "To maintain the legitimacy of my business stature with the Crown, I cannot be seen operating under the Jolly Roger."

"You won't be seen."

"If even one person escapes—"

"We aren't attacking a soul."

Coral was watching her like a hawk, but as far as he could tell, she was not lying. "I think it only fair to inform you that I've heard of your vessel, Captain. I've also heard that you're one of the most powerful pirates in all the Caribbean. And a pirate doesn't get that way without starting with small villages and raiding up the food chain to the larger towns."

She shook her head. "Pirating from the poorest villages is like kicking a puppy while it's down, and besides, it's not very profitable. But pirating from only rich towns would punish them for being successful, and that would depress the local economy, lessening our later pickings."

My God, what a mind she has! "You pirate from merchants, then?"

"Nah. No challenge."

"So who's left to pirate from?"

"We only pirate from pirates."

Coral raised a dubious eyebrow. "Didn't I hear of the TT—"

"Rraak! Teetees! Teetees!"

"—taking a massive haul of gold from the royal tax ship last year?" Coral finished as Captain Jackie silently picked up a cracker and flung it like a shuriken at her bird, almost knocking it off its perch.

"Tithe-takers may be legalized pirates, but they're still pirates," she answered blithely.

"So you say!"

"You disagree?"

"I do!"

"Don't they take your gold?"

"Yes."

"Do you have any say in it?"

"No."

"If you refuse, aren't you punished?"

"Yes."

Captain Jackie shrugged. "Taxing is pirating."

"But citizens get things for their taxes!" Coral protested.

"Oh? Like what?"

"Like ships to chase down pirates, and jails to lock them in," he challenged.

"Ah. And next year if business has been poor and you can't pay your taxes, those same ships that you so blithely paid for will come to take you to those same jails you also paid for." She smiled as he realized he could not come up with any further argument. "Nice extortion system the government has set up, wouldn't you say?"

Coral nodded slowly. "I find I have to agree: taxation is legalized pirating."

"Thank you."

He cleared his throat. "So, to get back to business, what specific purpose do you have in including me in your crew? You are planning on attacking another pirate's stronghold?"

The Captain shook her head, her long locks swaying gently. "No, it's not another pirate we're after this time. It's our own stronghold."

He cocked his head. "I don't follow."

"Like I said, we're a highly successful crew. We've

apparently gotten too successful: we've amassed so much gold that our home attracted a dragon while we were gone."

Coral rubbed his chin. "I highly doubt that."

"Oh? Why?"

"The last confirmed sighting of a Greater Caribbean Drake was two decades ago. They've been going extinct almost since we Europeans began to sail these waters."

"So cannon fire does work against them?"

"It would if dragons stood still, but they don't. Plus, you can't point a cannon straight up, and that's where dragons like to attack from."

"Then why did they go extinct right when we started arriving?"

"Sort of like you and your crew, they were too successful. They'd attack a ship, eat everyone foolish enough to come on deck, and then their stomachs were so stuffed that they couldn't fly all the way back to their caves. They drowned."

Captain Jackie's grimace told Coral what she thought of his story. "That doesn't bode well for us," she muttered. She reached for her guava glass, then set it back down when she saw it was empty. "Maybe I could put it around that we've been sunk, and let someone else—no," she decided. "We couldn't let our reputation take a blow like that, even if it was falsified. So, Wizard of the Eastern Caribbean, we return to my original plan: you. How can you get rid of this dragon that's plundered us from behind?"

"Rraak! Plundered her bootie! Plundered her bootie!"

Captain Jackie tossed another cracker at the parrot, but this was obviously a halfhearted attempt since she did not even take her eyes off of Coral.

The wizard leaned back contemplatively. "The Greater

Caribbean Drake is a more simple-minded foe than its European counterparts, or its North or South American Continental cousins. You're sure it isn't a mainland drake that's flown out here looking for new territory?"

"No," the captain answered honestly. "How would we tell?"

"If its scales are forest green or desert brown or another dark color, it's camouflaged for mainland. If it's turquoise or ocean blue or another light color, it's Caribbean."

"I don't know, then," the captain said. "We were sailing back at nightfall, and the only reason we saw the dragon was because it flamed where it stood atop the volcano."

"Hmm," Coral said. "So it's full-grown, then."

"How's that?"

"Young drakes can't flame."

"Oh, I could have told you that much," she said. "It was easily the biggest lizard I've ever seen."

As if warned by some hard-earned sixth sense, the captain raised a stern warning finger toward the parrot. The bird closed its already opened beak with a click, and sort of shuffled on its perch, avoiding her gaze.

Coral made up his mind. "If it's full grown, I suppose I should get a few things from the bungalow to prepare to meet this beast."

For the first time since their meeting, Captain Jackie looked less than sure of herself. "That won't be possible."

"Why?"

"We're already underway."

Coral sat bolt-upright. "What?"

"We didn't want to waste any time. We're almost out of food and ammunition, and we obviously can't resupply from our stronghold."

"But... you kidnapped me!"

She shrugged.

"We were under parley!"

"We still are under parley—a very, very extended parley. We'll not harm you. In fact, we're going to do everything in our power to make sure you don't come to harm. That's in perfect accord with the rules of parley."

He shut his hanging jaw. "Did you ever consider becoming a lawyer instead of a pirate?" he asked peevishly.

"It was a toss-up," she admitted.

Coral sighed. "Well, if we can't go back, then I'm going to be a bit more limited in what I can be expected to do. I can certainly provide consultation on the matter, but a direct frontal attack is out of the question. Drakes can recognize magic use, and unless I could kill it with the first blast... well, let's just say that dragons have traditionally found wizards to be rare delicacies."

"So you're agreed to be a part of the crew?"

"Until we get your stronghold back, yes."

She smiled. "I will go write up our accord and bring it back for you to sign. My writing utensils are in a chest in my office, so—"

"Rraak! Her chest! Rraak! Her chest!"

Captain Jackie threw another cracker at the parrot. "Perverted bird," she muttered. "Why I keep you around, I'll never know."

"He certainly is a fowl," Coral agreed.

Jackie tsked at him. "I'll be back soon." She sashayed out of the room.

After the captain had left, Coral got up and idly wandered around the cabin, looking at little knickknacks. Suddenly he leapt at the parrot and seized it off its perch.

"Alright, who are you really?" he asked.

The parrot wriggled in his grasp. "Rraak! Man overboard! Man overboard!"

Coral scowled. "You're not fooling me, my fine feathered friend. Now spill!"

"Rraak! Abandon ship! Abandon—"

In an ominous voice, Coral said, "Finish that repetition, and Captain Jackie will return to find her beloved pet has eaten its last cracker."

The bird stopped struggling and looked at him. "She'd know it was you," it said.

"A little electricity applied to your brain would keep you perched on your perch for several days, looking perfectly healthy."

The parrot gave a little sigh. "Okay, you win. How'd you guess?"

"As a general rule, parrots don't search out conversational sexual innuendo. They just repeat whatever was said." Coral thought it wise to keep to himself that the spell on the parrot made it stick out like a sore thumb to his eyes. "So? Who are you?"

"Roland the Magnificent."

"Oh, pull the other one."

"I'm not lying," the parrot insisted.

"Roland the Magnificent was the—"

"—most powerful wizard of the North American Atlantic Seaboard," the parrot said. "Yes. That Roland."

"He was killed by pirates over a decade ago," Coral scoffed.

"Uh huh. Which pirates?"

"The Black Island—" Coral stopped.

"Buccaneers," the parrot finished for him. "I'd made a fair-weather charm for their ship, and apparently it failed. They came back in full force at a time when I wasn't prepared for them, so when they busted down my door and shot me, I traded minds with my parrot."

"And you haven't tried to change yourself back?"

"With what magical tools? And who would I trade bodies with? Besides, it's not like living in plain sight in the dressing chambers of a certain lovely lady hasn't had its benefits."

Coral had a flash of insight into what this parrot's life was like. "You really are disgusting, you know that?"

"Yes, I do," the parrot said in a smug little voice.

Trying to get the pirates to leave their ship behind and attack a foe with cunning alone was like asking a toddler to leave its spoon behind and eat a bowl of pudding with chopsticks.

"We couldn't sail in there, guns ablaze!" Coral said to the rowing pirates for the fifth time, silently congratulating himself for not yelling yet. "If you were going to do that, you wouldn't need me, would you?"

"But if we haven't the cannons, how can we fight?" one pirate complained.

"We won't be fighting; Carl will!" Patch intervened from behind Coral. "We've promised Carl twice our share of the booty, and I say we make him earn it!"

"And to work my magic, I need to be on dry land," Coral followed up. "That's why we've come around the back of the island, so I can disembark and learn of this dragon's weaknesses. Then we will attack."

"Arr!" shouted the rowboat's crew vengefully.

Soon the boat was skimming over shallow water. Coral put a foot over the side to disembark.

"Nay!" Patch said. "Back in the boat!"

"It's sufficiently shallow," Coral said.

"There be sharks in these waters," Patch intoned ominously.

"You don't say?" Coral said.

"I do say," Patch said. "The Cap'n had 'em imported from Spain. Stronghold wouldn't be very piratical without sharks."

"I see. And they don't swim away?"

"Nay. The Cap'n's got 'em on leashes."

Coral tried to picture what sharks on leashes would look like, but gave up.

The pirates soon got out and picked up the boat, with Coral in it, to bring it onto dry land. When they were quite sure that nothing but a walking shark—or a flying reptile—could get him, they let him out.

"I'll be gone for a while, gents," Coral said. "I'll need complete peace and quiet, so don't come looking in on me, even if you hear or see something worrisome. Okay?"

One pirate raised his hand.

"Yes?" Coral asked.

"What if we hear a damsel in distress?" the pirate asked. "The cap'n's laid down the law about helpin' damsels in distress."

"Oh, all right. If you hear a damsel in distress you may check on me, but otherwise do not. Agreed?"

"Arr!" shouted the pirates agreeably.

Coral walked away from the group, who began to play at cards. He walked behind a rocky formation on the beach and went a little bit further just to make sure that he would have a little warning if any of the pirates got curious. He had not been lying to the crew when he told them he needed to be on dry land – demons could not be summoned over water.

"Sasisu," Coral said quietly.

There was a flash and pop from behind him, then a voice spoke. "My Master calls?"

He turned around. "Yes. I need—"

Sasisu interrupted him. "I smell sulfur. You've been

cheating on me, haven't you? Haven't you?!" The little imp was dancing from foot to foot in anger.

"You're probably smelling the dragon I've been hired to kill," Coral said mildly.

Sasisu froze in place, one foot in the air. He sniffed again. He said, "Oh."

"Yes."

He put his other foot down. "I suppose I overreacted a bit, just now."

"You could say that."

"Sorry."

"That's all right."

"You were saying?" Sasisu asked politely.

"I need you to go scouting for me. Find out the dragon's habits, what its weaknesses are, that sort of thing."

"Scouting? I don't recall that being in our guardianship pact, Master Reef," Sasisu said. "Do you wish to renegotiate?"

"No," Coral said. "Either you'll do it, or I'll do it. Of course, if I do it and I get killed, you lose your gateway to the overworld."

The imp considered Coral's words. One of the reasons Sasisu had given such reasonable terms to Coral's master's master a hundred years ago in London was because he enjoyed making mischief on the surface world. He had even put in the pact that he was to be passed on to apprentices, to make sure he continued to have access to the world. But Coral had thus far not taken an apprentice, so he had to be safeguarded until he did.

Still, Sasisu couldn't let Coral know how desperate he was, so he had to play hard to get. "But you're putting me in mortal danger, Master!" he whined.

"Mortal?"

"Okay, okay. Just danger."

"If you're about to be munched, I give you permission to pop back to the underworld."

"How will I report back to you, then? You can only summon me once a day, according to the Pact."

"You could come back on your own."

"No I couldn't. You're my gateway, remember?"

Coral made a mental note to write that down. "If you have to disappear for a day, I'll call you tomorrow and you can tell me what happened, or I'll finish things today on my own."

"Okay, Master Reef. I'll be back soon," Sasisu said.

The little imp nimbly jumped away on his scouting mission. Coral set about making himself more comfortable for the wait.

Though he would never have admitted it to the pirates, Coral knew very little about dragons. Since dragons were so notoriously evil-tempered they were always killed at first sight, little was known about them besides where each species could best be pierced with various types of weapons. Indeed, they had been thought extinct until Columbus had returned to Europe with tales of Indian dragon gold, sparking the westward migration.

Coral had barely finished turning a pile of rocks into a pile of pillows to recline in by the time Sasisu returned.

"That was disturbingly fast," the wizard muttered.

"There's not much to tell," Sasisu said.

"I'll be the judge of that. Tell me what you know."

"No freebies, Master. You get three questions, and that's it," the imp reminded him.

Coral had been hoping that, given the unusual nature of the situation, his servant might have forgotten about that part of the Pact. No such luck.

"What's the easiest way to defeat this dragon?" Coral asked.

"Nuh-uh," Sasisu said. "You can only ask about observable facts, Master. Try again."

It was worth a try. "What are this dragon's weaknesses?"

"That's still a matter of opinion. Facts only, Master."

Coral rubbed his chin. "How about this: where exactly are his armor's weak spots?"

"All over, actually," Sasisu said.

He crossed his arms. "That's not an exact answer, so I rule that you haven't answered my question."

"No, I really meant it!" Sasisu insisted. "His skin is baby-soft."

"Now that is intriguing," Coral muttered. "I wonder if dragons have to shed their skin every once in a while, like snakes. Maybe that's why the dragon decided to roost here, so it could shed its skin and let its armor grow back before returning to wherever it came from. If that's the case, all we have to do is wait a few days and it will go away on its own! Sasisu," Coral said directly, "is there a shed dragon skin on this island?"

"Nope."

Coral gave him an intense stare. "I find it hard to believe that you've looked over the entire island already."

"Didn't have to," Sasisu said cheerfully. "I know the difference between old skin and new skin, and this guy has old skin. He's just taken care of it, is all. He moisturizes...though he was a little dry and scaly along his spine," the imp added thoughtfully. "Not that I would have mentioned it to him, of course—that would've just been rude."

"Like a dragon would mind being told that it's scaly," Coral said wryly.

Sasisu made a face at him. "Just ask your last question."

"Hm." Coral thought. So it's not shed its armor, but it's soft all over? How? Why?

But then his subconscious, which had been screaming at him for about ten seconds already, finally got a word in edgewise.

"Wait a second!" he snarled. "You talked with him!"

Sasisu realized his mistake too late. "Oops."

"Sasisu, if you told him of our presence and that leads to the death of a single human being, then according to the Pact, I—"

"No, no! He's not like that!" the imp said hastily, cowering back from Coral's mounting anger. "He wouldn't harm a fly; he's vegan! ...Oops."

"What does vegan mea—ahem," Coral coughed. He had almost asked a question that he knew he could ask some other day when there wasn't so much at stake. He had learned enough from Sasisu's slip for today: if he said he was a pacifist dragon then no matter how hard it was to believe, he could believe it in full faith.

"Look, don't say anything?" Sasisu pleaded. "I told him I wouldn't tell anybody; it just slipped out!"

The idea of going down and telling the dragon exactly what Sasisu had said was rather appealing to Coral, but then he had a better idea.

"Attend to my last question, Sasisu," Coral intoned. "Would this dragon be willing to peacefully meet with me to negotiate at precisely sunrise tomorrow?"

The imp looked confused. "How am I supposed to know that?"

Coral shrugged. "I don't care how you find out the answer to my question. But I want my answer before the day is over, or else you've broken our Pact."

"But that means I have to go ask him!" the little imp wailed. "That's not fair—according to the Pact, you can't give me commands that aren't already negotiated in the Pact!"

"It's not a command. If you want to learn the answer to my question some other way, feel free," Coral said with a faint smile. "However, since you've already admitted that you can talk with this dragon, I'm afraid I won't be able to believe you if you tell me you don't know."

The imp stood there, his jaw hanging down, his hairless eyebrows drawn together in denial. Then he turned around and, dragging his tail along the ground and giving many a sullen backward glance, Sasisu trudged toward the front of the island once more.

Coral looked at the tip of the sun on the horizon. We're right on time, he thought.

"You're sure about this, wizard?" Captain Jackie asked again, keeping pace with him as he trudged along the beach.

"Completely," he assured her.

"And all of this folderol is necessary?" she asked, gesturing to the piratical baggage train that was trailing them.

"Most necessary, yes." Coral had raided the Topsy-Turvy for supplies, not answering a single question as to why he needed such odds and ends.

"Even my horses?" she asked wistfully.

"It all starts with the horses," Coral said. "No horses, no plan."

"They were supposed to be breeding stock."

"You can get more with the gold from the stronghold."

She sighed. "But no horses could ever be as wonderful as Goldie and Cut Lass."

"It's no use getting sentimental about creatures that are about to die," he pointed out.

Captain Jackie pouted at him. "You wouldn't understand."

Coral knew that Jackie was doubly upset about losing her horses because her parrot had flown off while she was sleeping. He guessed that Roland the Magnificent had been worried Coral was going to tattle on him, and he had decided to seek safer harbor.

"Arr!" Leg said reverently.

Coral looked at him, then looked in the direction he was looking. Off to their right, there was a huge, black soot-rimed footprint the size of a horse.

"Yes, we're coming up on him now," he said quietly to the group of pirates. "Dragons are well known to leave huge carbon footprints in their environment."

Leg clutched at the decorative wooden leg strapped over his shoulder like it was a teddy bear.

"All right, Captain," Coral said. "Lead us to this hiding spot of yours."

Just inside the entrance to the yawning, open-air volcano cave where the pirates made harbor, there was a pile of boulders. Jackie motioned for everyone to duck behind them—she had seen the dragon where it lay by their buildings further inside the cave.

Once everyone was set, Coral said, "Okay. Release the horses."

The pirate that everyone affectionately called Azure-Beard—for no particular reason—let go of the horses' reins.

The horses stood there.

"Poke 'em," Coral said. "Get 'em to run out where the dragon will see them!"

But all their poking and prodding only resulted in a few tired plods.

Coral shook his head. "When you want something done right..." He stood tall and clapped his hands together over his head, making a sound like thunder.

The horses gave a terrified neigh and ran into the cave.

"About time," Coral muttered, and quickly settled back behind the rocks to watch with the rest of the pirates.

The dragon's sleepy head had risen at the sound of the thunder, but then it saw the horses running into its cave, and it became far more alert.

"Goodbye, Goldie and Cut Lass," Jackie whispered.

The dragon batted its massive tail on the floor of the cavern, and in a big, deep, manly voice, squealed, "Oh my God, ponies! How darling—you even have ribbons in your manes! I simply adore long hair! There, there, now, ponies, the thunder's gone. Come on, let's find you some nice lush grass in a pasture out back. You'd like that, wouldn't you? I'm on a strict fruit and veggie diet myself, but grass is just the thing for a growing pony."

The horses had stopped their forward progress when the voice started speaking, but because of the echoes in the cave, they had not been able to figure out from where the voice was coming. But when the dragon suddenly swooped down upon them, they bolted. Too slow—they were both were gently clutched and flown up and out, right past the cowering pirates. The dragon kept gossiping the entire time, his voice booming out over the whump, whump, whump of his beating wings.

Then both horses and the dragon were out of range of sight and sound.

The pirates stood up and busily avoided one another's gazes.

"Arr," said Patch uncomfortably, scratching under his patch.

"Arr?" Coral asked him. There was only so far his Arr lexicon could stretch.

"He's a fairy!"

"No, he's a dragon," Coral corrected him.

"But he's a flaming dragon!"

"Most dragons flame, yes."

"I meant—Oh, never mind what I meant. What I mean is, we can't kill a big sissy! It'd be like kickin' yer baby sister!"

"Arr," agreed the other pirates disconsolately.

"Well, what are we gonna do then?" Captain Jackie wailed. "This dragon has everything we own! He even took my horses!" she added vengefully.

"Quiet, I'm thinking," Coral demanded.

"Oh, yeah, a lot of good your brain did us back there!" Jackie rejoined. "You sacrificed poor Goldie and Cut Lass for nothing!"

"I didn't sacrifice them, and as it just so happens, we did get something. Something very precious."

"What?"

"Information."

"Information?" Patch scoffed. "That's not precious—ye can't spend it!"

"But you can use it," Coral said. "Think, mateys: what did that dragon say it liked to eat? Fruits and vegetables. If I'm right and this is the rare type of dragon I think it is, we are in considerable luck."

Captain Jackie's ears perked up at the word 'rare,' since it usually meant 'expensive.' "What type of dragon?"

"A dragon that is allergic to meat."

The pirates traded disbelieving looks.

"Arr?" asked Leg dubiously.

"Arr," Coral confirmed.

"And what if you're wrong?" Jackie demanded.

"I'd be willing to stake my life on it," Coral said.

Whump, whump, whump.

"Then here's your chance," Jackie said, and shoved him out in front of the rocks.

"What?"

"Go parley."

Coral looked panicked. "What happened to keeping me safe?"

"You're sure that you're safe. Good enough for me."

"But—"

"Poke him, boys!" Captain Jackie leered, throwing Coral's words back in his face. "Make him run into the cave, where the dragon can see him!"

"Arr!" the pirates said piratically. They drew their cutlasses.

"Oh, all right, fine," Coral muttered.

The pirates crouched back down behind the boulders as Coral made his way forward.

Right when the dragon winged its way over his head, Coral cried, "Good day!"

The dragon's head swung around to locate the source of the voice. This had the unintended effect of unbalancing the rest of the great lizard's body, and it tumbled from the air into the water.

"Augh! Oh, cold, cold, cold! Brr!" The dragon lurched its way toward the cave's beach, and once it was out it shook itself like a dog. Only then did it look at Coral suspiciously.

"You're a wizard," the dragon accused.

"Yes," Coral said amiably. "I'm a wizard who just said 'Good day' to you."

The dragon was brought up short. Obviously not wanting to look like he lacked manners, the dragon replied, "Well, good day to you, too."

They stared at each other, neither quite ready to make the next move.

"I was wonder—" the dragon said, right as Coral was saying "By chance do you—"

"Go ahead," Coral said.

"No, no, you first," the dragon demurred.

"I'm sensing a bit of distrust between the two of us," Coral said finally. "I think we got off on the wrong foot. If I promise to not magic you, will you promise to not eat me?"

"Eat you? I promise to not do that anyway!"

"Ah, I can see that we're going to get along just fine," Coral said. "My name is Coral."

"Siegfried."

They bowed to one another, Coral from the waist, Siegfried from the neck.

"So, what brings you to this island, Coral?" the dragon asked.

"My clients, actually. They say that there's a squatter in their buildings, the ones over there. Have you seen anyone around?" he asked in a roundabout, non-confrontational fashion.

"Oh, dear," Siegfried sighed. "They probably meant me. I hadn't realized that this place was still occupied; I had thought it abandoned."

"I'm afraid not," Coral admitted.

"And this is such a nice island, too," he said wistfully. "I'd liked it! It even has ponies."

"Are you saying you're leaving?" Coral asked.

"Of course," the dragon said. "I won't stay where I'm not wanted."

"Come now, I didn't say that!" Coral hastened to assure him.

"What are you doing?" Jackie hissed quietly from the boulders.

"Look," Coral said to Siegfried, ignoring Captain Jackie. "You're a dragon. Humans tend to avoid dragons, right? And my clients seem to have a problem keeping unwanted visitors out of their stronghold while they're gone. Perhaps they might be interested in having you stick around and watch their home for them. And in return, I bet my clients would be willing to share their beautiful island with you."

"Hmm," the dragon said, gently scratching its neck with purple-painted nails. "It would be nice to have someone to talk with. I wonder if they might even be willing to moisturize my spine for me every once in a while? I can keep my skin from getting dry and scaly everywhere else, but I just cannot reach my spine!"

"I think that could be arranged," Coral said. "So do we have an accord?"

The dragon cocked his huge head. "That's a pirate word."

"My clients are pirates," Coral admitted.

"But pirates aren't very nice."

"Oh, these pirates are."

Siegfried considered, then decided. "Well, if pirates can accept a nice dragon, why can't a dragon accept nice pirates?"

"So you accept?"

"I do."

Coral turned to the boulders. "Do you accept?"

Captain Jackie stood up. "We do."

"Then I formally bind this accord," Coral finished.

"Arr!" shouted the pirates ecstatically.

Coral turned to Siegfried and winked. Unnoticed by the rejoicing pirates, the dragon winked back.

Coral walked out of the cave into the darkening night to let the pirates and dragon get to know one another.

"Sasisu."

Flash. Pop. "Yes, Master Reef?"

"How are things back home?" he asked.

"Actually, you don't have a home anymore." Sasisu

shrugged. "Sorry."

"What? What happened?"

"While you had me running errands for you here on this island, another wizard moved in and took over your island," the little imp said. "Maybe that'll teach you to not misuse me."

"Who?" Coral demanded.

"Roland the Magnificent."

Coral let out a stream of curses. "I'm gonna have me some parrot soup when I get back!" he growled. "With crackers!"

"Um... wouldn't that sort of be cannibalism?"

"Do I look like I care?" Coral shouted.

"Sorry, Master, but you've already asked your three questions for today," Sasisu said.

"Oh, that's all right," the wizard muttered. "I didn't have any real questions to ask anyway."

"Didn't you want to know what vegan meant?"

"I already figured it out, when I was writing out our script with Siegfried this morning."

"Oh?"

"Yes. Vegans are boy dragons who like to mate with other boy dragons."

Sasisu hid his snicker at Coral's naiveté. "You would know best, Master."

Coral settled down to take in the night. He could not get back home until the pirates had restocked the Topsy-Turvy, and by the sounds of the party that was starting inside, that would not be happening tonight, and would definitely not be happening tomorrow morning. He started counting the stars as they each became visible, and he listened to the pirates inside trying to teach the world's first pirate dragon their theme song:

We Arr! Pirates

(TO THE TUNE OF "WE WILL ROCK YOU" BY QUEEN)

Buddy you're a cabin boy, just a kiddie with a plan,
gonna be a first mate some day
You got salt in your hair, your skin's so fair, always
sailing, but you're never sure to where.

We Arr! We Arr! Pirates!
We Arr! We Arr! Pirates!

Buddy you're a young man, crewman, sailin, gonna
pirate from your very first ship today
You got blood on your face, you big disgrace, waving
your cutlass all over the place.

We Arr! We Arr! Pirates!
We Arr! We Arr! Pirates!

Buddy you're an old man, captain, sailin, got your
booty and you're gonna retire today
You got a shirt made of lace, patch on your face, wave
the Jolly Roger all over the place.

We Arr! We Arr! Pirates!
We Arr! We Arr! Pirates!
We Arr! We Arr! Pirates!
We Arr! We Arr! Pirates!

The God-Empress Of The Sea

By James R. Stratton

"No!" Kiku shouted and stomped her foot. She wore only tabi socks, so her foot made little noise on the tatami mat, but she didn't care. Some things demanded action: stomping, shouting or even breaking things. "I'm trained in the way of the sword just like any of your samurai. I'm twelve summers old now and I'm ready to join you in battle. I won't stay behind this time!"

Father sat rigid on his cushion by the fire pit, a cup of tea clutched untasted in his fist. She could feel the waves of anger flashing from him like heat from a kiln but she met his glare with her own clenched-jawed stare. Two of the maids, old Aiko and her daughter Hinata, knelt by the soji screen across the room, huddled together, obviously hoping to be overlooked.

"You're my daughter and will do as I say. I will not have a girl child aboard my warship. Especially when I'm going into battle with a Spanish Man-of-War. It will be dangerous." Father planted his other fist on his thigh and gulped down his tea. "I'll hear nothing more on this."

Kiku stamped her foot again and scowled. "Oh no! I won't be brushed aside like this. You trained me for battle yourself. You know I'm ready. I won't be ignored just because I'm a girl." She crossed her arms across her chest and glared. Dressed in a girl child's bright floral kimono, with her long hair tied back with lacquered combs, Kiku realized she didn't look the part of a warrior ready for battle. *I don't care. I won't be forced into spending my days arranging flowers and serving tea. I'm the only child of Murakami Takeyoshi, samurai and captain of the Atake Bune. I will be a samurai.*

Father's reply was cut off by her mother rushing into the room. Plump and matronly, Mother nevertheless had a will of iron that was flashing in her eyes as she glared them both into silence. "Stop it, both of you."

She nodded to the maids huddled across the room. "You're upsetting the servants. You are so loud half the village can hear you."

Father pursed his lips and sat up straight. "Then get your daughter under control. She is demanding to join me on this next voyage. It will be dangerous. I can't be fussing with a little girl while I'm hunting Spaniards on the open sea."

"Oh?" Mother also drew herself up and stared until Father, captain of a war galley, flushed and fidgeted. "I warned you of this when you insisted she should be trained on the bow and spear. What did you expect? You've said yourself she can match any of your own samurai with either. And she's of age now. The only reason she asks to prove herself in battle is because you put the idea in her head."

Mother's gaze swung around, pinning Kiku where she stood. Kiku felt her face flush hot and looked away. "But that does not mean she should be treated any different than any other young samurai. If she wants to see what a samurai's life is like, so be it. And I'll expect you to be very demanding with her, to show your men you do not play favorites."

Father's face twisted up. "But this voyage will be dangerous. She could be hurt."

Mother drew a breath and blew a shuddering puff of air out her cheeks, her eyes squinted up with worry. "I know. But she is your sole heir. She must prove her worth one way or another if she is to carry on the family name."

Father bowed his head and nodded. "I do not like it, but if you insist."

"Kiku-san, what're you doing? You'll ruin the fletches on that arrow!"

She froze in mid-scratch and slid the arrow from under her armor. When she turned to Father, the wind-driven rain splattered across her face and trickled down into her quilted undercoat.

She bowed carefully on the heaving aft-deck and wiped her eyes. "Sorry, but this rain's got my skin itching horribly. Why are we putting to sea in the middle of a squall? Mother Otsu says this storm'll end by first light. The Spanish galleon will be there in the morning. And why are we hunting the San Juan Bautista at all? It's armed with cannons and carries a squad of marine guards. We'll have a hard fight taking that ship."

Captain Murakami glared. Like her, Father was dressed in iron helm and lacquered armor, but with two samurai swords thrust through his sash. Kiku glanced at the matched swords bitterly before she looked away and bowed. When she asked, Father had refused to allow her carry any edged weapon. "You have not earned the right. Your bow will be enough."

Father stared until she returned his gaze red-faced.

"Girl, you'll address me as Captain Murakami Takeyoshi when we're at sea. You can save that tone for home! You're just another crew member when you're on board the Ataki Bune." He paused until Kiku looked up. "We chase the Spanish galleon on orders. Lord Yamada has gotten word that the Christian Daimyos are plotting with the Spaniards to make war on the other Daimyo. A written agreement is being carried to the Spanish king aboard the San Juan Bautista. If we can seize the document, we can bring proof to the Emperor's Court and put an end to the foreigner's influence."

He wiped away the water running down his face. "So you'll just have to ignore the rain like the rest of us. We're all as wet as you." He turned and nodded to the bustling samurai on the main deck below. The rowers were setting the oars as the samurai, dressed in full armor, tied baskets of weapons bundled in oilcloth to the railing.

Kiku nodded. "Yes, sir."

"And this storm works in our favor. That's the only reason the San Juan Bautista didn't sail on the tide this morning. Our best chance is to come upon the Spaniards while they are anchored waiting for the tide."

Captain Murakami stepped to the aft-deck rail and raised his red battle fan.

"Hai!" he shouted and the samurai below turned. "Cast off. We need to catch the San Juan Bautista before first light or we'll miss her. Captain Vizcaino will sail on the morning tide. And I don't fancy our chances besting a three-masted Spanish man-of-war under sail on the open sea. That means you'll be pulling hard in bad weather all night if we're going to come alongside before dawn. Are you with me?"

The samurai raised their fists and shouted, "Hai! Command us, Lord."

Captain Murakami bowed and his men returned it. "Go!" he shouted and returned to the helm as the crew pushed off.

The rowers lowered their oars and pulled as the squad leaders chanted a shanty. The galley surged forward, throwing Kiku off balance.

Captain Murakami caught her by the arm. "Careful, child. I can't have you injured before we even leave port. Now that we're underway, I can let you in on a secret." He flashed her a toothy grin. "You see, it wasn't just luck this storm blew in as the Spaniards prepared to sail. It was arranged. Now go below and make sure Mother Otsu is comfortable. If you're nice, she'll explain how she managed it."

Kiku stared. "What? She caused this storm?"

"Hush!" Father glanced around. "Not another word. My men will follow me into the Buddha's hell if I order it, but they're superstitious as old women. Talk of weather spells and Shinto magic will upset them. Now go."

Kiku paused in the doorway of the main cabin. Mother Otsu slumped in a chair, snoring. Kiku breathed a sigh and eased the door shut.

The old witch scared her bloodless. Kiku knew the horror stories she'd heard about witches and evil spells as a child were exaggerated, but even Father treated Mother Otsu with a deference he usually reserved for the Daimyo. And the woman herself was wretched to be with.

Kiku took a breath and shuddered. From the greasy, gray hair on the top of the witch's head to the dirt-crusted soles of her feet, she was the personification of filth. Even across the cabin, Kiku's eyes were watering from the smell. Like cold fog, the stench rolled over her so Kiku felt the foulness on her skin, making her itch even more than the rain. She tried to force the smell from her mind and failed, finally gasping open-mouthed and covering her nose with her sleeve.

The witch jerked up and her dark eyes seized the girl.

Kiku attempted a smile. "Captain Murakami sent me to see if you needed anything. I'm Kiku."

The witch unfolded a gap-toothed smile that twisted her face into a mass of wrinkles. "You'd be Murakami Kiku, the captain's daughter, eh? He said you may join us. Well, this bloody chair is torturing my poor old bones like a rack. I need a back rub or I'll not be able to stand. There's a robe in that trunk. Get out of those wet things."

Kiku hid her grimace behind a bow.

Kiku poured Mother Otsu more tea and returned the pot to the fire box. Ignoring the other chair, Kiku settled on a cushion.

"Father says you conjured this storm and spied out the San Juan Bautista's anchorage with your magic. Is that true?"

Mother Otsu frowned squint-eyed, heaved herself up and shuffled to a deep bowl of water on a stand. "I didn't create this storm, the God-Emperess of the Sea did after I asked her nicely. I suspect Lady Amaterasu enjoys plaguing mortals when she can, so I didn't have to ask too hard." She leaned over the bowl and chanted, then turned away with a smile. "And she was happy to tell me where the Spaniards dropped anchor, since the fools insist on ignoring her. She smashes their ships with wind and waves, and all the Southern Barbarians do is wail to their tortured god. Idiots!"

The old woman sank back in her chair with a grunt and slurped tea. "So why are you here? Captain Murakami doesn't need little girls to fight the Southern Barbarians."

Kiku hid her anger by examining her clothes drying over the sand-filled fire pit. "I could if I need to. I'm trained with spear and bow. I could brush aside your hair with an arrow at thirty paces without cutting you. And I'm trained as a samurai, daughter of Murakami

Takeyoshi. I'm here because I'm needed, just like his other warriors." Kiku yawned.

The old woman blew a puff of air out her cheeks and grinned. "If you say so. But you won't be needed for a while. There's a futon over there." Mother Otsu nodded to the far corner. "Get some sleep. I'll wake you when it's time."

The wind shrieked as rain stung Kiku's face, but she didn't notice. She stood next to Mother Otsu, gripping the rail against the heaving seas as the witch muttered and growled. Each time the old woman growled the wind howled back. Kiku shivered as the wind and the witch sang together. *Is she really talking to someone?*

Father pulled himself up the stair and walked hand-over-hand along the rail to Kiku. "The galleon is ahead. Make sure Mother Otsu stays safe. Have you kept your bow dry? Good! Don't hesitate if any of the Spanish scum board. Kill them!"

Kiku gulped and nodded.

He reached around Kiku and grasped the witch's shoulder. "The Spanish crew will be below decks. Give us ten strokes of the oars, and then end the wind. We'll need calm to fix grapples."

Mother Otsu nodded without halting her chanting.

A dark shape dotted with lights emerged from the rain on the third stroke of the oars. On the sixth, a three-masted ship loomed ahead, with lights gleaming from cabin windows and great lanterns blazing fore and aft. The main deck towered over the galley.

On stroke ten, the galley slid alongside and the samurai stepped forward with grapples and ropes in hand. Captain Murakami shouted and the rowers backpedaled, slowing the galley, then pulled in their oars.

At the same time, Mother Otsu sighed and shook

herself like a wet, muddy dog, spraying Kiku. Before Kiku could wipe her face clean, the wind eased and died.

The samurai hurled grapples over the galleon's rail and tugged them tight as the rowers took up the ropes, hauling until the galley bumped the side of the galleon. As the rowers tied the galley to the galleon, the samurai yanked out bows and arrows from oilskins and lined up with arrows notched.

An agonizing quiet descended. All Kiku could hear was the slap of the waves against the hull and the thump of the two ships rocking together. The rowers climbed hand-over-hand up the ropes with short swords gripped in their teeth, and hung like spiders below the galleon's rail. Beside Kiku, Mother Otsu giggled and clapped her hands like a little child. Ten breaths Kiku counted, the samurai poised to rake the galleon's deck with deadly fire, the rowers braced against the galleon's side waiting to swarm onboard.

Kiku stiffened at a voice above, Spanish words shouted in anger. "Roberto, you're insane! We're at sea in the middle of a storm. You hear pirates in every creak of the rigging. We bumped a log or something."

Silhouettes appeared overhead along the rail. Father waved his war fan and twenty bows twanged. The Spaniards fell backwards, screaming as the rowers flew over the rail. Father waved his fan again and half the remaining samurai swarmed up the ropes with bows and quivers strapped across their backs and clambered over the rail. The others stood with arrows drawn until their mates boarded, shouldered their bows and followed. Kiku watched open-mouthed as her father scrambled hand over hand up a rope and vaulted over the rail. Shouts and the clash of steel resounded from the deck of the galleon.

Kiku glanced around the Atake Bune, then remembered her father's orders. Overhead, shapes appeared at the rail in the flickering light of the great lanterns as she tugged at Mother Otsu's arm. "We've got to get out of sight. The Spaniards will attack if they see us."

Mother Otsu grumbled but followed.

Kiku spun at a shout from overhead and saw a man hurtling down. Another followed with a whoop. Kiku yanked out her bow and notched an arrow as the men landed with a thump, but didn't shoot. She could hear the Spaniards cursing, but could only see vague shapes in the dark, nothing she could target. She froze, waiting.

Mother Otsu gripped her shoulder. "Be ready," she whispered.

The witch muttered and light flared overhead. The two Spaniards stared squint-eyed, one in helm and armor kneeling with his hand pressed against the deck, the other unarmored but armed with a cutlass. Kiku inhaled as she considered.

Which man first? The kneeling man's armor's in the way, but they'll both be on me if I don't get them both. She glanced back and forth and aimed. *That one!*

Kiku exhaled and shot the kneeling man through the hand, pinning it to the deck. He screamed and clutched the shaft as she notched another arrow. The sailor glanced down then charged, howling, with cutlass raised. She shot, piercing his eye socket, splitting his brain, cutting off his shout as he fell, already dead. Behind him, the other knelt, gripping his pierced hand with his good one, dragging it up the arrow shaft. He looked up with tears streaming down his face and moaned when he saw her. "Please," he said and raised his good hand, pleading. Kiku shot again. Her arrow slammed into his throat above his breastplate. The Spaniard rocked back, gargling blood, then slumped down with his hand still nailed to the deck.

Kiku's heartbeat thundered as she glared about for enemies. She jumped when Mother Otsu touched her shoulder. "Well done!" the old woman whispered. The witch-light flickered and vanished. "You got them. We're safe." The darkness pressed in as Kiku forced herself to breathe, her heart hammering and the red haze of battle coloring her vision.

Kiku grabbed the witch's hand. "Come on, we need to get below before more board."

The old woman jerked back, standing firm. "No, we stay. If they board the Ataki Bune again, they'll scuttle her and we'll be stranded until another Spanish ship comes. We'll stand guard here."

Kiku breathed deep and nodded. *Yes, if we lose the Ataki Bune, we'll never make it back to port.*

She glanced up, looking for signs of how the fight was going, but couldn't see anything. A boom thundered overhead. Others followed. *They've got muskets!*

The Spanish guns were both loathed and sought after by most Daimyos. Samurai saw them as a graceless way to fight, a weapon any peasant could use. But the advantage they gave was too great to ignore. *Father and his men will be slaughtered!*

She glanced at the old witch and glared. "I've got to help them! Wait here." The old woman scowled but nodded.

Kiku slipped her bow onto her back and clambered up a rope to the railing. Through the rail all she could see was a chaotic crowd of surging Spaniards on the main deck. To the left, she could see that the raised aft deck was clear. Swinging along the rail, Kiku reached the aft deck and climbed onboard.

Below a mob of Spaniards with swords and armed with muskets faced Father and his men across the deck. Several samurai sprawled between with ghastly wounds to head and chest. Blue smoke drifted across the deck as the musketeers rammed ball and powder into their guns, preparing another volley. The sailors stood behind, shouting and shaking their cutlasses.

She could see Father and his samurai were gathering themselves for a charge when the musketeers shouldered their guns. *They'll run into the teeth of the guns. And die.* Kiku inhaled and notched an arrow. *Who first?*

Then a Spaniard in a gleaming silver helm raised his sword and shouted, "Take aim!" Kiku exhaled and shot him just under his helm, in the ear. The arrow tore through his head, half emerging on the other side. He pirouetted around to look, frozen with sword raised, looking up at her, puzzled, then toppled over. Kiku notched and shot again as the sailors below turned, shouting. One musketeer fired, sending needle-sharp splinters from the railing whizzing past her head. Kiku skipped sideways, loosing arrows as Spaniards fell screaming.

The musketeers fired a thundering volley, sending shot whining around her like angry bees as blue gunsmoke rolled over her. When she could see again, the musketeers were ramming powder and shot into their weapons. Kiku slapped her quiver for another arrow and found none. *Empty!* Kiku shook with battle-rage as she looked for another weapon, anything she could use.

All she saw was a sailor with cutlass mounting the stair, grinning. *And I'm unarmed.* Kiku took a breath and stepped to the rail. *So this is it, how I'll end my life? At least I'll show them how a warriors dies.* Across the main deck she caught her father's eye, smiled and bowed.

His face twisted. "No!" He raised his fan. "Now, at them, before they regroup!" The samurai shouted her name and surged forward. They were among the Spaniards with swords drawn before the sailors could turn.

Kiku stared at the swirling battle below, refusing to look to the sailor coming for her. *I can't let him see me afraid!* She stood with head down, hands gripping the rail white knuckled, waiting for the death-blow. She gasped when she was jerked backwards by gnarled hands as a blazing ball of light flew at the sailor. He backpeddled across the deck slashing at it with his sword.

"Good job!" Mother Otsu said. "But now I need you out of the way. I can summon help. Watch and learn!"

Mother Otsu began shouting and dancing, and the wind answered with shrieking force. From the swirling sea below a rumbling roar rose and the surface roiled. The galleon jerked sideways as the green seawater bulged and a massive head burst forth. Kiku stared into a mouth lined with a hedge of impossibly white teeth as the beast from below—no, the Empress of the Sea, Kiku corrected herself—rose like a waterspout, sea foam cascading down its long, scaled neck.

A dragon! A dragon as big as our galley! But it was a god as well, she saw, its scales glowing silver and red, its eyes flashing with fire from within. It crashed down until its huge equine head hovered at deck-level facing Mother Otsu. Black whip-like barbs from around its mouth twitched over the rail, enclosing the witch in a living cage.

"Lady Amaterasu, welcome!" the witch shouted as she clapped and bowed. "I am your servant, Fujimoto Otsu. I called you for help with these wretched Southern Barbarians. They're yours if you wish!"

The God-Empress rumbled deep in her chest and the long neck swiveled until the dragon faced the sailor on the stair, sword still raised against the flitting mote of light. The Spaniard froze, mouse before the snake, and then the great head snapped forward, jaws agape. The sailor howled as the dragon-god rose again with him gripped in her teeth, then his body spasmed as the dragon bore down until the sailor's ribs popped and crunched. Lady Amaterasu threw her head back and the sailor slid from sight, one hand scrabbling at the roof of the dragon's mouth as the other clutched a crucifix. A bulge coursed down the beast's long neck.

Mother Otsu laughed and danced. "There!" she shouted, pointing to the sailors below. "They are all yours, my Lady!" Father and his men stared wide-eyed and backpedaled across the deck, leaving the Spaniards huddled against the rail below the aft deck.

Lady Amaterasu's head arched back as her eyes flashed, pausing far above as she surveyed the trembling Spaniards, then she swooped down with fangs bared. Kiku jerked her gaze away as the Spaniards cried out and hid their faces in their hands.

Kiku panted open-mouthed, struggling to keep the smell of the dead from her senses. Father sat on his camp stool in the growing light of dawn, his armor scarred with sword cuts. Kiku could see he was hurting, but he sat tall, one fist planted on his thigh while waving his battle fan as if at a picnic. The heads of a dozen Spaniards stood upright before him on spikes so he could view their death grimaces. Grinning and nodding, he examined each in turn while his men stood by whispering and laughing. Kiku didn't understand why samurai enjoyed this dark ritual, or how they could stomach the smell, but it was a tradition always observed after battle. The viewing of the dead was interrupted when a squad of rowers emerged from below, shouting and dragging an ironbound chest.

"We found it hidden under the floorboards in the captain's cabin, Lord, just where you thought it would be. But there was no key." The chest was heavy brown iron, sealed with a lock as big as Kiku's hand.

Father blew a puff of air out his cheeks and called out, "Rikio, open this!"

A giant rower with muscles bulging strode over with a sledge balanced on his shoulder. Grinning, he raised the sledge high, and struck the hinges so hard Kiku felt the crack in her chest. After a few measured blows, the hinges shattered.

Captain Murakami sorted through clothes, candlesticks and bottles, before seizing up a silk-wrapped package with a shout.

Standing next to him, Kiku recognized the seal of the Christian Daimyo Date Masumune of Sendai Province sealing the package. Father slit the silk wrapper and flipped through a sheath of documents, pausing to read several, before smiling.

He raised the parchments high. "This is the proof we sought, what we came for. Lord Date is writing to King Philippe of Spain to ask for Spanish guns and conquistadors, to aid in a Holy Christian war against our Lord and many others. He would bring foreign armies to our land to use against us. There is much more here, all the proof our Daimyo needs to bring to the Emperor. Now we must work fast and salvage whatever we can. By midday, I want this vessel scuttled, and all traces of the battle buried in the deep with it. The Spaniards must not know of this until we choose to make it known. Go!"

Father turned as the men hustled about, dragging bales and barrels from below.

Smiling, he took her hand. "Kiku-san, you have proven yourself more than worthy of the rank of samurai. I plan to send word about this with Lord Yamada as soon as we reach port. I am proud of you. But I think this is enough. You have had your adventure. You duty to your family, and your Lord, will not allow any more of this. When we get home, I want to hear nothing more about you going into battle. You are my daughter and need to think about your life from here on. I need grandsons, heirs to carry on my name. You will marry and raise a family, keep your husband's house, be a good mother and wife. Eh?" He held her gaze with his own, squeezing her hand for emphasis.

Kiku felt father's words as if they were needles thrust

into her breast. *So that's it? I'm to be relegated to the kitchen and bedchamber now?* But she knew she had no choice. *I'm just a girl child, even if my father is an important samurai. I can't follow the way of the sword without his approval, and I won't shame him by refusing to obey.* Her gaze dropped to the deck even as tears welled. She drew a shuddering breath, preparing to say, "Yes, Father, if that's what you want." The words would burn in her throat, but had to be said.

A rumbling roar cut her off. All aboard froze and stared to the far rail where Mother Otsu still danced. The dragon rose slow and silent, towering over the deck.

"Lady Amaterasu, I thought you had left us. Welcome! What can I do?" The witch's face fell when the great dragon slid over the rail and coursed across the deck to halt before Kiku. She froze, hands trembling and breath caught in her throat, as the glowing eyes held her.

Behind her, Kiku heard her father hiss as he stood and grabbed at his sword. Kiku waved him back with one hand. "Please, Father, don't. I'm sure she means me no harm." She heard him step back.

The great muzzle loomed closer, gleaming white teeth showing behind the dragon's lips. The dragon snorted once, blowing her hair back, as its black barbs arched around her, touching her lightly, enfolding her in a living cage. Again she heard the Goddess' thunder, not words, but clear nevertheless. The Goddess was pleased with her strength, her courage. Kiku was to seek her own way in life, regardless of what others may want for her. She must choose.

Trembling Kiku bowed. "Thank you, Lady Amaterasu."

The dragon's gaze shifted for a moment and her father staggered, but then stood tall and nodded. Without further sign, the dragon pulled away and slid over the side, disappearing into the churning waters.

When she turned to face her father, he was staring. She

smiled. *I'm his darling daughter, he is my father. But he knows now, I must choose.* Kiku drew a breath. *But choose what?* She walked over and hugged him. *Father will know. He'll help me find the right path.*

Thar Be Magic

By Laurel Anne Hill

Myra set her ice chest down with a thud next to her suitcase on the porch. Rain tapped the overhang above her head. Damn Karl! He'd expended all his political capital this time. The bastard would never change. She pushed the creaky door to her vacation cottage open, fumbled in the dark and ripped a small framed photo off the wall.

"Rot in hell." She tossed Karl's portrait into a puddle in the unlit driveway. "Even Dutchie's better than you and he nearly drowned me twice."

Water lapped the cove's protected beach on the other side of the private roadway. The persistent rhythms of rain and tide evoked so many memories of those first weekends here with Karl. Eight years ago, her marriage to him had held such promise. Where had passion's magic gone? She sagged down to the door stoop and cried.

Such a fine pleasure to discover love and sensuality on a sofa or moonlit beach. Body chemistry could cast such marvelous enchanting spells. Now all that loveliness was gone, wasn't it? Washed away by Karl's meandering affections. The time to make a decision about her errant husband had finally arrived. No, after three affairs, it was long overdue. A new rush of tears flowed.

Myra stood. She stepped inside the darkened cottage and inhaled a damp, musty smell. A moldy cabin made an appropriate metaphor for a decomposing relationship. She sniffled. Not like she hadn't tried to make their marriage work. Black lace garters and fishnet stockings. Gourmet dining at home with her as dessert. What more could Karl have wanted? Myra winced. Obviously, this time, he'd wanted that brunette bimbo with the sultry eyes and pixie hairdo.

Why couldn't real men remain as faithful as imaginary ones? Captain. Her hero. He knew how to make her feel pretty and loved. Myra blew her nose. Maybe Captain would materialize tonight. He hadn't visited since before her wedding.

She didn't care to see Captain's dear old cohort, though, the apparition of the Dead Dutchman. Oh, Dutchie was a good one for telling scary stories under the bedcovers and giving her a mellow, warm shiver when she was safe in her own room, but he always smelled of rotting seaweed. Captain was better for hugging, despite the strong odor of rum on his frockcoat and mustache. Besides, Dutchie represented her warped fascination with the sanctuary of death. She dared not trust him around this cove, not after all that had happened.

Rather pathetic for a forty-year-old woman to sob on the shoulders of her childhood imaginary friends. Myra shrugged and flipped the light switch. No response. She hadn't anticipated a power outage. Probably the work of rats. She'd call an electrician and an exterminator tomorrow. Better get the BlackBerry out of her Lexus before bedtime.

Myra shivered. A fire would be nice. Karl had built her lots of cozy fires on weekend trips to this cottage. Daddy had, too. The corners of her eyes stung. She'd sobbed so much since the party yesterday, she ought to have used up all her tears. Oh, Karl.

"You asinine pig," she had shouted at him less than twenty-four hours ago. "You'd screw the neighbor's pony. You'll never see one dime of my inheritance from Daddy. Not one penny."

Daddy. Karl had once reminded her so much of him, writing silly little poems and bringing her long-stemmed red roses. Maybe she should retrieve Karl's picture from the driveway and bring it inside. If Myra got the BlackBerry from her car now, she could call him and promise to return, after all.

No! She could still envision that almond-eyed slut's flouncy blouse. Unbuttoned. Karl's hands massaging bare boobs as though he felt up two grapefruits at a discount mart. And after he'd promised to behave. Three affairs, and now this blatant romp. What an ass. She deserved someone better. Myra's shoulders slumped. His gray-blue eyes—thinking about them always melted her resolve. How could she still love him, care for him at all?

Myra needed light. She lit the candle in the hurricane lamp on the hearth. Despite her threat to phone her lawyer this weekend, nine o'clock on Sunday night was too late to call him. Divorce was a liberating but ugly word. This evening she should sort out her emotions and find inner strength.

Falling water drops drummed harder on the roof. She glanced through the open doorway toward her Lexus, parked on asphalt a hundred feet away from the front steps. Darkness and sheets of rain camouflaged her vehicle from easy view. Strangers rarely used the nearby road unless they took a wrong turn. Her laptop and BlackBerry would be safe and dry in the car. No sense in getting any wetter than she already was.

Myra switched on her keychain flashlight, clamped it between her teeth and lugged her ice chest from the covered front porch into the cottage. The magic of love was so intangible and fleeting, like the wings of transparent butterflies in a dream. What a pity. Best to let Karl's photo drown.

Myra leaned back in an armchair, rested her stockinged feet on the leather ottoman and closed her eyes. Under her gray sweatshirt, the tight waistband of her jeans pressed against her stomach. Middle-age flab in the middle. Well, she'd always been frumpy, a hump-nosed ugly ducking with lifeless brown hair. She should go on a serious diet someday. Who knew? Being skinny and homely might provide a refreshing change.

The warmth of the fire and a glass of cabernet enticed her mind to drift between consciousness and sleep. Burning pine logs spit and crackled. Sap. Why had she married such a sap?

Distant rumbling intruded. Must be thunder. She sat up straight. A flash of bright light illuminated the room, vanishing with the next clap of thunder. A ruby-red mist formed beside the flickering hurricane lamp now in the kitchenette. A three-cornered black hat floated above the haze. Captain? Another rumble of thunder arrived.

The sketchy figure of a man in knee breeches and a scarlet frockcoat gained form and substance, like a poor-quality TV image transformed into high definition. The man removed the pirate hat from his head and bowed with a sweep of his arm. Underneath his unbuttoned coat, a crimson sash held a flintlock pistol in place. A drooping mustache framed his broad mouth and thick lips. His sea-green pupils twinkled.

She could detect the odor of rum ten feet away. This was Captain all right, her self-delusion come to lift her spirits. Myra stood on the threshold to fantasy. Should she let herself succumb?

"It be good to see ye again," he said, returning the pirate hat to his head. Captain unhooked the scabbard from his belt and set his cutlass on the counter. He moved closer to Myra. His shoulder-length dreadlocks glistened and smelled of perfumed oil. "At yer service, me fine, fair wench."

Captain spoke in the pseudo-pirate lingo a seven-year-old Myra once had whispered to herself in bed at night. She always loved his familiar greeting. Who cared if he was a product of her imagination, conjured this time by life's bitter disappointments and wine? In Myra's childhood, he'd always comforted her in a way her oh-so-beautiful-and-perfect parents never could. Well, she needed more than ordinary comfort tonight. Karl had called her a nagging cow who didn't understand men. Myra needed an emotional miracle. She leaped up from the chair and hugged Captain.

"Were you waiting for me to arrive alone?" Myra said.

She laughed and stepped back. A tinge of gray infiltrated his black hair. Crow's feet accentuated his eyes. Otherwise, he looked the same as always. Oh, how Captain had captured her heart when she was seven—and still did.

"I be keepin' watch here since yesterday," Captain said. He pointed toward the window where a hazy light shone outside, then disappeared. "Thar be a rival pirate sailin' these waters. A scurvy dog."

A rival pirate? What did Captain mean, and had she imagined that light? She never would conjure a bad sailor, some thug from Somalia or a cutthroat from the high seas of history. Even Dutchie—helmsman of the fabled Flying Dutchman—wasn't evil. In the past, Captain had said many things she hadn't understood. At times, the cognitive part of her brain failed to decipher her own imagination.

The window remained dark, the momentary light didn't return. Perhaps someone had taken her road by mistake, reversed direction when he had realized his error. Easy to do in this weather.

"Ye best be eatin' some real food to go with that thar wine." Captain fingered the gold braid on his frockcoat's wide cuffs.

Of course, he was right about eating. That is, she was right. The sensible, life-loving part of her intellect—via Captain—was telling the dark and depressed part what to do.

She opened the refrigerator. A platter of food, covered with plastic wrap, sat on the upper shelf. Odd. Myra didn't recall cutting up those fresh vegetables and placing them on a plate. And when had she sliced that French bread and brie? But no one else would have prepared the food from her ice chest. She must have done so. How could a single glass of cabernet have sucked so much memory out of her mind?

"I be fixin' some vittles while ye be sleepin'." Captain grinned, exposing a row of crooked, yellowed teeth. He refilled her wine glass, then pulled a bottle of rum from a cupboard. A modern bottle, not his usual old-fashioned jug. He poured a mug of water and rum for himself.

"Mutiny be on the way to Pirate's Cove, me matey. This be the last grog for us both till the matter be settled."

Pirate's Cove. She'd named the nearby horseshoe-shaped beach Pirate's Cove when she was seven. But mutiny? What trick was her mind playing now? Perhaps Myra's imagination strove to transform the notorious Dutchie from a ghost helmsman of a doomed sailing ship into some sort of mutinous pirate. An icy chill rippled across her shoulders, as though cold seawater sprayed them. No mellow, warm shivers from Dutchie this close to the cove.

"I don't care to face down Dutchie tonight." Myra set the food platter on the kitchenette table with an emphatic clunk.

She found a butter knife in a drawer and spread fragrant brie on a slice of French bread. Why fret about Dutchie after all these years? She could resist his call across the water, couldn't she? After all, she was mature—far stronger and wiser than at age seven or eleven when he'd lured her down to the cove.

Cold, dark water closing over her. Small lungs gasping for air. At age seven, she'd tried to swim out to Dutchie's three-masted ship to play with him and nearly perished. Daddy had hauled her back to the beach, saved her life. At eleven, though, she'd gone to visit Dutchie for a darker reason.

"Argh," Captain said. "Dutchie be a fine friend if ye let him."

"Since when does an inner desire for suicide make a fine friend?" Myra mumbled through a mouthful of brie and bread.

She swallowed. This was ridiculous, talking out loud to someone who wasn't real. She dipped a piece of celery in hummus. Salty. Salt water. Myra shivered.

"Thumbin' yer nose at death," Captain said, "be makin' life more precious." He raised his rum cup in a toast and took a swig.

Myra closed her eyes. Sand dollars in the cove. A red flashlight. How easily some images of yesterdays surfaced. At age eleven, Myra had not fully comprehended death. She had not understood her best friend either, and the two sometimes had argued.

"You're ugly and stupid," the young friend had once shouted at Myra, as though Myra had purposely broken the sand dollars they'd collected.

Well, the past two days had broken more than sea shells. Still, Myra would not drop her flashlight in the sand tonight and race down the beach, crying, the way she had then. Even if Dutchie's square-rigger materialized in the harbor. Even if he stood at the helm, stretched out his bony arm and pointed his first finger in her direction. Promised her eternal peace, love and solace. She would not swim toward him ever again.

Myra fingered the teardrop pendant on a gold chain around her neck. The jewelry, a gift from Karl, wasn't as beautiful as the locket her parents had given her when she was ten. She'd lost the locket while trying to reach the Flying Dutchman, when hoping to sail away to a mystical land where she would become intelligent and beautiful. Dutchie wore her treasure now.

"I'll thumb my nose at death from this cottage," she said. How had an eleven-year-old Myra managed to swim back to the beach on her own that night? She'd probably never know.

She blotted her mouth with a napkin and wrapped her arms around Captain. He felt so warm against her, the flax shirt under his frockcoat so soft. The backs of her hands tingled. He could have been real.

"I've no intention of getting drunk," she added, "or trying to commit suicide because of—"

Karl. Because of Karl, the man with wiry brown hair and an infectious smile. The man with soft lips--the upper indentation pronounced, almost feminine. Compelling. His pupils were gray-blue with dark striations, not like Captain's at all. Myra hadn't meant to cry but tears came, as though she could purge grief with her body's salt water. She needed a husband with Captain's kindness and Dutchie's aura of mystery instead of the lout she'd married. Well, that would take a fair amount of magic, now, wouldn't it? If this were a decent world, there'd be enough magic.

Myra wiped the kitchenette counter with a damp cloth. Captain had vanished for the evening, and raindrops pelted the window panes and shingled roof. Time for bed. She opened a cupboard to put away her washed wine glass. A bottle of rum sat on the shelf, like the one Captain had used earlier to fill his cup. Yet Myra hadn't brought rum with her tonight. There hadn't been rum in this cottage for several years. No dust on the bottle. The label appeared bright and new. Furthermore, the bottle wasn't full. Approximately a half-cup was missing. Her brain wasn't set in imagination mode. How could this bottle be here? Things were turning too bizarre. After she called her lawyer tomorrow, she had better make an appointment with her shrink.

The nerve of Karl, fondling that woman at a birthday bash in their neighbor's home. The shameless bulge underneath his trousers had been no product of her imagination. He hadn't even bothered to lock the library door. Well, she'd turned forty this year. The inheritance from Daddy's trust was now officially hers. She wouldn't need anything from Karl's real estate business, although she deserved plenty.

Myra could still see the scribbled entries in Karl's business ledgers. You would have thought his accountant was a chicken. She'd computerized his books so an accounting service would handle them. Myra sniffled. Two years ago, that happened, and Karl never had properly thanked her. She was going to phone her lawyer in the morning, wasn't she? Yes, she would get the BlackBerry from her car now and set it on her nightstand.

Myra buttoned her trench coat and put on her wedge-heeled boots. The strong wind would blow an umbrella inside-out. Not worth the trouble. She stepped outside without one and into the building storm. She shouldn't turn toward the beach, toward the cove. Dutchie might be there, waiting. Well, let him wait. She wasn't about to kill herself and offer Daddy's money to Karl on a silver platter.

She retrieved the BlackBerry from the car, stuffed it under her long coat and into her jeans pocket. Such a tight fit. She needed a smaller BlackBerry or jeans with fatter pockets. At least the device wouldn't fall into a puddle, even if she stood on her head.

The wind howled a muffled name. Her own? No, the Dutchie part of Myra was doing that inside of her mind. Best to ignore him. On the other hand, she ought to at least wave to him from the beach, shout hello and goodbye to his imaginary form. Confronting Dutchie, while refusing to swim toward his ghostly ship, would demonstrate she was woman enough to accept herself, endure disappointments and move on to the rest of her life. A life without Karl.

Myra grabbed the handle of the halogen camp-lantern

on her car's back seat. She turned the knob to the high setting. Lamp held waist-high, she locked the door. Rain beat against her as she crossed the private roadway and strode through fine sand. Wind tousled her shoulder-length hair.

A moonless night and vertical sheets of rain veiled the cove. No iridescent green light emanated from tall black sails. No skeletal figure beckoned from behind a sailing ship's wheel. The Flying Dutchman wasn't even going to bother to appear and challenge her. She'd finally won the battle with that part of her imagination. How empowering. Myra grinned.

Then came a clicking noise behind her, distinct, even above wind and rain. A firm hand gripped her shoulder and an object pressed into the small of her back. What was—

"Keep walking," a male voice said, low and guttural, as though disguised.

A robber. This must be a robber. The pressure against her mid-spine. A gun? Myra froze.

"I said, keep walking." The man twisted her right arm behind her back.

Pain shot through her bent arm. That voice. Karl? Myra caught a hint of the familiar fragrance of aftershave. His aftershave. Yes, this was Karl. Her own husband threatened her with a gun? How long had he been here? The window. The light in the window must have come from his car's headlights. He'd waited for her to step outside, stalked her. Now he controlled her every move. Her heart thumped hard.

"What the hell are you doing?" she said, her mouth dry. Myra never had seen Karl with any gun. Maybe this one was a fake.

"Fulfilling your inner desire," Karl said, his tone re-turned to normal.

What was that supposed to mean, a new sort of game? That he'd force her to lie down in the sand, then make love to her? Cry about his unfaithfulness and plead to be forgiven? Be a proper husband forever after?

"You're going to take a nice long swim," Karl said, a nasty edge to his words. "One way. In the cove."

"Have you gone insane?"

She had to get help. Yet there was no way she could reach her BlackBerry and call 911 before Karl shot her. She clutched the handle of her lantern.

"Shut up and walk toward the water." The barrel of Karl's gun pressed harder against her spine.

Murder. This was murder. It made no sense for him to choose her death instead of divorce. This couldn't be happening.

"Why are you—"

"I said shut up," Karl said.

Thar be a rival pirate. Captain had told her, warned her earlier this evening. Pirates stole treasure. Her subconscious had worried about Karl all along. The inheritance from Daddy. Never see a dime. She had shouted those threats at Karl yesterday. Myra faltered.

"Don't try anything cute," Karl said.

One step, then another. Karl wanted her inheritance enough to kill her. She hadn't handled his accounting for two years. Had his business taken more of a downturn than he'd admitted? The sand, so wet, resisted Myra's footfalls now. Karl's moist lips, his hands on that sultry bitch. Had he intended for Myra to walk in on them? Hoped Myra would drive to the vacation cottage and check into Dutchie's watery domain? Had he married her only for money?

The water—he was going to force her to drown. They'd find her body washed up on the beach. Without any sign of violence, Karl would go free. She could almost hear the gossips now. "Crazy Myra killed herself this time," they'd say. "And what a shame with such a loving, handsome husband. Her being so frumpy and all."

But if Karl shot her, the entire scenario would change to one of foul play. Shooting her was not his Plan A. Wet sand squished under her feet. Dammit, she wasn't about to cooperate and become the ideal victim.

Myra stumbled toward the water. Could he even shoot straight? If she broke away from him, he might miss. The Internet. She'd read something on the net. The elbow was the strongest part of the body. Yes, that was it. If she could jab Karl in the gut and get away, run in a zig-zag pattern. Would such a maneuver work? She should have taken classes in self-defense.

Water seeped through the soles of her boots. The water's edge. If she didn't bolt soon, she'd lose all opportunity. Her muscles tensed. Now.

Myra dropped her lantern, thrust her free elbow backward at an angle and delivered the heel on one boot into Karl's shin. She wobbled and lunged forward. Soggy hair flopped in her face. Karl's hold relaxed. No more struggle than that? Myra darted ahead. Yes, she was free.

She broke into a run, or rather, a slog through wet sand. The crack of gunfire prompted her to duck and shield the back of her head with her hands. Her toe stubbed something firm. Myra pitched forward, went down and sprawled in the tide. A bullet wound would hurt a lot, wouldn't it? Then again, Karl was a lousy shot. How much ammunition did he have? A couple inches of water swirled around Myra. Would he step on her? Push her face into the sand until she suffocated? She turned toward Karl and braced to kick and fight any way she could.

Her husband stood motionless, twenty feet away, his

ankles in the low surf. Lamplight and shadows bathed his profile as he faced the sea. Karl's extended hand clutched a gun the shape of a revolver. A cutlass with a sturdy, curved blade floated in the rain-filled air, the weapon's tip inserted into the gun's barrel.

"Avast, ye scallywag," Captain said as his figure materialized, right hand clasping the sword's grip. His other hand held a signal lantern. "I be placin' the black spot on ye for Davy Jones' Locker."

Captain lifted the lamp, an old-fashioned one with a flickering flame. Several hundred feet off the shoreline, the three-masted Flying Dutchman rocked in the water. A skeleton at the helm, wearing a black robe, pointed his bony finger toward Karl. Dutchie. Myra tensed her arms around her bent knees. Seawater seeped into her undergarments.

"At yer service, me matey," Captain called to Myra. "What be yer pleasure to do with this landlubber? Have Dutchie keelhaul 'em?"

"Call them off," Karl cried. He dropped his gun into the water. "For God's sake."

Call them off? Karl could see them? He could see Captain and Dutchie? Those two sailors were—always had been—a product of her own imagination. What was going on?

Her spouse covered his face with his hands. Scared. Her imaginary friends scared the two-timing creep. What a coward Karl was. A lily-livered son of a biscuit eater, as Captain might have said. Captain and Dutchie—Karl actually saw them.

"Is he still to be yer husband?" Captain said, the tip of his cutlass against Karl's chest. "He be better mannered now."

No, Myra didn't want Karl for a husband, the bastard.

Still, she was better than he. Didn't lust to spill his blood, although she enjoyed watching him squirm. If only Karl would go away on his own. If only she could sleep for awhile, awaken fresh and start the rest of her life.

"I don't want him," Myra shouted. Rain pelted her face. "But don't kill him."

The rain subsided a bit, but blurred the outlines of Dutchie and the ghost ship more than before, as though the edges of the vessel and steersman dissolved. Captain, too, became less distinct, his cutlass and old-fashioned lamp translucent. Myra blinked. Pirate and ghost ship faded, turning hazy, then clear.

No, not entirely clear. A line of crimson light remained where Captain's sash had been. Two iridescent green orbs, the size of Dutchie's eye sockets, glittered above the water and raced toward the beach. Those manifestations of Captain and Dutchie danced atop Karl's head.

"Make them stop." Karl whimpered. He sucked his lips against his front teeth. "Please."

The ghostly lights vanished. Myra sat on her soggy butt. An outgoing tide stole sand from beneath her. Oh, to wash away the past two days, to scrub herself free from the memory of Karl and all the pain he'd caused.

Still, Myra needed to look at Karl one more time, to prove to herself she could resist his gray-blue eyes. Karl picked up Myra's halogen lantern and ambled toward her, his legs apart, as though he sought balance on a ship at sea. He extended his free hand. A gesture to help her rise? He'd just tried to murder her. She shook her head and clenched both fists. Myra could stand—and live her life—without the untrustworthy coward's assistance.

"Thar be magic," Karl said, his arm still extended, his voice rough and uneven. Water dripped from his sand-speckled windbreaker, mustache and goatee. He pointed his first finger at Myra. "When ye step o'er yesterdays."

How dare Karl mock Captain's quaint speech or Dutchie's beckoning stance. She shot him her best in-your-face disgusted scowl. But wait, Karl had blue-gray eyes. Now, in the lantern light, his pupils gleamed sea green. And what was suspended on the short, thin chain around his neck? A locket. Her locket. The one Dutchie had worn.

Karl had changed. This was his form but... Odors of rum, rotting seaweed and perfumed hair oil clung to Myra's nasal passages. She could almost taste the strong smells.

She opened one fist, permitting his fingers to entwine with her own. Such a mellow warmth. Bet he thought her pretty. Of course, she was—always had been—attractive in her own way. Shiver me timbers. The backs of her hands tingled.

A Treacherous Stone

MJ BLEHART

One minute he dreamt of flying, high above the hills and rivers, out to the ocean.

The next moment Malachi was, in fact, flying. But only the distance from his bunk to the wall across the cabin.

The pain to his shoulder from the impact with the wall made him aware he was no longer dreaming. He was in an awkward position on his hands and knees on the floor.

For a moment, all he saw was the wooden deck below him. The odors of tar and wood held an odd metallic tinge to them, as did the smell of the sea.

As he caught his breath, the sound returned to his ears in a rush.

Shouts, screams, cannon fire and the ring of swords clashing filled the air. He felt the deck vibrate below him, resonating with the running boots upon it and cannons lurching as they fired.

Painfully, he stood up, and saw that the starboard wall of the cabin was open to the sea. The bunk nearest to the hole was gone, though blood stained the remains of the floor there.

As he became more and more aware of his surroundings,

Malachi looked for his Master. He too had been thrown free of his bed, but having a lower bunk, not quite so far.

"Master!" he cried, leaning over his mentor.

His Master stirred, his head rising up. His long, white hair was mussed, but his clean-shaved face showed no signs of hurt. "Rook," he replied, addressing Malachi by rank. "We are under attack."

"Yes, Master," he agreed.

His Master arose, looking concerned. He pulled back his hair, surveying the damage to their cabin. "Come, Rook, we must assist our hosts. Bring your sword, and your tome."

"Yes, Master," he replied, and reached for his sword belt and the long, curved blade, as well as his leather-bound tome.

The Master did the same, and led him from the wrecked cabin.

The deck of the ship was chaos, and it was clear immediately that things were going badly. Men not in uniforms with swords attacked any of the crew who were armed. The sailors of the ship were fighting as best they could, but were being overrun.

The main mast of the ship was lying on its side across the deck. Clearly, it had been targeted first. There was other evidence of cannon damage across the ship, and the smell of burning wood and tar. He glanced off the starboard rail.

There was another ship there, keeping even with them. A large galleon with many cannon and three masts, not too dissimilar to the one they were now aboard. But it flew the flag of no nation...in its stead was a red flag with a black skull and black crossed swords below it.

Pirates.

Malachi felt his heart grow heavy with concern. He had heard many tales of pirates and the things they would do when they raided a ship. Rape, and plunder, and murder.

Men with no valor, men with no honor.

"Make ready, Rook," instructed the Master, his voice showing no sign of stress. "They will rue this day. They will not be expecting our kind here."

In that, he realized, his Master would be correct. Pirates attacking a random ship upon the seas would be ready for many things. But not likely ready for their kind.

Spellcasters.

He thumbed open his tome, pleased that he hit the precise page he'd wanted. Finding the spell, he focused his power, and his energy, and began to chant softly.

"Ah-lay ah-tay roh-vay mah-nay rac-khar per-tom suuk ver-doo lah-tem," he chanted, calling to each of the gods he named to grant him the power to cast the spell he desired.

The first time through called the gods to attention, the second showed them respect, the third requested their favor. And as he completed the third pass through the chant, he spoke the word that called forth what he desired.

"Illuminate!" he cried.

The clouds that had been hovering above suddenly began to glow, softly at first, then brighter, until it was nearly daylight beneath them.

That would give the pirates pause.

"Restore!" called the Master, having completed his chant.

The main mast shivered and arose off the deck, knitting back together at the point where it had been broken. In a matter of seconds, it was upright and fully repaired as though it had never been damaged.

Malachi braced himself, ready for the momentary drain on his energy that would always follow a casting. The sacrifice spellcasters gave for calling upon the gods to grant them power.

His head seemed to fill with heat and his body felt

as though it was full of leaded weights. He crumpled in on himself, but remained standing, as he felt all of his energy fall away. It was a terrifying moment, for if one pushed beyond their natural strength they might die.

Only a few seconds later, it passed. He rose up again, and took a deep breath. He looked over to his Master, and as always envied how little his spells drained him.

He looked once more towards the approaching galleon, and noted in the light he had made that the rail was painted a brilliant deep blue.

His Master reclaimed his attention. "Well cast, Rook. Now, we should..."

He knew why his Master stopped mid-sentence. He felt it, too. It was unmistakable.

There was another spellcaster out there. And he had just cast a powerful spell.

They were on a ship with other passengers and cargo... but they were the only spellcasters aboard. Which meant one thing.

The other spellcaster was with the pirates.

He realized there was nothing he could do. It was unexpected, and it was so powerful that even his Master was overwhelmed.

Once more all of his energy felt as though it was being leached out of him. And fight it though he might, he could not stop it.

Malachi sank to his knees, still fighting it, still trying to think. But it was to no avail.

He collapsed upon the deck, and the last conscious thing he remembered was hearing his Master hit the deck moments later.

The world went dark.

Malachi awoke. And he did not remember any dreams. Neither did he remember where he was.

The Rook blinked, and soon the room swam into focus.

He tried to move, but discovered his hands and arms were bound.

Then Malachi remembered.

"Well, boy," a voice said. He could not see the man who spoke, but his accent was unfamiliar. "An apprentice spellcaster. Quite the impressive tome you have. Either you are further along than most your age...or you have a trusting Master."

He stepped into sight now. A tall, lanky man, with a shaved head and a well-trimmed black goatee. He was dressed as a gentleman, in a fine linen tunic of deep crimson and a black leather vest atop it.

"I am Captain Anssem Thrall, and this is the *Glorious Sapphire* you are sailing upon," he stated proudly.

He had heard of Captain Thrall and the pirates of the *Glorious Sapphire*. Once a nobleman, he had turned to piracy half a decade ago and was nigh unstoppable. Many governments had sent their best to destroy him, but their best never returned.

He realized, though, that he did not need to fear. He would already be dead otherwise.

"I am Rook Malachi Spence," he told his captor.

"Ah," Captain Thrall commented. "A student of the Ah-suuk Way. You are far from home, young Malachi."

"Where is my Master?" Malachi asked, concerned.

"Master Karr is alive and well," Captain Thrall replied. "But silenced. A Master has many of his spells memorized in the event of capture, and cannot be allowed to chant, eh?"

Malachi would not answer that. He had been assigned memorization of certain chants, in order to call up special protections during this trip. He had not gotten far enough to succeed in that task during the week they'd been at sea.

"What do you want from us?" Malachi requested.

"Straight to the point. I like that," Captain Thrall said with a grin. "We have spared your life, and will spare that of your Master, if you will lend us some assistance."

"Assistance with what?" asked Malachi suspiciously.

"There is some strange thing going on with the crew," said the captain. "Some odd malady has been randomly afflicting them. A spellcaster to investigate this, since it seems most likely supernatural, would be best."

"You have a spellcaster," Malachi remarked. "Let him do it."

"Her, actually," intoned a feminine voice. A tall, very attractive blonde woman stepped up beside Captain Thrall.

"Rook Spence, meet Glory, my spellcaster," introduced Captain Thrall.

Malachi eyed her with suspicion. She was slightly taller than Captain Thrall, her hair long, wavy, and platinum blonde. She was slim but curvy, in a deep blue dress trimmed with gold. She was undeniably beautiful. "What Way do you follow, Mistress Glory?"

She smiled at him, and he could not help but feel comforted by that smile. "That does not matter, does it now, young Rook? And I am not a Master, so the honorific is wasted upon me."

"Lady Glory is a most impressive spellcaster," Captain Thrall stated, and Malachi heard the respect in his voice. "I have never met any like her before. But she has been unable to explain what is happening to my crew."

"My Master would be better suited to this, Captain," Malachi confessed.

"I don't think so," Glory replied. Her voice was low and soothing, and Malachi felt an unusual compulsion to desire her words whenever she spoke. "I have tested him, and while his mind is sharp, yours is more open. You would have a better chance of helping me to learn the truth of this affliction."

"I must see my Master, before I will help you," Malachi demanded.

Glory and Captain Thrall exchanged a look. It was Thrall who responded. "Very well."

Glory gestured and chanted swiftly, incomprehensible to Malachi, finishing with, "Release."

Malachi's bonds undid themselves, and he found he was free.

"Come," Captain Thrall commanded.

Malachi paused, watching Glory for a moment. Like his Master, she showed no weakening upon casting her spell.

They led him onto the deck and he felt the sun on his face. Seconds later he was led back into another cabin. Within, his Master was upon a table, bound as he had been, and gagged.

"Master!" Malachi exclaimed. "Have they hurt you?"

Master Karr looked to his apprentice, then shook his head no.

"Un-gag him," Malachi requested again.

"I think not," the Captain said. "A Master of such skill as he is too powerful to turn loose."

"And you know he will not swear before me to not cast spells," Glory added.

Malachi knew that no Master would swear such an oath. It would dishonor him or her, and force him from his Way. And nothing short of a sworn oath would convince anyone that a Master would not use his power in a situation like this.

"He will remain here, and kept alive, young Rook, so long as you help us," the Captain said.

"And if I do, what then?" Malachi asked, considering every angle.

"We will free you," Thrall stated.

Malachi placed his hands upon his hips. "And I should believe you why?"

Captain Thrall smiled. "You should not. But I swear, upon that which once let me be called Earl, on the honor of my father and the name I have soiled, that you will be freed."

"I witness this oath, and in the name of all the Ways, do pledge to see to it Captain Thrall will abide by his word," added Glory.

Malachi took a deep breath and looked to Master Karr. His Master caught his eye, and only barely nodded his head, suggesting that Malachi agree.

"Very well," Malachi said. "Where do we begin?"

Captain Thrall had excused himself, claiming the need to see to other duties. Glory led Malachi below-deck.

For all he had heard of pirates and their ships, the *Glorious Sapphire* was a surprise. The deck was immaculately clean, and every sailor Malachi espied was washed and groomed.

Glory introduced him to a very short but tough looking man with a thick red beard, dreadlocks, and pierced ears, nose, and upper lip. "This is the Quartermaster of the Glorious Sapphire, Symi."

Malachi nodded his head to the man.

"What's this boy here for, witch?" Symi asked, his voice hard and raspy.

Glory either ignored, or did not care about the insult the man had given her. "He's going to help me try to uncover what's happening to the crew. Since you encountered it first, I thought you should explain."

The man called Symi spat on the deck. "Evil," he muttered.

"Evil has many forms," Malachi said. "What is it you are seeing?"

Symi eyed him darkly. "What do you know of evil, boy?"

Malachi was nineteen, hardly a boy. And he was not easily intimidated. "I know enough of evil to know what is not. Now, please, do explain what is happening to the crew?"

Symi hesitated, then spat on the deck again. He eyed Glory. "So, now you believe, witch?"

Glory crossed her arms. "I never doubted you, Quartermaster. You know the crew of the *Glorious Sapphire* better than any other. So explain to my companion."

Symi growled. "It began a couple weeks ago, now. Grav, my assistant, just began to babble incoherently one day. He got louder, more frenzied...then collapsed on the deck in convulsions. Moments later...he was dead."

"That sounds vaguely like plague," Malachi commented.

"So we thought, at first," Symi conceded. "But there were no lesions, he had no fever, nor any of the other symptoms."

"Symi comes from a nation that has dealt with plague," Glory said. "He is a survivor, in fact. So none would know better."

Malachi had seen plague. Early on, when he first joined the Way, before he became a full Rook, they had visited a hospital with a ward of plague sufferers, and another of survivors. Spellcasters were immune to plague, but had yet to uncover a way by which to stop plague when outbreaks happened.

"The captain's cabin boy, Valk, fell next," Symi said. "He never would take leave to shore, and had no contact with Grav. Also, his death was nearly a week later."

Malachi knew that if it was plague, or a similar illness, that would be unusual. Deaths were usually hours, or maybe a day apart at most. And generally it was close-knit groups who would take ill at once.

"How many have taken ill?" Malachi asked.

"We have lost seven," Symi stated.

"Is there any pattern to their deaths? Some kind of connection?"

Symi spat on the deck again. "Evil."

"They were days apart, and disparate members of the crew," Glory said. "Symi, show Rook Spence where each man was lost, in order. Maybe he will discern something we are missing."

Symi looked to Glory unpleasantly, then growled. He glowered at Malachi. "Follow."

The short, unpleasant Quartermaster proceeded to lead Malachi all over the ship. They paused at seven different places, across random parts of the vessel, to see where each man had died.

Malachi immediately found nothing unique about any place where the deaths had occurred. Some of the spots were very public, constantly filled with crew coming or going, some very private, cabins or storage lockers or less traveled spaces. From that, he could discern nothing.

Symi returned them to Glory at the place they had begun after some fifteen minutes or so. "Thank you, Quartermaster," she said.

Symi growled something Malachi did not understand, bobbed his head curtly once, then stalked away.

"That was one of his more pleasant moments," Glory remarked flippantly.

She led Malachi back to the deck. "I presume the bodies have all been dumped overboard?" he asked.

"Of course," Glory commented. "The dead do not keep well aboard ship. Apart from being in perfect health before they died, there was nothing to mark these deaths."

Malachi considered that. "I wonder if it is murder?"

"Murder?" Glory repeated.

"Men in perfect health, suddenly falling ill and dying? It makes no sense," Malachi surmised. "Were they, per chance, among the most healthy aboard the ship?"

"No more than any others, no," Glory mused. "But certainly they were hale."

Malachi was nodding his head, considering. "There are some poisons, perhaps, that might produce the effect Symi described. But I am no expert on poisons."

"Nor am I," Glory said. "But I can consult my tomes, and see if I can find anything there."

"I could consult Master Karr," Malachi said. "He may have insight."

"I think not," Glory remarked. "I am sorry, my young Rook, but your Master must remain gagged and bound."

Malachi had expected that. But he had to try.

"I shall consult my tomes," Glory declared. "Go to the galley, Rook Spence, and get yourself a meal. Get to know more of the crew, see if you learn anything."

"Aye," Malachi replied.

They parted, and though he was sorely tempted to follow her, or to go and see his Master and try to free him, he realized it had been some time since last he ate, and he was hungry. He had concluded, additionally, that there was no way to escape.

Malachi did not have a lot of experience on ships. Once he had been aboard a small, coastal water trawler, before boarding the galleon with his Master that had fallen under attack. He found to his surprise that, as much as his situation was not a good one, neither was it proving unpleasant.

The smell of baking bread and some sort of fish stew made it easy to find the galley. Malachi ignored the looks the sailors gave him as he passed, accepting a bowl of stew and a hunk of the bread and taking a seat by himself near the port bulkhead.

He observed the crew of the *Glorious Sapphire*. All of them had clearly been in this life a while, each wearing the look of men who lived far more aboard ship than ever upon the land. But even though they were clearly veterans, they were, he noted again, not unclean. Even as gruff as Symi had been, he still was dressed in linen and cotton and leather, without patches or tears.

A sailor who had been walking past Malachi's table froze in his place a moment. Malachi wondered if he was about to turn and speak to him, when suddenly his eyes seemed to almost drop into his head, clearly no longer seeing anything around him.

"Ah-lay coor-vaj ah-tay gohr-mac roh-vay mah-rac-khar per-tom nor-pah suuk-nah ver-doo lah-tem caff-la mah-rekk vaash!" uttered the sailor softly at first, then more passionately, the last few words frenzied, shouted, as if he was spitting them out.

The sailor crumpled. He lay upon the deck, convulsing as Malachi arose, and activity throughout the galley ceased.

The sailor's convulsions racked his body, his boot heel slamming on the floor arhythmically, until he ceased and lay still.

Malachi did not need to look closer. He could already see that the sailor was dead.

Before another word could be said, on the other side of the galley, another sailor cried out and dropped to the floor, convulsing.

Sailors were, Malachi knew, a superstitious lot. That was all it took for them to forget their meals and to push their way out of the galley. Malachi stood over the body of the sailor that had fallen before him as others pushed past, hastily exiting.

Malachi could not deny his own discomfort, but he also recognized the influence of magic when he saw it.

The shouting faded to a rumble, and then aside from the creaking of the *Glorious Sapphire* on the sea and the smell of half-eaten meals, all else throughout the galley was silent.

Malachi had expected to see the second dead sailor on the far side of the cabin. What he had not expected was to find a total of six more bodies.

He walked over to the next nearest man, and bent down to examine him. Like the one who had fallen before him, he showed no signs of any illness, but lay dead nonetheless.

Malachi heard voices approaching, and looked up as Captain Thrall, Glory and Symi entered the galley. All three looked stunned as they took in the sight before them.

"By the gods," Symi cursed, spitting, crossing his arms over his chest with his fists balled, bowing thrice at the waist as if to ward himself from unseen spirits.

"Did you see?" Captain Thrall questioned.

"I did," Malachi remarked. "Just as Quartermaster Symi said."

"This is new," Glory commented. She was kneeling at one of the bodies. "There has never been more than one of these deaths at a time."

"I presume you found nothing about poisons in your tomes?" Malachi inquired.

Glory turned her eyes on him. "No. But you expected the answer to be no, did you not, Rook?"

Malachi was shaking his head. He gestured to the sailor whose death he had witnessed. "I heard him babble. It would sound incoherent to most. But to me...it sounded like a chant."

"A chant?" Captain Thrall asked.

"Like a spellcaster's chant," Malachi confirmed.

All was chaos aboard the *Glorious Sapphire* after that.

The sailors were demanding that the Captain bring the ship into port, some even going so far as to request a longboat, to be off the craft. It took all of the captain's command authority, the threats of the quartermaster, and the reassurances of Glory to prevent the crew from panicking.

"If you do not have a duty, remain in your cabin," the captain ordered. "Keep to the bunks when you have no duties. We will make a course for port, but know we are days out. We will do all we can to get to the bottom of this."

"How many aboard the ship?" Malachi asked of Glory.

"Sixty-seven," she replied. "Not counting you and your Master."

"We need him," Malachi stated, not missing a beat.

"I think not," Glory remarked. "I fear he will more likely add to our troubles than to assist us."

"I think, given the circumstances, he will not work against you," Malachi said. "He is strong and wise, and whatever magic this is, he will be best suited to unravel this mystery."

"Out of the question," Glory stated. "He is a Master of the Ah-suuk Way, a Warrior Spellcaster. He will be compelled to resist us, not to help us."

"And you know it, Rook," Captain Thrall added, having rejoined them. "I have encountered many of your Way in my time, and the Masters will fight to free themselves first and foremost. Let us have no more talk of this...what do we know?"

Malachi sighed. "The sailor I heard was not just babbling. I am certain he was chanting."

"Chanting what?" Glory questioned.

Malachi shook his head. "I do not know. There was something...familiar about the chant. But without my tome...I could not tell you."

The captain looked to Glory. "Should we allow the Rook to see his tome?"

Glory put her hands upon her hips, eying Malachi. "If I am with him, then yes. Maybe he will get a sense of what is happening."

Captain Thrall nodded his head. "Do it. See if an answer can be found there."

Glory led Malachi to her cabin. Once they were within, he observed that it was a simple room, with cabinets along each of the walls, and a cot next to a desk near the center. The room smelled of patchouli and other exotic, womanly scents.

"Sit," Glory instructed Malachi. He did, and she went to one of the cabinets. She opened and closed it swiftly, then turned and dropped Malachi's tome before him.

As he reached for it, she placed her hand upon its cover. "Do not think to try and trick me, Rook," Glory stated darkly. "If I detect any attempt to cast a spell, I will kill you without a second thought."

Malachi took a deep breath, and nodded his head. Glory removed her hand from the cover the tome and moved around to behind him. He heard her withdraw a knife from a scabbard, and knew hers was no empty threat. Steadying his shaking hand, Malachi reached out and opened the tome.

Again, he was pleased to see he was on the page he'd sought. He recalled most of what the sailor had babbled before his death, but not all of it. Malachi found himself perturbed that he'd not done a better job of honing his memorization skills.

He worked his way through the page, then flipped to the next. He paused at every spell that began with *Ah-lay coor-vaj ah-tay*, the words the doomed sailor had uttered before he died.

He found one or two spell chants that may have been close, but upon learning what they called for, he eliminated them. Surely this had nothing to do with accelerating plant growth or turning water to mead or ale.

He found a spell that seemed right. But something about it unsettled him. He leaned back in the chair, considering.

"What have you found?" Glory asked.

"I think nothing, yet," Malachi said, then reconsidered.

"There is a spell to call life energy to yourself. It is supposed to draw energy from the most minute particles in the air, or the plants and animals of the land. Not enough to harm them, but enough to allow the spellcaster to perform a magic that might otherwise be too powerful for him. But the sailor did not appear to gain energy...he seemed instead..."

Malachi paused, a cold lump in his stomach. "He passed his energy. To another."

"What?" Glory questioned, sounding concerned.

Malachi arose slowly, feeling ill. "I would not have such a spell in my tome...no one would. But...in theory, it's possible that one could call upon the gods to pass life energy to another...but spellcasters are touched, we are gifted with the ability to use spellcraft. Non-spellcasters could not do such a thing...unless..."

"Unless they were under the influence of a spellcaster," Glory finished for him.

Malachi had no words. It was unthinkable.

"I hardly believe there is another spellcaster aboard the *Glorious Sapphire*," Glory remarked, walking around the table and standing before him.

"This began before my Master and I were brought aboard," Malachi said. "And to what purpose would anyone take the life energy of another man but for evil?"

Glory was shaking her head. "But what sort of purpose would a spellcaster have for the energy of another?"

"We must find him or her...and find out," Malachi said. He froze, though, and looked to Glory, who still held a knife in her hand.

She cocked her head to the side as Malachi eyed her, and dropped her gaze to the dagger. She let it fall upon the desk, on top of his tome. "Come now, Rook...if I were behind this, would I leave you alive?"

Malachi let out a breath he did not know he was holding. "I suppose not."

"Come," Glory said. "We need to inform the captain of this. We need to search the ship and examine every member of the crew."

"We need my Master," Malachi pressed again. "A rogue spellcaster stealing the life-force of others will surely take priority over escaping the *Glorious Sapphire*."

"We'll see," Glory said. She opened the door to her cabin, and gestured Malachi through.

They moved across the eerily quiet galleon. The crew who were not performing specific duties were in their quarters. They made their way to the wheel, where the captain stood, surveying his ship.

"Glory, Rook," he addressed them. "You have something?"

"Yes, Captain," Glory said, gesturing for him to step away from the sailor at the wheel.

When the captain was near, Glory explained to him softly what she and Malachi had discovered. Thrall spat upon the deck and cursed.

"Get Symi," he ordered. "Go with him, Glory, and start examining the crew he trusts most. When you are done with that, search the holds, and let us see if we have a stowaway." He turned his gaze to Malachi. "I don't suppose you are yet strong enough, Rook, to simply feel the presence of another spellcaster?"

Malachi sighed. "No, not unless they are casting. But, Captain, I think if we explain what is happening to Master Karr, he will assist you in finding your rogue spellcaster."

Captain Thrall looked to Glory. She nodded her head to him.

"Very well. With me, Rook. Glory...you have your orders."

"Aye, Captain."

They parted ways, the captain leading Malachi towards the cabin holding Master Karr.

Captain Thrall sighed. "I do hope we can resolve this

soon. I grow weary of the delay."

"Delay?" Malachi queried.

Captain Thrall sounded despondent. "I tire of this life. We have made a vast fortune, and I wish to retire. Yours, in fact, was the first ship we have attacked in many months."

"Why did you choose to attack us?" Malachi asked.

Captain Thrall shrugged. "I felt...compelled. Your ship was alone, and clearly not military, and I guess it was just too good a target to pass up. And unless they are ashore, the crew does get restless."

Malachi considered that, but he had no answer.

They reached the cabin, and Captain Thrall unlocked the door and led the way inside.

"Master," Malachi spoke. "I know your first thought will be escape, but hear me out."

Before he could continue, Malachi noted the state of Master Karr. His back was arched, as though he was in agony. He was muttering hoarsely through the gag, his eyes squeezed shut, his face stained with tears.

"Master?" Malachi asked, rushing to his side. "Master, it's me...can you hear me? Master?"

But Master Karr continued to mutter through his gag, and his posture did not change.

Malachi did not know what to do. He went to remove the gag, but Captain Thrall stopped him.

"No, Rook," the Captain said. "This is something wrong, something evil, and I do not know that removing that gag will help or harm him. We need Glory."

Malachi was torn, but accepted that the captain may be right. "Yes. We should seek her."

They departed the cabin, and returned to the deck.

Malachi was shocked when he noted that all was perfectly still. The creaking of the ship upon the ocean, and the smell of saltwater were all he observed.

At the base of the main mast, they noted the first

bodies. All around, the sailors were dead, showing no signs of any illness, but no signs of life, either.

"All hands!" cried the captain. "To me! To me!"

They stood in the center of the deck, upon the ghostly quiet galleon. None replied. Malachi felt his skin crawl, and an unbidden shiver ran down his spine.

From below-deck Glory, Symi, and two others emerged. They all looked stunned.

"Report," Thrall ordered softly.

"We...we are all that be left," Symi said, unable to hide the fear from his voice. "We found everyone else dead... or dying. And now...we are all that remain."

"Did you find anything?" the captain asked.

"We searched the ship from fore to stern, and there is no one here but our crew," Glory replied.

"Lady Glory, go with the Rook to his Master," Captain Thrall commanded. "Symi, Dorn, Potyr, let's prepare a longboat."

"Do you mean to abandon ship, Captain?" Glory asked.

"I do," Thrall replied. "There is something evil afoot, and I believe we must away. We will await you. But hurry!"

Glory and Malachi rushed to the cabin in which Master Karr was held.

He was still as Malachi had left him, his back arched and his face decrying his agony. His hoarse muttering continued, but was now no louder than a whisper, his voice spent.

"What can we do for him?" asked Malachi.

Glory chanted so softly and swiftly that Malachi could not hear her spell at all, save the word "Release." The bonds at Master Karr's hands and feet fell off.

His posture was unchanged, but now his arms flopped upon the cot, banging violently against it. Malachi feared his Master would shatter his limbs.

Glory reached for the gag, but before she could remove

it, Master Karr arched back even more, a sickening crack coming from his spine, his arms and legs going rigid. He gasped, and collapsed back onto the cot, limp and still.

Malachi stepped closer, but there was no need. His Master was gone.

"What has happened here?" Malachi whispered, walking about the cot to cradle his Master's head. "How can this be?"

"Perhaps...perhaps the usurper was using your Master as a conduit," Glory mused.

Malachi considered that. But such spells were far beyond his knowledge.

It dawned on him, then, that Captain Thrall seemed to know quite a lot. In fact, as Malachi considered it, for a non-spellcaster, Anssem Thrall seemed rather literate in magic.

The answer came to him. Captain Thrall had amassed tremendous wealth, and he claimed he wished to retire. But what of his crew? Could he just leave them? Or would he need to make certain that, once he was no longer aboard the ship, they would not get in his way?

What better way to insure that he could retire in peace?

Without a word, Malachi was on his feet, and racing out of the cabin and onto the deck.

He moved quickly, pausing only to take a sword from one of the fallen crew. There was an ominous feeling to the air, an unnatural calm. Malachi saw where one of the longboats had been lowered, being prepared to depart the ship.

As Malachi reached the rail, he froze in his tracks. He could scarcely believe what he was seeing.

Symi and the other two sailors were lying upon the deck, dead. But to his horror, so was Captain Anssem Thrall.

"What?" Malachi asked to the air.

"Rook," said a voice behind him. It was Glory.

Malachi turned to face her in disbelief. He still held the sword, and stared at the beautiful spellcaster, her blond hair framing her face, the only other survivor, before him.

"What have you done?" Malachi asked, gesturing towards the dead.

"What I had to," Glory replied.

"Why?" he asked, his mouth having gone totally dry.

Glory sighed. "They would not fight. They had become content to just sail the seas, and contemplate returning to land. But the energy of combat...I need it. I need it to sustain me. Without it, I was dying...so I took their energy."

"You," Malachi could scarcely believe. He had come to not only trust, but to respect Glory. "I...I don't understand."

"And you won't for some time," Glory replied. "I sensed him, Master Karr. And I remembered him...he made me. Long ago, now. When he was a new Master. He would not remember...I have changed a great deal since then. And with his energy, I was able to draw them all into me, and I will be sustained until I find a new crew."

She gestured to the longboat. "Go now, Rook Malachi Spence. You are not a part of this...and I promised you would be freed, as per Captain Thrall's oath. I am sorry to have deceived you so...and one day, you will understand."

Malachi was at a loss. Glory produced both his and his Master's tomes, and threw them into the longboat.

Without another word, Malachi climbed aboard the small craft. He stared blankly at the pair of tomes before him as he was lowered to the sea below.

He felt the small boat rock as it touched the sea, and looked up at the galleon. It was a mighty ship, and now he noted again the deep blue painted along its rail. Truly, it was, as its name, a *Glorious Sapphire*.

As the longboat drifted away, Malachi looked up to

the deck of the galleon. Glory watched him, and raised a hand to wave farewell. In his shock, Malachi reached up his hand and returned the wave.

He blinked...and Glory was no longer upon the deck above him.

Malachi took the oars, and began to row the boat. He paused and reached forward, adjusting the tomes so they would not get wet. He gave the oars a few more strokes, then looked back once more.

The ship was still there...but it was a galleon no more. Now, sailing away, he saw a two-masted brigantine, its rails painted a deep blood red.

Master Malachi Spence tapped out his pipe, his bones aching with the winter. The hall smelled of leather furniture, pipe smoke, and the fire burning on the hearth.

He eyed the youths before him, having recounted the tale of how his Master was lost. It was a test, to see what questions they might ask. One of many such tests he gave potential Rooks in the eighty years since he'd made his way home, and himself become a Master of the Ah-suuk Way.

The youngest, a boy called Joran, stirred. "Master... what became of the ship?"

"That...is another story," Malachi informed the young Initiate with a wry grin.

"Master?" asked the Initiate with the most potential, a girl named Aria, with long, straight black hair. "What of Glory? Did you learn why she took the life force of the crew?"

"I did, in fact, learn the answer."

He paused, letting the memory wash over him again. "I was at sea many days, before I was rescued. I studied my tome, and Master Karr's, and when I returned home I had learned enough to become a Master."

Malachi reached for more leaf and began to stuff it into his pipe. "I consulted with Master Karr's contemporaries, and I asked about his early years. One told me of a project my Master and others had worked on...spellcasting to enhance a ship, to make it more efficient, to use fewer crew. Enhancements to protect it from attack, to make it stronger, and more fearsome. Master Karr and a half dozen others spent years devising spellcraft for that purpose...but abandoned it. None remembered if they had had any success."

Malachi finished stuffing leaf into his pipe, and lit it. He took a puff, then blew out the vanilla and orange smelling smoke, remembering. "I had to go to the archives, to find the old notes, for Master Karr had been the last of the six who had performed those experiments. It took me months...but I finally learned what they had planned. And what they had tried to do. They thought they failed...clearly, they had not."

"The experiment to enhance the ship came to fruition," Malachi continued. "And the ship they chose was a sloop named the Glorious Onyx. They failed because they concluded that the ship would need a source of continuous power to permanently hold its energies...and all they could harness was life energy itself, or conflict energy. Considering the experiment a failure, they thought that the Glorious Onyx was destroyed...but it wasn't."

"Master Malachi, I still do not understand...who is Glory? And why couldn't Master Karr sense her?" asked a freckled face initiate.

Malachi shook his head. "There was no sorceress to sense. There is no Glory, boy...only Glorious, be she Onyx, Sapphire, Ruby or Jade."

History in the Making

By Tera Fulbright

My first sight of Grace O'Malley was at the point of her cutlass. Her sea-green eyes flashed dangerously as her long red hair whipped violently in the wind. A storm gathered across the horizon beyond the ship. My first thought was History got it wrong. She's not an Irish Rose at all, and it's not black hair and blue eyes. Her hair was the color of the sunset, her eyes the color of the sea.

"What magic is this? How did ye get aboard me ship?" she asked.

I could hear the anger in her voice through the thick Irish brogue. I took a deep breath and raised both of my hands in the universal gesture of surrender. Kneeling on the rough-hewn wooden boards of the deck, I looked up at her, perhaps the most famous Irish pirate, and said, "Would you believe me if I said I didn't know?"

She gave a short, barking laugh. "Either you're incredibly stupid or you really don't know." She glanced around the ship. The rest of the sailors were all standing around staring at us. The woman known as the Pirate

Queen looked suddenly fierce.

"Bah, I don't have time for this." She looked over at a tall, bald pirate. "Take her below, I'll deal with her later." She then turned on the remaining sailors. "What are you doing? Are we out for a sail? Back to work, ye layabouts! We have a ship to find!" At her words, the pirates snapped into action, moving the sails and ropes swiftly across the ship as the sailors themselves dodged beneath, between and behind them.

The large, bald pirate grabbed my arm and yanked me to my feet. "With me," he snarled as he dragged me across the deck and down below. A short trip down a set of stairs and he unceremoniously tossed me into a small cabin. "Herself'll be down to deal with ye."

"I'm surprised you're not taking me to a brig." I said confusedly as I looked around the cabin.

"What brig?" the pirate said. "We don't waste valuable cargo space on passengers...even ones that appear out of nowhere." Then he slammed the door behind him and I heard a key click in the lock.

The small cabin was sparsely furnished. A hammock hung in one corner. A captain's desk stood against one wall and a small chair, covered in fine tweed wool, leaned precariously against it. A large trunk rested under the hammock. On the desk lay several pieces of parchment, sea charts, a feather pen and inkwell and a small leather-bound journal. The only light came through a small porthole in the side of the cabin but a half-filled oil lamp rested on the desk ready for evening.

I took a deep breath as I looked around the cabin. Finally, I pulled out the tweed chair and sat down on it. I had not been lying when I told Grace O'Malley that I had no idea how I ended up on her ship. To be honest, the only reason I was reasonably certain it was her, besides the fact it was an Irishwoman captaining a ship, was that I had just been researching her. Interestingly, I noticed that the one discrepancy between the stories I had read and what I saw above deck was her hair. It's always described as black, but the woman I saw had hair the color of flames. I ran my fingers through my short hair and began rubbing small circles at my temples. Back to thinking about how I got here, the last thing I remembered before finding myself at the point of the Pirate Queen's sword was examining a sextant that had supposedly belonged to her.

The sextant had been a gift from my husband. We found it in an antique shop near the Academy, where we'd met for lunch a few days ago. We had spent the afternoon watching the ships and walking around the antique stores and other shops. The day had dawned bright and clear but cold, I remembered wishing I'd brought my gloves as we'd walked around.

The sign over the shop where we found the sextant had read "Erie's Charms" and the owner of the shop was a young girl who said her grandparents had been Irish immigrants. Most of her antiques were English and Irish pieces. As we looked around, I had spotted the sextant tucked in amongst some long-forgotten jewelry. As I reached for it, an old smooth voice spoke near my shoulder...

"You've got a good eye on ya, ma dear." I turned to see a man with sparse white hair, dressed in a tweed suit. His eyes sparkled merrily beneath bushy white eyebrows and he gave me a happy grin. "That there piece has a ghost story attached to it!"

I looked at him and raised one eyebrow skeptically.

He reached past me to pick up the tarnished piece. "See here, it's engraved," he said, pointing to the piece and passing it in front of my face. I could see markings but could not read them before he took the piece back to look at it himself. "This sextant has been passed around from woman to woman for generations. It used to belong to the Dark Lady of Doona, that'd be Grace O'Malley, don't ya know."

I nodded warily.

"Its last owner was a witch from Salem; she escaped the hangman's noose and came to Annapolis. She passed it on to her grand-daughter's grand-daughter who eventually sold it to me." He leaned in close and whispered. "It'll bring good luck to any strong-willed woman who owns it," he said. "It's supposed to show you the right course, no matter how far off ye get."

The young girl approached and overheard the last bit, "Now, Grandpappy," she said. "You know you're supposed to be resting." She gently took the sextant from him and handed it to me. With an apologetic smile, she guided him away from us and back toward the other end of the shop. When she returned, she said. "I apologize. If you listen to Grandpa, every piece in here has a story to tell."

"As it should," said my husband, an avid historian, who had walked up as the old man was speaking. "I think we'll take it. How much is it?"

She looked at the piece. "Well, it is a bit worse for wear, isn't it? Let's say $650."

"Sounds fine," my husband had said.

"We can't afford that!" I had exclaimed, futilely as it turned out. He had just smiled and handed the young lady his credit card. Shortly after, we walked out of the store with the sextant in hand. A few days later, I had decided to take a break from my research and pulled out the sextant to look at it, and had suddenly found myself aboard the pirate ship.

Now, in the solitude of the cabin, I pulled it out of my bag and looked at it again. The sextant was made of heavy gold that had tarnished with age. The wheels and gears remaining still worked but it was clear that pieces were missing. Faded engraving could still be seen on it but time had worn the words so that all I could make out were "history. We will."

As I stared at the sextant, the door to the cabin slammed open and Grace O'Malley stood framed in the light from the hall. She still had that angry look about her. She was dressed for practicality rather than to impress anyone. Wearing a simple man's shirt in bright yellow and cropped sailor's pants in a faded blue or green, she was barefoot, her feet gripping the wooden floor; her stance easy on the rolling ship. She had thrust both a pistol and cutlass in her belt. The lady pirate looked at me sitting in the chair and raised an elegantly curved red eyebrow. I leaped from the chair and stood behind it, placing the sextant back in my bag as I did so.

"Better," she said. She walked into the cabin, turned the seat to face me and pointed at the hammock. I tried to sit down gingerly but the hammock continued to move with the ship, swinging away from me. She looked at me. I gave up and just sat on the floor. Once I was seated, Grace's eyes traveled from my shoes, up my pants, lingering for a moment on the bag at my side, then continued up to my face. Her green eyes locked with my own, and I suddenly knew then the reason her men followed her without question. Those eyes seemed to reflect something, some magic that I had never seen, seeming to promise me all my dreams and desires if I but obeyed her, followed her. I broke contact first and glanced over at the small captain's desk.

Grace sighed and leaned back into the chair crossing one leg over her knee. "So," she said. "What are you called?"

"My name is Colonel Brianna Ni Riain," I said. "I'm a pilot. I fly spaceships."

"You do what?" She looked skeptically at me. "People do not fly, Miss...what was it? Ni Riain?"

"Colonel Ni Riain and it's not that I fly," I said. "Rather, I pilot starfaring craft."

"I wouldn't joke," she said. "Your life may depend on your words."

"I'm not joking," I replied. I was surprised at how calm I was.

"Hmmm." She said the word with a casual wave of her hand that I took to mean, "Go on."

"No, honestly, I truly don't know how I ended up here."

"Well, how you got here seems obvious enough. You must have stowed away aboard on one of the carts and then were carried aboard in one of the boxes."

"I did no such thing!" I said, my voice rising angrily.

"What is in the pouch?" she said, changing the subject abruptly.

Surprised, I took a deep, calming breath. As I did, I took off my messenger bag and laid it across my knees. Did I dare pull out the laptop? Time travel and paradox had never been one of my strongest areas of understanding. Though unofficially happening within the military's black ops, I still couldn't wrap my mind around the paradox issues. In fact, I still was not sure what I was doing here or for that matter how I even got here. My brief hesitation seemed to anger her and with a movement so swift I was caught off guard, she pulled the laptop bag up from my own knees and on to her own.

"Ugh. That's heavier than I expected," she said. She pulled the small black computer from the bag and looked at me. "What is this?"

"It's called a computer." I said, "It's like a journal, a calculator—umm—that's a way to add numbers quickly, and a map in one."

"Show me," she ordered.

I hesitated again.

"Show me," she said again. Her voice was firm.

"Aye-Aye, Captain," I said, a hint of sarcasm in my voice. She raised an eyebrow again.

Deciding that perhaps I had pressed my luck enough for the moment, I stood up and walked over to kneel beside her. Her eyes watched me the entire way, her hand near her pistol. I opened the laptop and turned it on. The familiar music started and she looked at it surprised. "It plays recorded music as well," I said.

She looked at it wonderingly as the background appeared. I was glad I had chosen a simple path through the woods as my wallpaper. I hesitate to think of what she would say to the pirate artwork of Don Maitz or the space shuttle launching in air.

"May I?" I asked as I slid the laptop from her legs onto the captain's desk. She moved her chair to allow me better access but still kept herself between the door and me. I pulled up a word document of one of my mission reports and showed it to her.

"More."

I showed her the calculator, followed by a spreadsheet of numbers from a flight recorder, then showed her one of my PowerPoint presentations with pictures.

"More."

I showed her how to type letters, more perfect than

by hand and neater than a printing press. Grace typed tentatively—two fingered, at first but soon found her own rhythm and system.

"More," she said after a few minutes of typing.

I showed her some of the PDF articles I had published on flying. She read them almost greedily, absentmindedly pushing that long red hair out of her face.

"More."

I opened the music player and introduced her to the recordings of Rush, Beethoven and Count Basie.

"More."

"I'm afraid I don't know what else to show you." I said. Rocking back on my knees, I put my hand on my lower back and pressed. Looking up at the pirate, I waited for her response.

She leaned back into the chair and looked at me appraisingly. In the silence, I could hear the rain on the deck as the storm I saw above deck reached us...or we reached it.

"You said you were a pilot? Not a magician or witch?" she finally asked.

"Pilot, yes. Not a mage or witch, though I do believe in the Gods and magic. As has been famously said, 'There are more things in heaven and earth...'"

"...Than are dreamt of in your philosophy. Shakespeare."

"Yes."

"I like his plays." She gave a half-smile and looked at me again, "You really do not know how you arrived here?"

"No, only that I did." A loud clap of thunder punctuated my words.

"Yet, you carry magic greater than I have ever seen." Grace looked up toward porthole as she spoke.

"It's not really magic; it's just, well as another famous author once put it: 'Any sufficiently advanced technology is indistinguishable from magic.' It's a bit complicated to explain."

"This is technology?" she said pointing to the computer.

"Yes." I said.

"It's still magic to me." She picked up my messenger bag and dumped the rest of the contents onto the desk. Pens, pencils, several small notebooks, a media player and the sextant all fell across the parchment and maps. She looked through them, touching each briefly, and then glanced at me.

She seemed to take in my clothes again, as if seeing me for the first time. I was wearing my dress whites: white pants with gold stripe down the leg, white jacket with all my ribbons and the single dress cutlass at my hip. "Only one weapon," she said matter-of-factly.

"Yes...I," I hesitated again. "I believe I could use the sword if I had to. I can shoot a pistol. But I'm a pilot, I fly, I don't typically climb into a ship armed. Bullets do bad things inside pressurized cabins."

"Hmmph," Grace gave that elegant wave of her hand again; it was obvious she had stopped listening halfway through my explanation. Looking at the items on the desk, she shook her head, handed me back my bag and gestured at my stuff. I took that as the okay to put it all away.

She then stood and began pacing back and forth in the small cabin. I took the time to shut down the laptop. How much actual battery power I had left, I did not know. As she paced back and forth, I listened to the sound of the rain on the deck above me. The sky outside grew darker, as did the cabin.

Finally, she stopped pacing and looked at me. She

pulled a tinderbox out of a pouch on her belt and lit the hurricane lamp on the desk. The small flame from lantern shed a flickering light in the cabin, creating shadows that played across the walls and floor.

"Tell me what you know of me," she said, returning to the chair. I sat down cross-legged on the floor, my bag beside me, leaning my back against the cabin wall.

"Ummm...you're Irish."

She laughed—a ringing sound. "Anybody could tell that by me accent. Tell me something most people wouldn't know."

I racked my brain. "You've been sailing since before you could walk. Your father owned your men and your ships. He left them to you when he passed. Your men trust you and follow you into battle willingly. You raid the English, trying to prevent them from conquering Ireland."

"Good. Now, again, why are you here?"

"I don't know. I was researching you when I suddenly found myself on your ship."

"Aha, perhaps there is something there. Why were you researching me?"

"My CO recommended it. I have an opportunity to command the first interstellar space exploration vehicle—the Corvette, Enterprise." I shook my head. I still couldn't believe they named it the Enterprise.

"CO?" Grace asked, a look of confusion on her face.

"Commanding Officer. Ummm. A captain's captain?"

"Ah, like the O'Malley or O'Donagh," she said.

"Yes."

Grace looked down at me, "So, you are being given a ship to captain? This is a good thing, yes?"

"Yes. But I also have a family; a daughter and a husband that I love with all my heart. If I accept this assignment,

I will be gone from them for at least four years, maybe longer."

"Have you discussed it with them?" Grace asked.

"Of course, and my husband supports my decision. He knows that NASA and the space program have been my dream since I was a child. I'd flown the space shuttle before its retirement and the disbandment of NASA. I am now a pilot for the Schooners, the ships that replaced the space shuttle, in the newly formed Starfaring Navy. The chance to fly the Corvette is an incredible opportunity."

"NASA? Starfaring Navy? What are these?" Grace put her elbows on her knees and leaned forward toward me, placing her chin on her hand; her face had an intense serious look.

"I guess you could say they are the organizations that allow me to fly. They provide the funding, the gold as it were, needed to keep exploring."

"Ah, I see and what does your daughter think of this?" Grace asked.

"She is young and I don't know that she really understands yet what it means for me to be gone that long. She just thinks it's cool that Mommy flies spaceships."

"You've mentioned these spaceships before, what are they?" she asked.

I thought about trying to explain space travel or faster than light travel and decided that I had better keep it simple.

"You know space—where the stars and moon are?"

"Of course, we navigate the seas by them."

"A spaceship allows me to travel to them and explore the unknown, much like you sail the sea."

She nodded. "I understand. So why do you hesitate to accept this honor?"

"A lot of reasons. The timing. My daughter is getting

ready to start school for the first time. If I am gone, I will miss most of her elementary years. My husband and I have been together nearly twenty years; I do not think anything will come between us. I worry about the public pressure. This is a major undertaking. The fact that I've been nominated means my entire military career as well as my personal history is up for review. And modern journalists are particularly good at finding potentially embarrassing facts."

"Do you regret anything you've done?" Grace asked.

"Not really. I have pushed the limits of some rules. I have more administrative letters in my file than most other woman in the service. But I get results and that, I think, is what matters."

"Sounds like me," said Grace, as she leaned back, almost relaxing. "I was never one to sit at home and watch the children. I wanted to be on the seas, exploring, sailing, and fighting. I think I would have never survived if I didn't have my ships and my men." She gestured at herself deprecatingly. "Pirate, men call me. And pirate, I am. But I am good at it."

"I can relate to that. I love the men I lead. And I think they respect me as well. I know I'm a good leader but leaving my family is asking a lot. I don't know that I want to give up the love of my husband and family for the chance to explore space."

"Wait! Whoever told ye ye'd have to give it up?" asked Grace, "My Hugh and I lived and loved for several years before his death. He never stopped me from sailing. He understood the call of the sea as much as I did. And never tried to keep me from her. But I always came home to him. Hard choices, we have all faced."

As she spoke, she caught my eyes with her own—that feeling of following her to the depths of hell and beyond came over me again. I shook my head and looked at her again. A faraway look had come into her eyes. She almost seemed to be somewhere else when she spoke again. "I found him, ye ken? My Hugh. Murdered by the MacMahons, his blood staining the ground. His eyes were closed. He looked peaceful, as if he was simply resting in the field. But I knew something was wrong. I could see from the wounds and the bloodstains on the ground that he was gone." I could see the loss of her lover was still a recent wound to her.

She got a fiery look in her eyes and I began to realize where she got her reputation as a fierce warrior. "But the MacMahons had failed to hide their trail. In my Hugh's hand lay a scrap of their colors. Hugh was the love of my life, but a nobody to most, a sailor I rescued from a sinking ship. He had no claim to land or property. He was not worth anything as a hostage, so they murdered him. And I could not let it go unavenged. I gathered my men and asked if they would support me. Of course, my men agreed. I found out where the MacMahons were going, sailed after them, found and killed them. Perhaps that is a bit of an understatement. We followed their trail. We attacked them on the Holy Island of Caher. Though I am sure that I will be punished in Heaven for what I did, for we attacked them on pilgrimage. The fight was bloody and fierce but I do not regret a single death. Even then, I was still not satisfied, for the MacMahons had no cause for my Hugh's death.

"So my men and I set across country to Doona Castle and captured it for my own. I know that perhaps revenge is not the greatest of things but it was all I had. My love for Hugh was greater than any other love I'd felt, even that of the sea. And his death nearly took it all from me. But I know he would have been disappointed in me if I hadn't returned to the sea. So I did and in the sea's waves found him again." She shook her head. "Bah, I'm getting melancholy in my old age." She smiled and then grew serious. "And now, now, I fight for my children."

"The meeting with Queen Elizabeth the First?"

"Now, how did ye know about that? Are ye a spy after all?"

"No, no," I said, shaking my head. "It is simply one of the stories that make you famous in my time. A meeting between two strong female leaders; neither of whom were known for giving ground."

She looked at me carefully, "Hmmm...you know, you could be useful. You say in your time this meeting took place."

"So history tells us."

"And you said you were a pilot?" she asked.

I nodded affirmatively.

"Can you navigate the waters?"

"I might be able to."

"Good. Then I have an idea. You will be me."

"I will what?" I must have looked utterly confused.

"Richard Bingham is a useless twit who has been given control o'er Connacht by the Queen. He thinks he owns my ships. He does not. He has waged war o'er my lands. Now he has gone so far as to kidnap me sons and holds them hostage for my behavior. Her Majesty has not seen fit to agree to my demands for their return though she agrees to meet with me should I win a challenge set before her."

"A challenge." I said flatly.

"Aye. Her Majesty has promised to order Bingham to release my family, if I can find a ship that she's hidden in a cove along the Irish Shore...before her chosen champion, Sir Francis Drake, can find it."

"That sounds challenging." I said.

"It will be. It will take time to find the ship. But you will help. You will be my decoy. I will set you aboard my flagship, the galley. You look enough like me that from a distance, it would work." I watched her pace back and forth in front of the faded wooden walls of the cabin. "My quartermaster will stay with you to help you run the ship. While you sail the waters in an obvious manner, I will take one of the caravels and find this hidden ship. If Drake and the Queen think that I am out here, any delays they send will come at you, not me, and it'll give me a better chance at finding the ship faster."

"But I don't sail. I fly. Your men don't know me."

She made a short chopping gesture with her hand. "But my men know me." She looked at me. "And I trust my men. Even if you were a spy for Her Majesty, which I do not think you are, they will keep my ship safe. You will be the perfect bait."

I watched the shore of Erie pass by as the ship edged around the island. The storm had passed and clear skies could be seen for miles. From my vantage point at the bow of the ship, I could see the tall cliffs of Ireland, the white and green and black of the stone faces that wind and salt had carved into the crag. Grass and shrubs in shades of green and yellow covered the tops of the cliffs but I could see no tall trees to stand guardian against the winds. It seemed a harsh land, even from our distance; I could hear the waves as they crashed up against the rocks.

"Sails ho! A stern," cried the lookout from the crow's nest high above the deck.

I turned from my position at the helm and opened the spyglass. Peering through it, I could see two ships-of-the-line closing in on us—very large three-masted ships with a double row of cannon. They were very imposing looking.

"Can we outrun them?" I asked, turning to the sailor who stood beside me, her quartermaster, the tall bald pirate who I found out was named Sean. Sean was the epitome of a pirate. Wearing loose pants and not much else, scars covered his body. He rarely smiled and spoke in short terse sentences. I don't think he agreed with Grace's decision to leave him behind.

"Perhaps," he said. "Close-haul them sails, boys."

"What will that do?" I asked.

"Hopefully, move us closer to the wind and able to run faster. Ships-of-the-line are heavy. They carry a lot of weaponry. We might outrun them."

I looked back at the two ships. Suddenly, a thought came to me.

"You said they were heavy."

"Aye."

"Does that mean they are low in the water?"

"Aye."

"Are we as heavy?"

"Nah, Herself likes a fast ship. We draw less water."

"Then, if we could get closer to the shore, could we run them aground?"

Sean looked appraisingly at me. I think he was trying to decide if my suggestion had merit or if I was completely insane. To be honest, I did not know which was correct.

"Hey, it always works in the movies." I said, thinking that I had no idea if it would work in real life.

"The what?" Sean asked.

"Never mind," I said, shaking my head. "Do you think it'll work?"

"Assuming our charts are accurate, yea. Mind ye,

that's not a particularly good assumption." Sean gave a short, sharp nod, and turned back to the helm. "All right, men, grab your swords and hang on. We're going to ease toward the shoals of Erie and see if we can't run them English bastards aground."

Our ship slowly began to move closer to the shoreline. Even as it was, the two ships-of-the-line continued to close with our galley.

Suddenly, I heard a very large boom followed by a splash of water that covered my face. I looked back to see a puff of smoke rising from the ship closest to us.

"Did they just fire on us?" I asked.

"Warning shot only." Sean said. "Terms of the sea mean we should heave to and wait for them to close."

"What do you think?" I asked.

"The longer we make them chase us, the longer Herself has to find that ship."

"Right." I said and looked around at the other pirates, who seemed to be waiting for a decision.

"Keep running, men! We'll make them chase us!" I shouted.

Cheers rang out from the sailors at my words. The pirates rushed about the ship, adding sail here and trimming sail there, doing everything they could to get a little more speed from the ship.

Over the next couple of hours, the two English ships would sail in close and cannonballs would splash into the sea. The men would pause in their work and look to Sean and me. Sean would shout at them to return to their work and they would jump to it quickly.

Suddenly, a horrible sound filled the afternoon air: a mix of a dying scream and terrible crash at the same time. I looked back to find that one of the ships had stopped moving. We had actually run one of them aground.

Shouts and cheers rang out across our deck, while small figures ran around in complete disorder on the sand-barred ship. I was not sure if the second ship would stop or not, and it seemed its captain hesitated as well. We continued to gain distance on them for a while, but then his ship began moving after us. He must have decided that catching us was more important.

As day moved into night, the pirates managed to remain just outside the reach of the English cannon fire.

Suddenly, a shout rang from the crow's nest. "Sail starboard!"

Reaching again for the spyglass, I looked toward the coastline. In the dim light, I could see two ships. Handing the spyglass to Sean, I waited for his response.

"It's Herself!" he said joyfully. "And the other ship, she be flying English colors! It must be the hidden one!"

The cheers again rang out from the pirates. I found myself joining in, and then blushing furiously when I realized it.

"Head towards those ships." I ordered. Glancing back, I saw that the remaining English ship must have seen the sails as well, and it begin tacking toward the moored ships as well.

As we sailed the ship closer, I could see Grace O'Malley aboard the English ship; her bright red hair and colorful clothing stood out amongst the red and blue uniforms. When we anchored beside her caravelle, one of the sailors shouted down that Sean and I were to row over to the English ship.

We soon did, and I found myself standing next to Grace as she yelled at the captain of the English ship.

"Now, as I was saying, I found you fair and square. I want the letters of proof from Her Majesty."

"That won't be necessary," said a female voice from

behind the captain. A cloaked woman had walked up to stand beside him.

I would not have recognized Queen Elizabeth I if it were not for Grace's reaction. When the cloaked woman pulled down the hood, her stern face was cast into the light. A gold circlet lay nearly hidden in her reddish blond hair. Grace's anger at the captain of the ship seemed to diffuse and she nodded toward the woman.

"Majesty," she said.

"You have done well," said the Queen. "We suppose We should be surprised that you reached Us first, but We are not. When family is on the line, one does what is necessary. Isn't that what you said?"

"Yes, Your Majesty."

"We will order Bingham to release your family. These papers..." she nodded and a small clerk, who I had not noticed before, rushed forward and handed a sheaf of papers to Grace, "deed control of your lands and ships to you directly. Of course, you are still expected to pay taxes."

Graced nodded. The Queen moved forward. As she did, another clerk handed her a small black box. She handed it to Grace O'Malley and leaned forward to kiss her on both cheeks. She whispered something so that only those closest could hear. "And We trust that you will limit your raids to Enemies of England from now on. Go with Our blessing."

Grace nodded and with a glance at me, she walked back to her ship. I followed her quickly. Once back aboard her galley, she turned to me with a joyous look, "We won!" she shouted. Her men cheered, more loudly than I had ever heard.

"Yes, yes, you did!" I said softly.

She leaned over me and I suddenly found myself in a

warm embrace. Our eyes met and another flash of that power, the need to follow her, came over me. When I shook myself, I realized I was lying on the carpet of my office. Had it all been a dream? Surely not. I stood up and walked over to the coffee pot on the sideboard. After pouring myself a cup, I looked back at the desk and noticed a small black box to one side. I opened it up. There in bright, shining gold was the engraved sextant. This time when I pulled it out and looked at it, I could read the words.

G o'M: Well-behaved women rarely make history. We will make history. QEI

As I stood staring at the sextant, I realized the old man was right; its magic was true. It was not that it transported me to Grace O'Malley's ship and showed me how her men followed her without question. It was not even her telling me the story of her loss and revenge. Its true magic was in showing me Grace's willingness to take risks, to step out of the roles assigned to her, to follow her dreams...and most importantly, to put her trust in others even when they arrive unexpectedly.

I chuckled and placed the sextant back in the box. I then closed the books, leaving them neatly stacked on my desk to return to the library another day. I walked down the long hallway to my CO's office and knocked.

"Enter."

I entered and saluted the commander. "Can I help you, Captain?" he asked.

"I'll do it, sir."

Author's Note: Special thanks to Laurel Thatcher Ulrich for the inspirational quote. This story is dedicated to all the women of space travel but specifically to Sally Ride and Eileen Collins. Thank you for leading the way.

Mister Adventure in Neverland

By Davey Beauchamp

Act 1: The Lost Boys

All children, except one, grow up. They soon know that they will grow up, and the way, were the last words Alex, as Mister Adventure, remembered reading aloud to the orphans, when a shimmering dust came flying out of the book and hit him directly in the face. It was quite shocking. Things quickly went fuzzy, a blur, and he thought he had heard voices of the orphans calling out to him, or were they just random thoughts, or something else entirely? Then came the falling into the cold darkness of unconsciousness.

First there was only silence; followed by...
Voices
Booming

Screaming
Pain

It was the pain; that was how Alex realized he was beginning to regain consciousness. Confusion quickly followed as the darkness that filled his head became bright amorphic blobs of color and sound. It felt as though he had gone a round or twenty with one of Doc Tech's mechanized marvels and it had gotten in a few lucky blows to his head.

"Who...he?"

"...y is he wearing a mask...the Captain?"

"He must...pirate captain!"

"A...captain that might be...take the Hook!"

In unison they cried out, "Tie him up! Tie the pirate up!"

"Where is Tinker..."

Voices

"... the rope."

"Look, there's a note!"

"Let me see it!" Spoken with authority over the others.

"Quickly, before he wakes up."

Little by little, Alex's sight began to return. The blurs became a light tunnel, forms gained a reality of detail about them and his other senses also slowly became more coherent. He could tell that he was poorly tied to a makeshift chair of some sort. For the moment, Alex was going to see how things played out, because... Were those children's voices he heard?

"It's in fairy!" the voice said, annoyed.

"He will not be able to break through that," another voice said confidently.

"Let me see," the tiny squeaky voice said. "I can read fairy."

"Look, he's starting to wake up!" two similar voices said in unison.

"No one can read fairy but girls and fairies."

"And me!" A round crimson form said, trying to make himself sound as though he had some sort of authority.

"Fine!"

"That wouldn't be something I would admit to," the voice said. "Except this one time, since it might help us find Peter."

"What does it say?"

It amazed him that they weren't even trying to hide their numbers with their chaotic chatter that sent their conversation everywhere. He had to wonder, *Do they even know who I am?*

Alex could tell there were six people in the room: all young, all boys by the sound of their voices. These were by far the worst henchmen he had ever encountered in all of his days as Mister Adventure. They almost made him laugh—and Alex might have, if he didn't think it would just add to the pain in his head. And all of this talk about fairies and pirates just added to the humor of it all.

The tunnel of light faded and all appeared as it should be. Alex finally saw the boys who had captured Mister Adventure. He went from wanting to know just how they had captured him—if they even knew who he was—to being dumbfounded in a split second.

Six boys, a very motley crew, gathered around their captive, apparently still not sure what to make of him, with one staring at a crumbled up bit of paper no bigger than his hand.

Shaking his head, Alex couldn't believe what he knew he was seeing. They were all there: Tootles, wearing crudely constructed red wings that flapped in opposite directions when he moved; Nibs, dressed in a gray shirt and black pants filled with holes and covered in dirt; Slightly, wearing a tweed coat with a pair of pants held up by crudely crafted and aged suspenders. Curly looked more like a washed up mad scientist's assistant than a Lost Boy. And the twins: one was dressed in a white night gown and the other in a black one.

He knew who these characters were, as well as he knew his own friends. Alex, as Mister Adventure, had read the story of Peter Pan and his adventures with the Lost Boys and the Darlings countless times to the children of the Sapphire City Orphanage. That thought quickly brought to mind there was no sign of the Darlings, Peter Pan or Tinker Bell.

"Look out, the pirate is moving!" Nibs said excitedly.

"Hey there, guys," Mister Adventure said kindly, knowing how to deal with frightened and scared children. "I am not a pirate. I am Mister Adventure."

"What's a Mister Adventure?" Curly asked, eyeing the stranger up and down, still fairly certain he was a pirate. Because everyone knew that all adults in Neverland were pirates—except for the Redskins, who could just be as frightening.

"He looks like a pirate to me," the First Twin said, followed by the Second Twin, who said, "He wears a mask like the Hook does."

"Trust me, I am no pirate," Adventure said with a smile. "I take it I am not in Sapphire City anymore."

"This is Never—" the Second Twin tried to say before being cut off.

"Don't tell him that!" Slightly exclaimed. "You never tell a pirate nothing."

"Well, if he is a pirate," the First Twin said, "he already knows this is Neverland."

"But—" Tootles tried again but to no avail.

"STOP!" Curly yelled.

"Why?" the boys said in unison.

Tootles had had enough and was going to be heard. "The letter from Tink explains it all," he said, then added, "I think," because he didn't want to be the one to free a new pirate to the Jolly Roger.

Peter is missing.
Looking for him past the second star to the right.
This man, no pirate.
He can help find Peter if the pirate has him.
                                                          Tinker Bell

The boys looked at Mister Adventure, and Alex looked at the Lost Boys. He wished that Kid Adventure was with him, but then again, he was no longer a child. Alex knew he just had to gain their trust and he had read Peter and Wendy enough times to hopefully do it.

"Do we trust him?" Nibs asked, looking at each one of the boys one by one, until his eyes fell to the man in the tied to the chair.

"Do you ever trust a pirate?" Slightly said at the top of his lungs.

"No!" they all said in a unified voice.

"But Tinker Bell said he wasn't a pirate and he was here to help us," Tootles said, getting his wings caught up in the roots of their hideout.

"Can we really trust Tinker Bell?" the First Twin said, followed by the Second, "She is a fairy after all."

"The one thing Tink cares about is Peter," Nibs said.

"So maybe we can?" the Second Twin said.

"What do you say, pirate, can we trust you to help us find Peter and maybe Tinker Bell?" Slightly said, eying Mister Adventure.

Alex was just amazed by all of this. It was like being in an unwritten chapter of the book. He just wished he knew what the point of all of this was, because there was always a point to these bizarre trips. Alex had to wonder who was behind this little trip to Neverland and what was going back on in Sapphire City, but at least he knew the League was there to take care of the city in case anything was happening in his absence.

"If I am here to help," Mister Adventure said, "then I am here to help."

The boys just looked at him.

"Do you always say things twice?" the Twins said.

"No, I think it's adult speak," Nibs said.

"Could one of you please free me from these ropes so I can help you find your missing friend," Alex said. He figured the sooner he found Peter Pan, the sooner he would be able to return home.

They all scattered, looking around for a knife to cut the ropes, while the Twins tried to unite the knots. Both parties were failing at their tasks.

Alex just shook his head. "Stand back, please." As he stood up, he couldn't believe what happened. He was prepared to break through the ropes, but they fell off of him. They had been tied too loosely or not all. Alex smiled. He had no idea what was going on, but it brought a smile to his lips nonetheless.

And with that smile, something else hit him. It was the smell of this place. It smelled of boys, and not just any boys: boys who went out and adventured. Boys who weren't afraid to get dirty and play in the mud and muck. These were boys who lived in the moment. The smell reminded him of Kid Adventure's vacant room at the brownstone.

Act 2: The Jungles of Neverland

Alex was having the time of his life as he ran through the jungles of Neverland. It had been far too long since his last adventure in the jungles of South America with Dr. Stone. And for some reason, the jungles of Neverland reminded him of those times, right down to flora and fauna; it was like this place came from his memories, but he hadn't run into anything directly from them. Like the head hunters the two of them had accidentally stumbled across while trying to track down Michael Azteck.

As he ran, Alex got a wild idea. He grabbed a low-hanging vine and swung up high into the air, landing on a nearby tree limb. A smile crossed his face as he realized he had just done it. Alex leapt towards another vine, grabbed it and swung higher into the air and let go. For a single moment, he was flying through the air and it was so much different from leaping from building to building in Sapphire City.

Alex figured time was on his side here. When he had left the Lost Boys' underground home, he had not seen Wendy's house and since Tootles was still a boy and not a judge, it was safe to say all of this was happening before the Darlings came to Neverland. He figured he had a little bit of time to sightsee in this unwritten prologue.

Vine after vine and tree limb after tree limb—Alex was Tarzan and it gave him a freedom he felt he had lost over the past couple of tragedy-filled months. Alex grabbed another vine and flung himself upwards, breaking through the canopy of the jungle, and he could see all of Neverland. The view was exhilarating; he could see the whole island, including the Jolly Roger. Alex let out a roar of excitement.

The roar gave all the animals and inhabitants of Neverland pause. It was a sound unlike anything they had ever heard a human make before. They knew something had come to Neverland that had never been there before, and maybe never should have.

Alex came crashing back down through the canopy; tree limbs and branches broke from the force of his descent. He didn't reach out for vine or limb; with a loud thud, he landed on the jungle floor and took off running without a second thought, heading towards the Mermaid Lagoon.

But nothing was ever as easy as that, especially in Neverland, where one couldn't travel from point A to point B without passing through points X, Y, and Z first.

A giant furry black-and-grey-striped arm came out of nowhere, knocking Alex to the ground. Dazed, Alex shook his head, trying to clear it. He had been so focused on where he was going and the fun he was having that he forgot to keep an eye out for any surprises that might pop up. In Sapphire City, such a mistake could cost him or another their lives. Or worse.

But before Alex could grasp what had just happened to him, a large dark furry mass fell upon him with a throaty, squeaky, chirpy roar. The weight of this creature knocked the wind out of him.

The mass of fur rose up off of Alex as though it hadn't noticed him. Alex took a quick deep breath and filled his lungs once more with air. It felt like he had just gone yet another round with the AtomiK Fist, taking an atomik punch to the gut. Alex rolled to his right, making sure that if the mass of fur fell back again, it wouldn't be on him.

There was a second roar, different from the first, but sounding very familiar to Alex. It reminded him of the time Mister Adventure was in the Pacific Northwest dealing with the Red Aliens from Saturn and their attempt to mechanize the Sasquatch that lived there in order to conquer and colonize the Earth. But then again, it also reminded Alex of a time before Mister Adventure, when he went to the Sichuan Province to hunt pandas.

Instincts took over and Alex became Mister Adventure. He leapt to his feet and lunged at the mysterious and massive form before him, performing his patented Mister Adventure one-two punch. One, Mister Adventure hits you and two, you hit the floor! But the power of his punch was defused, thanks in part to the creature's massive furry exterior. And it felt as though he had just punched into one of New Moon's or Full Moon's gravity walls.

A brief moment of pain crossed Mister Adventure's face as he tried to decide what he was going to do before becoming dinner for these monsters. "I have no idea what you are or who made you," Adventure said, cracking his knuckles, "but I am going to take you down."

Two highly different furry forms turned towards him, apparently noticing him for the first time. Adventure leapt out at the skinnier of the two furry forms. It easily leapt up over the man and landed behind him. "Hey, watch out there!" A chirpy high pitched voice said.

Adventure's eyes widened and shook his head in disbelief as he saw what exactly had attacked him. It was a giant panda and raccoon. The two of them looked quite as surprised as he did.

"What are you?" Adventure said.

"The same could be asked of you, sir," the giant panda said, grabbing a piece of bamboo from the jungle and beginning to chew on it. "After all, you did interrupt us."

What is going on here? I am certain that that bamboo wasn't there a moment ago, Alex thought to himself.

The raccoon smiled. "I think we can forgive him for interrupting our romp. After all, he can't be all bad, not with his great taste in facial wear."

Mister Adventure's stern hero face returned to the softer and now perplexed Alexander Venture's face; his jaw hung wide open. And his body relaxed a bit, now no longer looking for a fight or a bit of heroic action. This had to be the strangest sight he had ever experienced: a talking raccoon and panda and they were acting just like people. He wondered if he had left Neverland and stepped through the looking glass.

"It looks like you might have broken the man," the panda said with a soft deep tone to his voice.

"Or could it be a cat got his tongue," the raccoon said, with a look in his black beady eyes that said he wanted their romp to begin anew. "Though I haven't seen Mister Tiger around lately."

Alex's hunter's instinct took over and he began to back away from these two wild animals. He didn't want to get caught up in their romp.

The two animals could smell the slight scent of fear coming off of him, along with other scents they had never smelled before. They turned towards him as though the romp would now continue with three. The panda tossed aside his piece of bamboo and cracked his neck just by turning his head.

Alex began to back away. "Look, gentlemen, I really don't want to join your romp."

They looked as though they were about to pounce upon him, but instead fell to the ground in laughter. Alex just knew he had this dumbfounded look upon his face and wondered, *Where is the Mad Hatter's tea party?*

"It is okay," Raccoon said.

"We just like to have fun with the newcomers to our jungle. The Lost Boys just love it," Panda said. "So is there anything we can do for you this fine evening?" He grabbed another piece of bamboo and began chewing on it.

A look of utter and total surprise came across Raccoon's face. "Where are our manners? We forgot introductions."

"Yes, proper introductions are in order," Panda said with a snort. "I am Mister Panda and that is Mister Raccoon."

"Hi!" Mister Raccoon said, in a quite excited voice.

"I am Mister Adventure," Alex said, offering an outstretched hand. The trio all shook hand and paw.

"It does seem we have quite a few Misters here," Mister Panda said curiously. "Though there was a time I thought about being a doctor. Doctor Panda."

A smirk appeared on Alex's face at the thought of this panda dressed up like a doctor.

"But where are you off to?" Mister Raccoon said.

"I was heading to the Mermaid Lagoon before I accidentally interrupted the two of you," Alex said, still not believing he was having a conversation with two animals that would never meet naturally in the wild and one that he had hunted.

Mister Raccoon looked him up and down. "Why would you want to go there?"

"Yes, those mermaids are dreadful, wicked, I would say. Quite foul," Mister Panda said with a shiver. "Quite, quite foul. I am thankful that my bamboo doesn't grow anywhere near that place."

"And I have to deal with them every time I want to eat some crabs or clams," Mister Raccoon said, his nose wrinkling.

Panda looked curiously at Alex. "Do you mind if we walk with for a bit with you? It is just I have never met one such as you before."

"Sure, the more the merrier," Alex said.

"Would you do us the honor of telling us more about this land that you come from?" Mister Panda asked politely. Alex was more than happy to oblige, so he told the two of them all about Sapphire City and all the wonders the city held. He also told them all about many of his exploits as Mister Adventure, from his battles with the Master of Zombies and his ghoulish creations to the time he met a multitude of Sir Walter Raleighs gathered from an infinite set of realities to save all of creation. Then Alex couldn't help telling the two about his adventure's against the Martians, where he lost yet another friend and ally.

Raccoon and Panda were just amazed by these tales, but before they knew it..."It looks as though we are finally here," Mister Panda said, putting a halt to the conversation.

The three of them stood looking out over the lagoon. The Jolly Roger was set off in the distance, anchored for the coming night. The mermaids lay nestled on their rock outcroppings.

"Well, this is a disappointment," Alex said with a sigh. "I was really hoping I was going to come out over by the cliffs."

"Why would you want that?" Mister Raccoon asked, not fully understanding Alex's love of adventure and daredevilry.

Alex really couldn't think how to put it into words that Raccoon might understand. So they stood there in silence as he thought about it. Raccoon's attention quickly got distracted as it turned to all the tasty things waiting for him in the lagoon and he forgot he had asked the question.

On some level, Panda understood—he could see it in Alex's body language. "Remember this is Neverland and it appears as how you perceive it," Mister Panda said. "Adventure is always just around the next tree or behind the next rock."

Mister Raccoon danced about the water and saw what he was looking for.

"And sometimes you don't even have to go looking for it," Panda continued.

Alex laughed because that was so true even in Sapphire City. Rarely did he ever go looking for the next adventure: it always had a way of finding him.

The ground rose instantly around him and the water was no longer at his feet. Alex just looked down and smiled.

Mister Raccoon had barely grabbed onto the cliff's edge as it rose out of the water and leapt back onto solid ground. Panda just stood, interested in seeing what Alex was going to do next.

"Now that is more like it," Alex said with a huge smile, and then fell forward.

Raccoon and Panda just looked at one another. Panda believed they had just met someone who was even more foolhearty than Peter Pan.

"Do you think we should have warned him that the croc was near?" Raccoon asked.

Mister Panda just shook his head. "Do you really think such a warning would have made any difference to that one?"

Raccoon looked down at the water and all the tasty treats he wasn't going to have. "No, I guess you're right. It wouldn't have."

The two of them then turned and headed back into the jungle without a second thought for the man they just met.

The land returned to what could be said was normal in Neverland as a giant crocodile slid into the waters, looking for its next meal.

Act 3: The Croc and the Mermaids

The lagoon couldn't have been any more perfect, from temperature to clarity. It reminded Alex of another time, a time before Mister Adventure and Sapphire City, when he didn't have a care in the world and was vacationing in the Caribbean. He was definitely a different person back then, a person who only carried about himself and no one else. How he had changed since the World's Fair, for better or worse.

He shook his mind free of the memories of the past, because he had a feeling the real fun was about to begin. With everything Alex had faced as Mister Adventure, he had never had the chance to go up against real life pirates and he was quite excited by the thought. Alex was quite the fan of Errol Flynn's Captain Blood.

There was no warning as the snout of the crocodile hit Alex in the back, disorienting him and knocking the air out of his lungs. The croc quickly swam back around to clamp its powerful jaws on its meal, so it could drag its prey down to bottom of the lagoon to drown it and to save it for later.

Alex felt mind-shattering pain shoot up through his leg as the croc clamped down on him and began pulling him down. Panic filled Alex's mind, and in a slight moment of clarity, he couldn't believe he had been so dumb. This could be how Mister Adventure went out, far away from Sapphire City: by a crocodile in a story book.

Darkness once more began to claim Alex's conscious mind and he wondered if the League of Adventurous Heroes would ever know what happened to him.

A sound appeared through the darkness and pain, echoing in Alex's ears: he could somehow see the words tic, toc, tic, toc of the clock inside the crocodile.

Neverland was what one perceived it to be and Alex was once again breathing air and not choking down water. His body spasmed between coughs as his lungs burned. Time seemed to slow down as Alex realized he was now falling out of the sky, back towards the water of the lagoon below and the waiting jaws of the croc.

Alex reentered the water with a splash and a velocity which sent him straight down to the bottom of the lagoon.

The croc was highly confused; one moment it had its next meal secure in its mouth and then it was just gone, only to reappear with a splash at the bottom of its home. It was not about to lose this one again. It darted off after its meal.

As the croc closed in on Alex, he was already swimming towards the surface, and for the second time he heard the tic, toc and didn't wait for the animal to grab him. Alex just appeared at the Lagoon's surface treading water. In the back of his mind, Alex figured this was how Dr. Specter must feel with the ability to appear and reappear wherever he wanted.

He waited for the croc, because he knew the beast would not stop coming at him until it had him as its next meal. The tic-toc became louder and louder and Alex managed to avoid the croc's snout this time, but he did roll along the side of the mighty reptile. The rough scales of the croc shredded his shirt.

"That's it! I had it with this croc," Alex yelled, becoming Mister Adventure once more and diving under the water, looking for the croc. He waited for the monster to come at him again and as he did, Mister Adventure readied his patented one-two punch. He also knew time was of the essence here because once the sun finished setting, he wouldn't be able to see the croc in the lagoon. It appeared the crystal blue water was turning a murky black ichor and the croc would then have the full advantage. One Mister Adventure didn't want to give it.

The showdown came as the sun was about to pass into the darkness of night. Mister Adventure had to partially rely on instinct and the movement of the water as the croc approached. With all the might Adventure could muster, he dove underwater and the two connected. Adventure's fist struck the croc's snout, sending the massive creature flying out of the water. He quickly rose to the surface to catch a glimpse of the croc landing deep within the jungles of Neverland.

Amazement hit Alex, who couldn't believe what he had just done. "I guess all the laws of physics go out the window here. Now all I have to do is save Peter Pan from a boatload of pirates."

Alex swam over to the mermaids' rocks to catch his breath and pulled off his shredded shirt; it was no better than wet rags. The mermaids didn't say a word, because they didn't want to mess with the man who had defeated the tic-toc croc with a single punch.

Act 4: The Pirates

Night had finally come to Neverland and Alex quietly swam over to the Jolly Roger. He had lucked out or it could have been Neverland reacting to his wishes, but clouds had obscured the moon, helping to hide his presence. All appeared quiet on the deck of the ship. Alex made his way along the hull until he reached the anchor chain. Grabbing the chain, Alex quickly pulled himself out of the water and used the chain like a ladder. Silently, he slid onto the deck giving a pause to see if his presence had been noticed.

Across the deck Alex could see a cage and a form within that looked like Peter. It could always be a trap for the real Peter Pan or for him, though. Someone or something had brought him here and this player still remained hidden.

Was it a break that there was no one on the deck to guard the prisoner or a piece of the trap to lure him or others into a false sense of security? But then again, if it was Peter Pan in the cage, who was left to defy Captain Hook now? Alex knew the Lost Boys wouldn't and couldn't. They were not organized enough to do so without Peter's leadership. The Redskins wouldn't bother Hook as long as he left them alone. Hook would now have free rein over Neverland and its waters if he played it smart.

But regardless, it was time to fall into the trap. Alex once more shifted into Mister Adventure and walked over to the cage, in the open, to find nothing more than a silhouetted figure held within. It was flat, translucent and without true form or mass, but it was moving around on its own. Mister Adventure knew it could only be one thing: Peter's shadow.

A voice rose out of the darkness and in that moment Adventure knew he had walked into the waiting trap. The voice possessed a thick British accent. "I knew that by capturing your shadow. In the end I would finally capture you, Peter Pan!"

The deck lights and hooded lanterns began to glow, illuminating the ship, the crew and Hook. The captain was taken aback to find someone other than Peter Pan standing before him. "You're not Pan!"

Mister Adventure turned around to face Captain Hook. "No, no, I am not."

Hook looked over the man before him, trying to discover the game he was playing at. Adventure did the same thing to Hook, whose demeanor quickly changed from triumph to surprise to curiosity and finally to good spirits. It was an odd course of emotions to go through. Hook's face spoke volumes or at least the part which Adventure could see thanks to the long flowing handlebar mustache traveling the man's face. The captain wore a highwayman's mask hiding the upper portions of his face, which now made sense as to why the Lost Boys thought he was a pirate, but Alex had to wonder why this fact was never in the book.

"Well, then, who are you?" Mr. Smee said with a thick Irish accent. "Don't keep the captain waiting now."

Mister Adventure wasn't exactly sure how to answer the question and he knew it was only a matter of time before he was in the fight for his life against a ship full of pirates. His fists tightened. There was only going to be one option that would allow him to free Pan's shadow and get this story back on track.

"Mister Smee, can't you see?" Hook said with a grim smile, obviously annoyed by his boatswain's ill manners. "We have gained another able bodied man to help us tame this wild land of Neverland."

"Are you sure, Captain?" Smee said in a groveling tone, cowering as to not be inflicted with another beating or worse.

"You," fire and anger filled Hook's eyes, "dare question me, Mister Smee!"

"No, Captain," Mr. Smee groveled. "How do we know this isn't some trap sent by Peter Pan?"

"Mister Smee, do you really think Peter Pan," he said the name with disgust as he glanced down at the hook he now had for a hand, "would seek help from an adult? The boy is too prideful for that."

Adventure did not want to waste this opportunity, so he used it to his advantage. He never understood why villains would talk so much, giving Mister Adventure the time he needed to stop their plans or thwart their doomsday device or save the damsel in distress. It must be the villains' fatal flaw. Adventure spun around like he had countless numbers of times and kicked down on the padlock, shattering it underfoot.

The remnants of the lock fell to the deck with a rain of clanks, which stunned the pirates.

Smee burst into excitement, bouncing around. "See I to—"

"Shut up, Smee, unless you want us all to face the plank," Starkey said sharply.

With the lock gone, Adventure opened the raw iron cage. The shadow quickly fled, leaving Mister Adventure and the pirates to face off against one another.

"Well I think that clears up why I am here," Mister Adventure said with a smile, posing himself for the onslaught he knew was about to come.

An unseen force of Neverland or another aspect of whom or what Hook was, that could not be consciously be explained, caused the highwayman's mask to fall away from Hook's face and it brought Alex back for a split second. Alex should have been surprised by what he saw, but he wasn't. He was beginning to gain a handle on what it was like being in Neverland. It appeared the face Hook was hiding behind the mask was that of Alex's own father's. Alex didn't give the face a second thought and once more was Mister Adventure.

"I now see you for who you really are," Hook said with disgust, spitting on the deck. "You are Peter Pan. And you are mocking me by wearing that mask. Did you think I could not see through such deception!"

Adventure thought about it for a second and figured the ruse could only work in his favor with dealing with this madman. "Yes, I am Peter Pan!" A grin appeared on Mister Adventure's face as he stood there in his best Peter Pan pose.

"Pirates, kill him!" Captain Hook yelled at the top of his lungs, drawing his cutlass.

Pirates emerged all around Mister Adventure, coming from every convincible nook and cranny the ship possessed. This was just like any other venture into a nemesis' lair and facing off with all the minions they could throw at him. And this was the moment Adventure lived for.

The pirates charged Adventure with all manner of weapons in hand, beginning a dance which Adventure had done one too many times to count now. He had to give the pirates a nod because they were holding their own. These were the best trained henchmen Adventure had faced over the years in Sapphire City and abroad. It was actually a nice change of pace for him, but not a challenge that he would allow to overcome him.

By the time Mister Adventure was done with the pirates, they were scattered all over the deck and some had been sent flying into the water. Hook looked confused.

"Hook, I have to give you this," Mister Adventure said, a bit winded. "Those men are some of the best I have ever fought. Well done, sir. So I am really looking forward to see what you have to offer me."

"Indeed," Hook said, leaping down from the upper deck down to the main deck where Adventure awaited him. Adventure grabbed the closest sword to him and the two met with a loud clang of cold steel.

The sun began to rise again as the two continued their climatic battle. Alex couldn't be happier: this was everything he had dreamt it to be. The only thing he wished was that the sails were down so he could have slid down one with a knife. He was amazed by the stamina

Hook had at his disposal, but that could have been the fact he was nothing more than a fictional character in a book. It would also explain why all the other pirates were still just laying there on the deck defeated. Adventure figured he would never be able to beat Hook in a straightforward sword fight—that just wasn't how it was done. He needed to defeat the captain in a clever and unique way.

An idea leapt into Adventure's mind. There was only one way to defeat Captain Hook and that was with the captain's own ego and pride. Mister Adventure jumped back from the captain and smiled. "Come on, old man, is that the best you got? I remember how easy it was to beat you when I just a mere boy and now it is even easier. Where is the challenge?" Adventure laughed mockingly at Hook, maneuvering him into position.

"Old man! Old MAN!" Hook screamed, with fire and vengeance in his eyes. "You are the only one who has gotten old!"

"Then let's see what you got, old man," Mister Adventure said, still laughing.

Captain Hook charged Mister Adventure with the cutlass leading the way. Adventure smiled and then leapt high in the air just before the captain would have run him through. Hook suddenly found himself in the cage which had held Pan's shadow. Adventure landed, shutting the cage door with a loud slam and inserted his sword into the u-lock latch of the cage. He bent the sword in the latch to slow the captain's release.

"I am going to kill you, Pan," Hook screamed at Mister Adventure, who had stopped listening to him. The more pressing concern for Alex was that he suddenly began to glow a bright white and began to fade from the deck of the Jolly Roger. The sound of Hook screaming faded, though the sound of nothingness was just as deafening.

The next thing Alex knew he was once again standing in the orphanage reading room as a fully clothed Mister Adventure. The book Peter and Wendy lay at his feet.

Epilogue

Looking into the orphanage, through the bay windows of the room in which Mister Adventure reappeared, stood two men that no one else could see.

"So why," a raspy phantasmagoric voice asked, "did you have me send him into the book?"

"Doesn't the smile on his face say it all?" Adventure Lad said turning to Doctor Phantom.

"I know not what you mean," Doctor Phantom said with a hiss.

"When was the last time you saw Alex smile like that and just have fun?" Adventure Lad said, "Alex as Mister Adventure has been through so much lately and I know he still blames himself for what happened to me. He has forgotten what it is like just to have fun being Mister Adventure."

"Fun..." Doctor Phantom said inquisitively, "I believe I remember the word, but not the feeling. Though if you say it was what he needed, then it was my honor to bring it about."

"Thank you," Adventure Lad said with a smile.

X Spots the Mark

By Michael A. Ventrella

Irad poked at the lifeless body.

"He ain't gettin' any more dead, Cap'n," said Bart.

"Aye, I suppose you're right." Irad sighed, tossing aside the gnarled stick. "He was a good man, he was, and a brave one, too. Greenie! What be his name again?"

"Daniel, sir," Bart replied, clenching his teeth at his captain's refusal to learn the names of any of his recent crew.

"Daniel, eh?" Irad scratched at the five days' growth of beard that had become a new nesting place for the small sandy bugs that infested the island. "Not exactly a name to strike fear into yer enemies. Ah, well, here's to ye, Daniel."

The three remaining pirates raised their hands in salute to their fallen comrade, and Bart licked his lips wistfully, wishing for a drink to make an honest toast. The relentless sun burned their skin, and the Caribbean wind extended little reprieve. Bart rubbed his brow with a dirty cloth and glanced at his captain.

Captain Irad's long untidy mane of golden-red hair swirled in the breeze like a cold fire engulfing his head, the steely resolve in his eyes guaranteeing no mutiny would deter the mission. Sweat drenched his fine linen shirt and days of climbing over rocks, crawling through quicksand, fighting giant scorpions, and surviving a series of strange explosive traps had taken a toll on his usually immaculate appearance. It would be difficult to perpetuate his reputation as the lady-killing "Kissing Pirate" in his current state; the women would seriously resist his advances, as opposed to merely feigning protest.

Irad knelt and spread the parchment wide between his hands, the two remaining staring over his shoulder.

"Blast and bugger, it still says the same thing!" he spat. "Ye'd think Daniel's death would have satisfied it."

Bart bit his lip and glanced at the first mate who, as usual, remained deathly silent. "What was supposed to happen?" he asked.

"Arrr, I don't know," Irad admitted, scratching at his unshaven face. "But every other time we did the right thing, the next clue would appear on the bloody map."

"I don't trust it." Bart shivered. "It be terrible voodoo magic."

"Aye, 'tis indeed," Irad said, eyeing the young lad. "But if that's what Rummy Jack made, then that's what it be."

"How do ye know it be his?" Bart asked, backing away from the dreaded magic.

Irad stood with a bit of difficulty, leaning slightly against his cutlass for support. "Ye don't know, do ye?"

Bart shook his head. "I follow orders, Cap'n, and don't ask no questions. But it's been five days now, and a dozen dead. I don't wanna be the next, and I'd like to know what makes you so sure this ain't a trap."

He stared defiantly at Irad, who tilted his head, pursed

his lips, and looked down at the young sailor. Bart had recently agreed to join the captain and his crew because of the promise of great treasure, but nary a doubloon had been sighted. Instead, the young sailor watched as one after another of his fellows died from a variety of strategic and mysterious traps. To make matters worse, the captain seemed to care little for the lost men. Bart, the youngest and newest member of the crew, had been instantly dubbed "Greenie" for both his inexperience and the color of his favorite cap. The constant use of the name had soured his enthusiasm for this seemingly foolish quest.

Without turning his head, Irad gave a glance to his first mate, whose dark skin glistened under an oversized hat. A boyish grin filled the first mate's face, soon accompanied by a shrug.

"Right ye are, lad." Irad smiled, turning back quickly. "Ye ain't been with me that long, after all. Ye don't know the bloody truth."

Bart wiped his filthy hands on his filthy pants and blinked uncomfortably, unsure of his captain's intent.

"Rummy Jack's been sailin' these waters for years, as ye know," Irad began. "Stealin' from the Spanish and Dutch but mostly stealin' from me! These be my waters, and he knows it! The Pirate's Code be nothing to this scurvy villain!"

Bart nodded, aware of the rivalry.

"So when I discovered that he had buried his treasure and had a voodoo queen make a magical map, well, I says to myself, 'Irad, that treasure be rightfully yours,' I says. 'Twasn't that hard to have Betty get that map for me when Rummy be visitin' her one night."

"Betty?" Bart asked. "Ye mean Buxom Betty?"

"Aye, ye know her then?"

Bart smiled broadly. "Everybody knows her."

Irad gave a quick snort of a laugh and continued. "I paid her quite a few doubloons for it, and she delivered. Had the map in me hands faster than a rat jumps a sinkin' ship. But when I open it up, the map be blank. All it says is 'ye need the right key.' 'Twas a clue, no doubt."

"The right key..." Bart mumbled as he stared at the ground, brows furrowed.

"Key Largo, ye damned fool!" Irad spat. "The easternmost key, farthest to the right on the map."

Bart nodded. "Aye, that be brilliant!"

Irad smiled. "There's a reason I be captain, ye know."

Rubbing at his sunburned nose, Bart asked, "But if it be just a map fer himself so he can find the treasure again, why did he set up all these traps and puzzles?"

Irad slapped the lad across the back of his head, propelling Bart face forward into the sand. "Ye bloody dinghy boy! Rummy knows how to get by all these things. He needs the map to remember where they all are. The scallop sucker probably will have that voodoo witch with him when he comes fer it, too. She made most of the traps so she can conjure up some way past 'em." He grinned and added, "Ah, Greenie! Wish I could see Rummy's face when he learns the treasure ain't where he thinks it be."

Bart rose slowly, keeping his distance. "Right, but what now? Daniel be dead from the dart. I'll not be touching that rock to get one fer myself. Cap'n," he added.

Irad stared at the map, brushing off pebbly sand. Each time a clue had been figured out or a barrier passed, more of the map became visible. Following the clues required crisscrossing the island in random directions.

The grizzled captain ran his dusty finger over the sandy parchment, tracing the path. "Skull," he finally muttered.

Bart leaned forward. "What?"

"It be a skull!" Irad proclaimed. "Look here! The trail we made be the outline of a skull, and right now we be where the nose be!"

With a confident smirk, Irad marched to the large incongruous stone blocking their way. The others joined him, certain that they had reached their goal, for the huge stone did not fit the topography of the island. Irad reached out his hand, and ignoring Bart's cries, confidently traced an outline of a skull. Not a glimmer of worry crossed the captain's face, as if he had done this sort of thing many times before.

"No dart," Bart whispered.

"Aye, but now what?" Irad asked, glancing down at the map which remained unchanged. "That should have—"

A low rumbling interrupted the pirate's words and the three jumped back involuntarily, staring at the rock. Like sugar flushed by rainwater, the solid stone softly crumbled and dissipated into the ground. Within seconds, no sign remained of its presence.

"Voodoo magic!" Bart gulped.

Blue lichen illuminated a tight path leading down into a salty cave; a cool inviting breeze washed over their faces. Irad nodded to his first mate, who handed him an already-lit whale oil lamp. Without a word, the pirate captain rolled up the precious map, held the lamp high and took confident steps forward. The two followed cautiously.

Cave walls sculpted smooth by years of moving salt water made traversing the narrow passageways tricky, but Irad marched on, unconcerned with the danger. Bart blinked nervously and struggled to keep up, while the first mate sighed disapprovingly and occasionally gave him an encouraging shove.

Key Largo itself was barely above sea level and as the trio dogged the twisted trail they soon passed below the ocean. Turning an anxious eye to every shadow, Bart whispered, "There be no caves in the keys. 'Tis voodoo..."

"Voodoo... voodoo... voodoo" echoed back his voice from a distance.

The cave abruptly widened and the lamp illuminated a broad and tall grotto. Salty water dripped down its edges and stalactites, into a small pool in the center. The steady droplets into the pond matched the three's heightened heartbeats. Irad held the lamp low and crept toward the pond.

"There! See?"

Bart's heart pounded so loudly he thought he'd wake the dead. Moving cautiously, he peered into the shallow pool. Caught in the lamplight, a large red "x" shimmered on the bottom, prancing in the water.

"Rummy Jack's treasure!" Irad licked his lips. "It be here!" He moved forward, only to be held back by Bart's strong arm. "What be this mutiny, Greenie?" he demanded. "Leave me go!"

"It be a trap!" Bart cried. "A big red 'X'? That be too obvious! A trap, I tell ye!"

A voice echoed through the chamber. "Listen to Greenie."

Irad whipped around, the lantern high above his head throwing wildly dancing shadows against the walls. "Who be there? Show yerself!"

Bart drew his weapon and quickly took position beside his captain, staring nervously from side to side. From a corner of his eye he could see that the first mate had done the same.

Light flooded the cave from a dozen lamps and torches. Slitting his eyes in the brighter light, Bart turned to find a motley group of pirate scum leering at them from all sides. Three very large and smelly brutes, each armed with a sharp sword and a sharper smile, blocked the only exit.

Above them, with one foot propped on a ledge, posed a heavily tanned pirate with a prominent scar decorating a freshly-shaved cheek. A bright purple overcoat hung to his knee over a flowing white shirt that was buttoned low to accentuate his ample muscles. Long black hair fell in ringlets down his shoulders and his broad smile reflected the lamplight off numerous golden teeth.

"Well, keelhaul me first born if it not be Rummy Jack!" Irad said with a forced smile. He lowered the lantern to the ground and drew Toecutter, his jewel-laden cutlass.

"Ye don't think ye can fight yer way out of this, do ye?" Rummy taunted, looking immensely pleased with himself.

"I ain't planning on being yer prisoner and I don't think ye plan on lettin' me outta here alive," Irad replied. "Revenge fer that incident in Tortuga if nothing else, I suppose. But I don't see why ye didn't stop me earlier, before I destroyed all yer traps."

"No, ye wouldn't understand, would ye?" Rummy grinned. He stretched his arms and gave a fake yawn to prolong the moment. Irad rolled his eyes.

"The 'Kissing Pirate' has been a boil on me arse for years; ye know that. You and yer crew be cruisin' my waters fer too long, taking what be rightfully mine." Rummy Jack paused to allow his enemy to argue the point, but Irad held his chin high and refused to give Rummy the satisfaction. After a few seconds, Rummy continued. "Now, I could have attacked that scurvy colony ye call yer ship outright, but that would have meant puttin' me own ship and crew in danger, as well as costin' quite a few gold to repair the damn thing and replace the dead crew members."

Irad raised Toecutter above his head and shook it violently. "Ye didn't attack because ye knew who would win, ye cowardly black-souled son of a jacksnipe!"

Rummy merely smiled at his prisoners and continued on as if never interrupted. "Instead, 'twas much cheaper to pay that blasted voodoo queen Sonia Laveau to make a fake magical map and a series of traps. Buxom Betty played along, too."

"What be this treachery?" Irad screamed. "A fake map?"

"Well, of course." Rummy grinned, to the delight of his crew. "I knew yer greed would get the better of ye. Ye paid for the map—thank ye for the gold, by the way—and then ye went about searchin' for a treasure that ain't there."

Irad held his hand against his chin but his eyes never lowered from Rummy Jack's. "It be a mighty complicated way to get me trapped in here."

"But so satisfyin'!" Rummy laughed. "And much cheaper, too. Men and weapons and ships and battles cost money, ye know! The map and some traps be nothing in comparison, and look what I get! Yer entire crew is dead save these two swine, and I didn't have to lift a finger to wipe them all out. Didn't waste one bullet; not one saber needed sharpening. I just watched from afar as they died one by one."

Rummy Jack's crew considered this the height of humor, their twisted laugher echoing through the cavern.

"The rest of my crew has by now taken yer ship that be moored on the other side of the island," Rummy continued. "Ye only left two to watch it, so I'm sure the half dozen I sent over could handle 'em. Yer weak-kneed guards probably surrendered as soon as they saw 'em." He chuckled. "I've defeated ye without losing even a cabin boy."

Bart slowly looked around the cave. Triumph glowed in the eyes of their captors, who cackled spitefully. He counted fifteen of them but knew that more could be hidden in the shadows. He growled deep within himself and turned to his captain. Now was not the time for caution.

"Cap'n," he whispered, leaning in close. "If we run for the cave opening, we'll only have to deal with a few o' them afore we can block the door an'..."

"Quiet, Bart," Irad whispered back. "I'm captain here."

Taken aback by the captain's use of his real name, Bart retreated a few steps and waited for an attack order while eyeing his captain warily.

Irad sheathed his weapon and placed his hands on his hips. "Brilliant," he said, looking up at Rummy Jack. "Quite clever indeed. Destroy me crew and steal me ship with no risk to yer own."

"Aye, 'tis clever, ain't it?" Rummy laughed again. "So why make it more difficult? I'll let the last o' yer crew live if you give yerself up. They can work for me. I'm impressed they've lasted this long. Might be a good addition to me crew."

Irad turned to the two remaining crew members. Bart stared back, steely resolve in his eyes. The first mate was, as always, unreadable.

"'Tis a reasonable offer," Rummy added. "Ye have already caused the deaths of the rest of yer crew. Ye should be punished fer yer mistake, but ye can at least show some honor in yer death."

Irad paced, staring at the ground. "Aye, I suppose that would be a fine deal indeed," he admitted. "Except..."

"Except what?" Rummy snapped.

Irad shrugged. "Except none of me crew be dead."

Rummy Jack's eyes narrowed. "What be this lie? We

watched them leave yer ship. We watched them die. Ye left a trail of them across the bloody island!"

Irad shook his head slowly. "None of those be my crew. Like Greenie here, they be just a group of mercenaries I hired about a week ago. I don't think most of 'em knew their aft from their stern, bless their dearly departed souls."

Bart stared at his captain, mouth agape.

Rummy shook his cutlass angrily. "So where be yer crew, then, ye scalawag blowfish?"

Irad shrugged again and looked at his fingernails. "Well, I don't know fer certain, mind ye, but I'd say they came up from hidin' below decks to kill the few men ye sent over to take me ship."

A low growl rumbled in Rummy's throat.

"Aye, and once they done that, they likely traveled to the piece of garbage ye call yer ship and captured it from the small group ye left behind," Irad added. "Meanin' I still have me own ship and I have yours as well."

Rummy's scream nearly drowned out the uneasy mumbling of his men. "Ye lily-livered swab, are ye mad? Even if that be true, do ye think ye can defeat all of us by yerself? As soon as yer sad bones be decoratin' this cave, we'll take both ships back."

Irad yawned. "Oh, aye, except that me crew has by now blocked the entrance to this cave, sealing it forever."

Growls and curses resounded through the chamber. Light and shadows played tag against the crags as fists shook lanterns in anger. Bart looked at his captain aghast as his fingers tightened on his cutlass.

"What be the meaning o' this?" Rummy yelled above the noise, cutlass and fist raised high.

"Ye damned fool, ye think ye can own everyone!" Irad growled. "Ye think a few coins here and there solves everythin', do ye?"

Rummy glared back, anger smoldering in his eyes. Bart looked from one to the other and once more began to formulate escape plans.

"Suppose, just fer the sake of argument, that Sonia Laveau didn't like you very much," Irad said. "I know, it be something ye can't imagine, but it be true—ye have to admit yer a bit of a bastard. Now let's say that the voodoo queen decided to go ahead and take yer money and make yer map but that she also decided to share this information with someone a lot more likeable." He grinned as Rummy's eyes narrowed.

"So let's suppose—just fer the sake of argument, mind ye—that this handsome fellow decided to play along, and that he hired some scoundrels to pretend to be his crew, no-goods who were certain to die in these traps... all just to mislead ye."

Bart marveled at the way Irad had siezed the advantage while he simultaneously hated knowing that Irad considered him so disposable. However, when Irad glanced in Bart's direction and winked, the captain's charm captivated him once more and he watched in fascination as Irad paced the cave, explaining the plan.

"Can you imagine the triumph of that handsome hero when he finally trapped ye, ye rotten bastard, in yer own magical cave?" Irad laughed. "Just imagine! Fer the sake of argument, of course."

"Ye bloody fool!" Rummy exploded. "Can ye not count? If what you say be true, then we all be trapped here, and there be only three of ye, and there be five times as many o' us! We'll tear ye apart and then we'll all die and where will that leave ye?"

Irad feigned surprise. "Shiver me timbers!" he said, with an exaggerated widening of his eyes. "Ye be right!

Why... to get out of here alive, I'd need... magic!"

A broad floppy hat sailed across the cavern. Irad's First Mate stood tall and let out a laugh that echoed eerily through the cavern. Cascading curls escaped to frame a bright smile against a dark face. A sly wink greeted Rummy Jack's stare.

"Sonia Laveau!" he gasped.

"Nice doing business with you, Rummy," the voodoo queen said in a heavy Creole accent. A bright flash exploded from her outstretched hand.

When Bart's eyesight returned, he found himself standing on the sandy shore of Key Largo. A cool breeze whipped salt spray across his face, as Captain Irad and First Mate Sonia Laveau stood nearby, laughing and slapping each other on their backs.

"Come on, Bart," Irad said, marching off down the beach. "Time to celebrate!"

"Aye aye, Cap'n," Bart grinned. "But call me 'Greenie.'"

In the Runes

By Danielle Ackley-McPhail

The waves pummeled the shore as the longboat went to ground. The sharp bite of salt—with a fainter hint of decay from flotsam—flavored the air and the timbers creaked as they left the cradle of the sea to settle on land. Three men remained sitting while the rest of the mates scrambled to pull the vessel more firmly onto the beach. Their low grunts were accompanied by the scrape of sand against salt-soaked wood and the moon cast their soft shadows across the shore like the writhing ghosts of great hunched beasts.

"You will wait here, Morrow, until we reach halfway to the trees, then follow," ordered the man with the short braid of dark brown hair down his neck. "Do not come within fifteen feet with your mumbling or I will cut your tongue from your head."

Morrow nodded but did not flinch as the two men moved off—the mate, Cragg, with a spade over his shoulder, and Captain Tulo clutching a burlap sack the size of a small ham. The runecaster did not even stand until they were halfway across the prescribed expanse.

The moment they passed it he set off, keeping both pace and distance, his lips moving in a barely heard invocation, his expression serene despite the recent threat.

The captain did not mean it, surely. Morrow was good, but he was useless without his tongue; his runecasting required him to vocalize, which was better than most, who must sketch the marks on air, water, or even paper, to work the cast. Very few had the skill or the strength to do so purely with the mind. Or, more accurately perhaps, the focus for it. Yes, Morrow was under no illusion: he was better than most, but not than all. And any of their kind were rare. He was safe from the captain, though, mostly because he was not stupid. In his hands he held a raw gemstone, roughly the size and shape of a small lemon; he was knowledgeable enough of his craft that it was the only one that would be imprinted by his casting.

Letting the tug of his magic flowing into the stone soothe him, the runecaster followed Captain Tulo and Cragg, the only other sailor trusted with the secret of the runestones. Technically he was first mate, but the captain was stingy with his power and none aboard the *Devil's Get* held rank that they did not earn—and keep—amongst themselves. Morrow had only to think of the razor-sharp collar about his own neck to be reminded of the captain's ruthlessness. The runes holding the edge from his flesh were placed there—clearly—by another, as Morrow would not have enslaved himself. They could be spoken away by Tulo at any time, from any distance. Some day Morrow would find his way past the binding. Until then, he was the model runecaster.

Ahead he noticed the others slowing and adjusted his steps accordingly, all the while murmuring the runes that imprinted their path into the stone. When he was done, the captain—or anyone else given the trigger word—would have the means to find the treasure they buried this night.

The breeze ruffled Morrow's hair and sandy soil shifted beneath his feet as he followed them. A sudden chittering high in the palm fronds to his left made him jump, but he was careful to keep his voice steady and constant as he spoke the runes. With his hind brain he readied his defense, should more than monkeys or song birds come down from the trees. Of all the spells he knew, this was the strongest and the most closely guarded; passed down to him by his granddame, known by none but those that were a part of his family. He dared think that it would protect him from even god or devil, were they small enough. Spell in place but for the speaking, Morrow brought his attention back to his task.

Ahead, the captain and first mate stopped, the latter lowering the spade. Morrow ended his runecasting well before the distance the captain dictated, the path to the clearing complete and a reversing end-rune added, binding the return path to mirror the way in. The stone was now spelled to lead to and from this spot for as long as the strength of the rune lasted, though looking around, he could not imagine why anyone would do so. It was pretty enough, but what was the likelihood there would be much of a harvest here? Yet the captain claimed the place was regularly used by rune-witches from a nearby island. Maybe, maybe not. It mattered not to Morrow. The pirates would bury their cache of stones and any spell worked in their vicinity would be captured in the closest runestone at the moment of its casting, with the witches none the wiser that they hadn't merely misspoken the spell, as sometimes happened. They would leave this clearing ignorant of the theft.

The thought was sour in Morrow's mind, having had more than just a spell snatched away. It galled that his efforts were used against others of his kind. No matter, though; he was not responsible for anything more than his "muttering." 'Twas the captain that stole the runecasting of others, not Morrow, though not all would see it so. Some would call him a traitor. Let them. He had little choice for he liked his skin too much to part from it on principle. From the day he woke with a shiny new collar after 'casting a protection rune on a pouch for a customer, this had been his involuntary life. But he watched and tested and someday he'd be free. For now, he did as instructed.

"It is done, 'caster?" Tulo called out, adjusting his coat as the first mate began to dig.

"Aye, sir," Morrow answered, stepping forward, runestone held out. It glowed softly with the magic of his casting.

The captain looked at it and gave a familiar smirk with a hint of a sneer in it. The first mate stopped digging. He straightened, then raised the blade of the shovel, a grin revealing teeth gone yellow and breath flavored with rum. Morrow looked back to the captain. Confusion reshaped his features. And still he could not believe...

Then he dropped the runestone as the jungle erupted around him. The underbrush thrashed, as did the fronds overhead. Yells sounded close by, the men's voices echoed as demons' howls in Morrow's heart, and before he could duck away a hard shove sent him forward and to his knees, closer to the captain and Cragg. He reflexively uttered the runes of his defensive spell as a blow took him between the shoulders.

Nothing.

A second clipped the base of his skull, another, his kidneys, none with a killing force, though brutal enough. He curled as best he could and frantically muttered the rune again, and again, all his will and arcane strength behind it. Still nothing. He kept muttering brokenly until a familiar tugging registered with his addled mind. His eyes went wide and his body chilled, shaking as a kick jarred him loose from his ball. He angled a horrified glance toward the sack of stones. Stones he'd already set with Tulo's trigger words. They glowed faintly through the burlap, confirming his master's betrayal even as Tulo spoke *that* word and the runes about Morrow's neck faded.

He felt the bite of cold steel as the collar closed on his flesh.

There was no more muttering. Morrow stared up at the empty palm fronds rigid with horror until Tulo leaned over him, obstructing his view. Then the runecaster floated free, looking down on his empty shell and the man that murdered him, senses intact, though muffled and without substance. He was a shadow, but he could hear and see as Tulo mocked him. "There are a half-dozen like you in every port," the captain said with disdain as Morrow's soul began to drift. Hatred supplanted horror.

The pirates laughed and sang coarse songs as they went away with a sack of stones imprinted with his family's blast rune.

Morrow felt himself fade as the breeze pushed at him.

He panicked. Reached out. Latched his thoughts on the dropped runestone, which lay forgotten on the ground, tumbled beneath the undergrowth. His magic, his essence, still warmed it with a faint glow. He felt a familiar tugging.

A dragon rode the thermals lacing the tropic sky. Her belly gently mottled in shifting patterns that mimicked her backdrop, complete with starbright glimmers from the occasional diamond scale mixed among those midnight blue, deep amethyst, and sapphire, her wings bowed and billowed like the surrounding wisps of night clouds as the air cooled. She circled in lazy arcs, her neck craning, her gaze sweeping the far-below shore. Faceted eyes narrowed, the earthfire kindling in their depths. A snarl like thunder shook her throat as in her heart she felt the fading echo of as much as a score of emberlings even now moved beyond her reach.

Her belly roiled with an unvoiced scream but she locked her muzzle shut on it. Let mankind dream and wonder, tell their terrible tales around the bottle and the bar, let them scurry from doorpost to arch, but never must they know for certain that dragons were born from more than foolishness, or whiskey vapors and bad beef. If that knowledge were common, she and the dragons that would one day rise from the emberlings she succeeded in returning to their earthfire nests would be hunted down and their flames banished. She shuddered at the horror of that thought.

Camirel stilled her cry and searched on. With a desperate hope, she let her eyes sweep the land below once more, reaching out with will and wish for some sign any ember yet remained. Ear ridges lifted and fanned, a scarlet frill feathering an elegant head shaped somewhat like an antelope, delicate despite the massive size. Swiveling, the ridges confirmed what her flicking tongue already tasted on the air: no human heartbeat pulsed within a league, though primates peered at her from the tallest palms below, cowering beneath the fronds. Lower she swooped and they scattered, chittering through the trees and into the brush, revealing what had been too faint for her to sense. In the heart of the islet jungle laid a tiny, muted spark.

Triumph was much harder to rein in than rage.

Cami didn't bother, belling as she soared down from the sky, skimming surf and sand until bronze claws gripped the anchoring reef bared by low tide. There was no one nearby. She lay herself down upon the rock, curving muzzle to flank, and breathed with the rhythm of the waves, let herself cool, then gently pushed the earthfire back below to cradle in the deep pumice hollow her draconic senses told her was there. A shudder. A ripple. Then the magic currents snapped.

She rose on two legs. Moonlight briefly glimmered off of naked flesh the next moment clothed in a loose, dark cotton robe. No rune was murmured, none etched in sand or water or air; it simply was. Camirel had always been gifted that way. More so since her rebirth. The young woman thought nothing of it as she hurried unerringly through the brush, her hand going through a slit in the side of the robe to an empty pouch bound around her waist. It never left her person, not even during the change, thanks to the spell she'd wrought on the leather. Its emptiness weighed heavily on her. But perhaps with fortune's blessing it would not be empty long.

Striding faster, following a trail of broken foliage, along the way she passed two large lizards fighting over the carcass of a man. The remains were much abused, but around his throat she spied a glint of metal sunk into the skin clear around, like a necklace gone too tight. Her own throat tightened in sympathy until a hiss called her attention back to the scaled contenders. The lizards had united, scurrying forward to force her away. The emberling hard in her thoughts, Cami took no convincing at all to leave the brutal sight.

Once more hurrying through the brush, she soon came to a nearby clearing disturbed by digging, lizard tracks... and violence—though no sign remained, beyond a few crushed ferns and a darkened patch of damp soil that smelled coppery even to her lesser nose. She closed her eyes. Shut out the signs of disturbance. Shut out the memory of the poor soul she'd passed on the trail. She stilled her thoughts and turned a slow circle, letting her heart seek the glimmer too weak for her mortal sight to see. There was a flicker, like heat lightning. It was too slight for her to latch onto. The circling stopped.

Cami shook off frustration and let her head fall back

until her throat was straight and her closed eyes faced the sky. Deep breaths brought calm to her heart while the warm island breeze riffled her hair. Around her, the jungle sang a lullaby full of *sushing* fronds and sleepy monkey sounds. She let it calm her further until not one muscle was tense and her legs sank her to the sandy soil. Head still back, she let her tongue trill against her teeth, echoing deep in her throat, blending with the night-song until it carried her call to the one she sought.

The resonance was muffled, the earthfire dim, but Cami felt it like a weak sunbeam against her neck, slightly off to the left. Her head lowered and turned, her eyes opening languidly until a nearby gleam winked at her from the underbrush. Slinking forward, she stared intently at the gemstone hidden beneath a leaf the size of her head. To the unknowing it appeared as any other uncut jewel, only rather larger than most. To a runecaster, or any other in tune with the earthfire, it was something magical, but nothing more. To Cami—adopted daughter of the Last Mother—it was a dragon egg stolen from the earth much before its time.

She frowned. Something was wrong with this emberling.

A sullen glow emanated from the stone's heart. Almost as if she stared at the ember through a haze of smoke or shadow, roiling and dark, smothering. Perhaps the Last Mother would have known what was wrong, but she was gone. Not for the first time, Cami cursed the fact that she had nothing left to guide her but instinct.

In this, she was conflicted.

The thought of gripping the stone made the skin of her palm ripple and twitch away from the wrongness she sensed. Yet this was her sacred charge: to find and reclaim the embers of the earthfire, to return them to their molten nest deep within the First Mother that they may learn and grow and rise from below the earth to sing their songs, restoring true dragons to the world.

Her duty was stronger than her doubt.

Her fingers closed around the cool, dark stone, felt etching upon the surface, and this time her whole body arched, her grip tightening until the rough edges cut her flesh and the swirling chaos of death slashed at her mind.

Cami fell senseless to the jungle floor.

"Haul anchor and away!" the captain bellowed before the longboat even cleared the rail. He leapt to the deck, the heavy heat of the sack thumping his back. The masts and timbers creaked as pirates scurried into the rigging and the ship yawed with the pounding of the surf against the hull. Tulo shifted his stride with the pitch as he went to secure the stones. At the door of his cabin he uttered a word to turn the knob; another locked it secure behind him. Inside, guided by the sun streaming through the windows of his cabin, he immediately carried his burden across the chamber to a chest beside his bunk. It was made of thick cypress planks bound around and anchored to the floor with heavy bars of iron. A different word, barely whispered, lifted the lid on a small cache of assorted stones, no more than eight, three gleaming rubies spelled for healing, and five other mixed stones each bearing a different set of runes: one for light, one for causing pain, the emerald was a death curse, and the last two summoned wind for the sails. All captured runes, none of them as powerful as the twelve newest, each and every stone etched with the legendary blast rune known only by Morrow's line. A priceless treasure indeed, with pending war whispered of in every port.

Without the sack, the inside of the chest revealed more bare wood than rough gems. This night's work brought his total to twenty, for the sacrifice of but one; more than enough to fill the coffer with gold coin several times over.

He would dole out a few runestones once they reached Callais; not too many, or it was worth his life. For a rare few and the promise of more, Devon and his hag would pay; for a haul like this they would do violence and take them, much as he had with Morrow. Tulo stowed the stones and brought down the heavy lid, binding word spoken before the thud ended.

He whistled as he returned to deck, already planning a trip to port. Wine and women and gold to be had...oh, and a new runecaster. Idly he caressed the pommel of his dagger, where a smallish runestone was nearly hidden by gold filigree. No, mustn't forget the 'caster.

"Cragg, set course for Callais."

A mass cheer went up from the rigging.

Cami woke to a monkey tugging at her hand. He grumbled and shrieked alternately, prying at her fingers in a manner that should have snapped them, then yanked at her arm as if that might instead come free. Summoning a flicker of earthfire, Camirel growled with her dragon voice.

Such screaming she had never heard. The creature—and its more timid companions in the trees—fled. The screaming continued, echoing in her mind. Still linked to the earthfire, Cami sniffed and probed, searched for any sign, any at all, that she was not alone. Plant life and decay were plentiful; as were the monkeys. But, other than a scattering of birds and reptiles, there was nothing else that drew breath on the islet. Slow and careful she set the emberling on the ground before her and stared at it intently. Unlike the others she had found before this, it was marred, changed. Something etched the surface and the heart was clouded. The Last Mother had said to bring all emberlings, but she'd said nothing about the tainted. Cami did not know what to do. She had reclaimed so few;

which was the greater risk, taking this one, damaged as it might be, or not?

Don't stare. The words sounded in her head, gruff and masculine, tinged with ill-concealed unease.

With a squeal that morphed into a growl, Cami drew harder upon the earthfire, and rose to a crouch. The cotton robe she'd magically donned earlier was now barely enough to contain her; she changed with the sudden heat of the 'fire until a half-human, half-dragon melding loomed above the emberling, with human arms and legs and the beginnings of a dragon's muzzled head beneath the sweep of her dark gold hair. Jewel-scaled skin reflecting the colors of the jungle wrapped her flesh like armor.

Again, the screaming in her head.

It was followed by an odd muttering until Cami felt a faint ripple, as if someone attempted to draw upon mage energy, but nothing came of it. The glow at the heart of the emberling flared and pulsed in time with it. She had felt death's touch before, shocking and brutal, unyielding, as the Last Mother sacrificed herself for Camirel. She felt it now at the heart of the stone, a second soul disconnected from the earthfire.

"Hush," she hissed softly, aloud, her voice faintly reminiscent of the lizards that had been fighting over what must have been his body. Cami loosened her grip on the earthfire until only the protective scales remain, sheathing her own form. The anger was not so simple to let go. A shudder rippled her skin and her hands flexed; the tips of her fingers were suddenly capped by short, curved talons as instinctively she drew the earthfire close once more. The dead had no rightful place among the young. That such had touched the tender emberling... who knew what effect that would have?

"You have taken a place not yours."

A sense of hesitation as the glow flickered wildly.

I did not mean to. I did not know. I'm sorry...I cannot say how it is even possible...

"You have mutilated and scarred our young."—for Cami spoke also with the echo of the First Mother when earthfire was within her.

The gem flared then dimmed to a bare glow. It seemed to tremble against her hand as she stared at the runes etched into the surface. What effect would they have if she nested the emberling? The runes themselves could wreak havoc, let alone the sundered soul.

Young?

Camirel did not answer. Secrecy in this had been a part of the song she'd absorbed before her rebirth, along with the knowledge all dragons shared from the inception of their kind until the death of it. Both were vital if she was to resurrect the species, but was this unseated being any kind of threat to that? Hard to say; she could end him easily enough, though at the sacrifice of the emberling... she still could not say if that would be a bad thing. *Perhaps it was worth the risk,* she thought. *If the usurper had knowledge of the others.*

"This stone you are in," she said, her voice low and as sharp as her talons. "There were others here. Where have they gone?"

Her question was met by silence.

"Do not think to lie. I can sense they were here."

I do not intend to...I do not know...but... The man's thoughts held an edge of guilt, his presence strengthened as he thought the matter through. *Tulo, the captain of the Devil's Get, he will not horde such a treasure long. If he heads anywhere, it will be to Callais. 'Tis his preferred port and we...we have been quite a while at sea.*

Cami's heart quickened and she felt the earthfire answer. Before it was too late she scooped the stone into her talons and deposited it into the pouch even as the change sank it beneath scaled hide.

What were you called, man?

The voice was silent, as if it searched for the answer. She sensed his confusion and felt pity for him. Death was indeed unsettling. *Morrow, m'lady,* he finally answered, subdued. Still suspicious of him, she did not return the favor. "M'lady" would serve nicely, though it was far above her current station.

To Callais, then, Morrow, she thought toward the stone with fiery vehemence. Then she launched herself into the sky, leaving below screaming monkeys, churned earth, and felled trees.

The Whiskey Cask was not your typical dockside haunt. It was quiet and dark, and several streets over from the main concourse. No women sold drinks or themselves; no rousing shanty songs disturbed the night. Cragg leaned alone against the bar, more staring at a pint of ale than drinking it. Captain Tulo sat at a table in the far corner, beside the hearth, the remains of a plain meal and a full bottle of whiskey before him, but his eye on the door.

Another hour passed before it opened. The man that walked in was clearly too clean and hale for the common clothing he wore. A smile on his smooth face even revealed a full set of teeth. As if any man on the docks had any such thing...or reason to smile, without a doxie to hand. Tulo would have laughed if he weren't so furious. He had been waiting hours. Devon played at subterfuge as if necks would not be stretched if they were caught. The fool.

Now, entering behind him, hunched and sloven and looking much attuned to the atmosphere of the docks, the hag Zia drew a more respectful look from Tulo. Perhaps she played as well, but she had an air about her that spoke of cunning and power. If she played, it was to a purpose. Tulo stood and made a show of drawing out a chair for her, meeting her disturbing yellow eyes as if they did not unsettle him. She gave a shrill laugh and made a show of settling into the seat, more grace in the act than Tulo would have thought her capable of.

"The stones," Devon said as he settled into his own seat, hand already held out across the table, his eyes gleaming eagerly. He spoke low, his words carrying just enough for them alone to hear. Tulo laughed at him with equal softness. Dangerously.

"Come now, I don't have them with me any more than you have the coin you would pay me with on your person." The captain sat back in a show of calculated insolence, his lip faintly sneering as his voice emphasized the word pay.

Devon again betrayed his noble birth, straightening with well-exercised offense and entitlement, hand reaching for the pistol surely beneath his coat. Such weapons were costly, pretentious, and nowhere as reliable as steel or magic.

Before tempers won out, the hag's ritually scarred hand darted out to smack the lordling's down. "Don't be a fool." Her voice crackled with age but her words had strength behind them. "What proof have you then, rogue?"

Tulo pulled a scrap of parchment from his pocket and spread it across the table. The crumpled sheet bore a carbon rubbing of one of the stones, only partial, but enough that the rune for Morrow's clan was clearly evident.

The hag nodded as Devon seethed beside her. She ignored him. "Fair enough," she said to Tulo. "And terms?"

He refolded the parchment and slid it away, then leaned forward. Then he looked toward Devon, who, after all, held the purse. "For the three I can give you, one hundred gold each."

"I am reminded of the difference between a thief and a pirate now," Devon said in a tight voice. "The thief robs you in secret, the pirate, face to face."

"It is not my war," Tulo answered. "I merely thought to aid where I am able. If this is too costly for you, I am sure there are others that would be grateful of my... assistance."

"Three are hardly worth my time." Devon affected a dismissive pose, good at the play when he bothered to take it seriously.

Tulo held back the smile the comment drew. He had him. "Well, I have but three right now, but I can secure more over time, should they be of use to you...."

Devon's eyes went bright and he unconsciously, barely perceptibly, leaned forward. "More?"

"A few."

"Done!" Devon forgot putting on airs in his excitement. "And where shall we collect?"

"Why, tomorrow is market day, is it not?" Tulo grinned and took a swig from the whisky bottle now that the deal was set. "I'll have a man bartering wares near the dock entrance to the market square. Hand him this mark," the captain laid a blue-painted chip between them on the table, "and ask to see his war god carving.

"Have the payment in full," Tulo continued. "Even should you somehow manage to make off with them, the stones are useless without the trigger words, and those you must have from me."

Devon's face flushed and his brow furrowed as he came to his feet. Before he could speak, the hag rose as well, drawing Devon down by the collar of his coat. She murmured low in his ear as she nodded and led the noble out the door.

The pirate captain laughed and capped his bottle. "They are so amusing when they scheme, they'll have a shock though, if they try to play the pirate at his own game. Come, let's find some place a bit more rousing," he said to his man, and they too departed.

The timbers of the masts creaked and swayed as the dragon circled high overhead, stirring the winds. Her tail lashed the clouds into tatters as she eyed the *Devil's Get,* waiting and watching.

I do not care for this. She growled deep in her belly, like a rumble of thunder.

We must wait or you will fail.

Her tail lashed with more violence, the rumble went deeper. Below her the muffled glow of her emberlings was like a small sun beckoning from within. The urge to dive and crack the timbers like an oyster shell was overwhelming. She gathered herself, muscles tensing and earthfire hardening her scales like the purest iron. The angle of her wings tilted, her body dipped, ready to take the *Devil* down, when Morrow cried out, *No!*

The mental shout disrupted her focus, instantly, brutally, yanking her out of the dive. She shuddered and swayed and nearly roared in challenge. *No! Don't, m'lady!* She felt urgency in Morrow's thoughts. It softened her fury toward him.

You mustn't, Morrow warned her. *Tulo is the key, you must wait until he returns or your emberlings will never be safe. He hunts them like a pig finds truffles, like he has some sense for them. None other that I know of, save the captain and his man, Cragg, have the secret of the runestones, finding them...making them; take those men and that knowledge dies with them. Take the stones and leave them free and you will face a constant battle.*

Camirel continued to circle, tail still thrashing, wings cutting the air until the sea writhed and whitecaps battered the harbor and the ships at dock. Her muzzle twitched as she quietly muttered with impatience.

Finally, a few hours before dawn, two forms swaggered the length of the pier. *It is them,* Morrow whispered into Cami's thoughts. As she descended she slowly released her hold on the earthfire, her form dwindling as she came lower. Cami felt a mental gasp from Morrow as she thought the runes to hide her from all senses.

You mustn't do that! Not again, never close to him. Frantic images of a gaudy blade and steel collars accompanied Morrow's thoughts as Cami settled to the deck, sliding into the shadows as the pirates stepped onto the gang plank.

Morrow babbled on, thoughts darting erratically, forcing her to winnow through for what was relevant and block out all else. *Speak a rune in his proximity and Tulo will enslave you. The stone in the pommel of his dagger, it is one of your emberlings, spelled to bind runecasters. Speak a rune and the stone flares. If Tulo speaks the trigger word your thoughts, your body, are bound as if by iron. He will capture us. You will wake with the gleam of a sharp new necklace circling your throat.*

Cursing, Cami instinctively dropped back deeper into the shadows, though the pirates could not sense her even had she stood boldfaced before them. Morrow never shared the details of his ending, but she had seen his remains and the manner of his death. A growl rumbled deep in her belly.

Cami doubted such a thing would have effect on her, but she could not risk the testing of that conviction. Tulo had stolen her children, abused and twisted them, sought to sell them. He would not escape her wrath.

All runes, or just a new working? she asked.

New only, he seeks to bind any runecaster he can, to profit from their skills. Set runes are too common, and do not guarantee those bearing them have an ability for 'casting. Catch too many of those and the scheme is revealed.

Satisfaction sharpened Cami's features. Runecasting was the least of her talents. Unlike most of mankind, she was not restricted to runes; her will was enough. Since her rebirth she was directly linked to the earthfire. She drew on it now. This close to the water—the natural rival to fire—it was an effort, but she increased her will and once more transformed into an armored version of herself, a melding of woman and dragon, armed with talon and teeth, muscle sheathed in scale no man or beast could pierce.

It was unlikely the pirate could even sense the working. Only one person had ever challenged her, before the change or after: the witch, Malizia. More than once she had sought to steal the emberling Camirel had guarded before she'd even known its secret. She'd nearly succeeded. It was because of the witch that the Last Mother was no more. The woman was unnatural and ruthless. She was driven to eradicate dragonkind from the world; but for the emberlings and Cami herself, she had achieved her goal. Zia's power was peculiar and had no link to the earthfire. She consorted with leviathans, creatures whose power was born of water, the single beast that was a threat to a dragon. Malizia's magic was the only thing Cami had encountered capable of disrupting her own, unless she shielded against it.

Camirel put the woman from her thoughts as she watched Tulo cross the deck, waited boldly by the door to his cabin, knowing it by the presence of the emberlings within. A smirk twitched her lips as he murmured his trigger word to open the portal. The rune was a simple one she could have easily broken but it would have cost her time and she could not risk being wrong about the dagger spell, linked as it was to an emberling. It was beyond simple to slip in behind him, though, and to block the counter word meant to lock it tight again.

The man crossed the cabin and sank into a crouch

beside the chest, chuckling in a self-pleased manner. His hand ran over the planks, caressed the iron bands until he swayed slightly and chuckled some more, releasing whiskey vapors on each breath. He murmured a word expectantly. Cami could hear the syllables slur, sensed the flaw in the magic even before he cursed and brought a fist down hard on the chest. Gently and unnoticed, she used her mind to steady him. He muttered and twitched as if some part of him sensed her. She wondered at it; he should not have been able to. Tulo shook his head and turned back to the chest before him, betraying no sign that her efforts tripped the binding rune. Cami relaxed and watched closely as the pirate breathed deep and tried again. This time there was a click and the lock fell open.

In the silence of her mind, Morrow gasped. Cami barely noticed as the lid to the chest rose. Her heart cried out and her voice joined it.

Something was horribly wrong.

The captain spun about at her cry, his back to the chest and a plain boot dagger in hand, already casting it before his eyes focused upon her. She hissed and flinched as the blade sank into her shoulder, striking scales that had softened to thick hide. So focused on her goal, she had not noticed the earthfire dampen.

A wicked, throaty laugh sounded from the cabin door as a curse came to Cami's lips.

"A lovely bonus then, quite unexpected!"

"Malizia," Camirel growled even as the captain called out "Zia!" in a voice both confused and angry. Cami screamed and half spun herself, one hand clutching the hilt of the dagger, as she forced her will through the other in a mage blast meant to shred the witch's focus. The effort was a waste; between the water below and the witch's influence the blast was barely a warm breeze ruffling Malizia's hair, which slowly morphed from an old woman's scraggly grey, to a youthful woman's full ebon locks.

Even as the witch reverted to her true form, the last of Camirel's scales faded away until she found herself naked, bleeding, and vulnerable before her nemesis. Cami had time only to grip the emberling pouch bound round her waist before the witch's fingers flicked in her direction. In deep contrast to the warmth of Morrow's stone, a chilled stream of magic lashed her, binding Camirel's limbs like the cold grip of the sea's deep currents. To add further insult, Zia then turned away, as if she were of no further consequence.

"Cragg!" The captain bellowed, shocked sober and steady. "Rally the men!"

Malizia laughed again, even more wickedly than before, and sent another tendril to bind Tulo. She sauntered forward and brought up her finger to silence his lips. "Best not to disturb the dead, *captain*. They are so unsettled when newly made."

"Witch!" he cried and strained against his unseen bonds.

"Why yes, pity you are only now so observant." She purred and wrapped a single hand around his throat, casually crushing it with all the weight of the ocean below. The expression on her face as she let go was obscene. She stared over her shoulder a moment, catching Cami's eye, and then leaned past his crumbled corpse to lift a stone from the chest. "A few moments sooner," the witch confided, "and I might have had to work for my treat. This way...easier, perhaps, but less satisfying."

Zia turned until Camirel had clear view of the emerald emberling held aloft.

At that moment, Morrow stirred with the mental equivalent of a caught breath. *The stone she holds... the rune it is etched with is a death curse! Murmur this word...* He spoke the trigger into her mind, but Cami hesitated; would the rune work its magic against the witch or would her shielding block it? Who then would the curse target? Camirel herself? An innocent beyond this vessel? Through the open door she could hear the sounds of the docks coming alive for the day, providing targets aplenty, should the spell fly wild.

Say it! Before she comes. Morrow's thoughts were frantic, as if her safety mattered to him. Perhaps it did, if only in relation to his own. It didn't matter, really, her indecision already faded, too weak to stand against her vivid memories of past dealings with the witch. There was no doubting the evil Malizia would inflict on the world if left unchecked. Rather than speak aloud, Camirel thought the word as clear and willful as she was able.

Green fire lit the room. The air sizzled and snapped, the sound oddly in harmony with Malizia's screech as the curse hit her. Her body jerked and her fingers, clenched about the stone, shriveled. With a snarl the witch focused her will upon the limb, halting the curse at the wrist before turning her gaze on Camirel. Such fury Cami had never seen, and Morrow's stone trembled against her thigh.

Damn! The failure was bitter, though her fears had been unrealized.

The witch's yellow eyes blazed with the promise of slow retribution and her expression twisted vindictively with glee. But first she pursed her lips and blew a stream of water magic until her hand and the stone were encased in ice. Zia brought it down hard on the edge of the chest until both hand and stone shattered. Magic sealed the wound.

The earth cried out through Camirel as the emberling died; grief blistered her throat and hot tears etched her cheeks and with that her link to the earthfire grew a little stronger. The faint echo of talons formed at fingertips that crushed the pouch as her hand fisted protectively over the emberling containing Morrow. The fire in her grew as Malizia lifted another runestone.

"No." Camirel growled low and tight, wrath burning off the chill of her mage bindings. She flexed and felt the flow of scales creep across her flesh, closing her own wound. She willed the scales flesh-tone even as she drew harder on the earthfire, linked through the emberling in her grasp and those blazing across the room. She prayed the link stronger, but feared it was not enough to overpower the witch's spell.

Malizia sneered and summoned her water magic, slinked closer and pursed her lips, ready to send a second spell stream to extinguish the young she held in her remaining hand.

Camirel roared and fought her bindings. She could not yet work her magic beyond her form and her arms remained locked, but her body rocked and her eyes narrowed. She waited for the witch to draw near. With the whisper of a breath, she murmured a promise, loud enough for Malizia to hear, but not make out.

Venom in her gaze, the witch moved closer until her face filled Cami's vision. "You are a splinter beneath my nail, *girl*; it will be a pleasure...." Cami rolled her eyes and slammed her head forward, cutting off Zia's prattle. The emberling dropped as the stunned witch crumbled. It landed beside Cami's foot against her flesh. At its touch the earthfire in her flared brighter. She flexed and expanded until the water bonds shattered, even as Zia stirred at her feet.

Cami lunged down; her right hand closed around the emberling first, her left shoved the witch away. They grappled and fought like common wenches, neither possessing enough control of her magic to summon a strike. As they wrestled around the cabin there was the sound of footsteps coming up the plank, followed by an outcry as whoever boarded discovered Malizia's deeds. Cursing, Camirel thumped the witch's head against the cedar chest, once, and then twice before her opponent lost her one-handed grip on Cami's throat. Shoving the evil woman aside, Camirel lunged for the open chest, grabbing the emberlings and thrusting them into her pouch.

Her magic completely restored, she turned to deal with Malizia. The witch had gained her feet and some command of her own magic. She stood between the Last Mother's champion and the door. Hatred was thick in the air, turning it rank and sour.

Camirel felt the weight of realization: One of them would not leave this cabin. She readied her defenses, sank the pouch and its precious contents beneath dragon hide, and called forth the lethal power of earthfire. Across from her, Malizia similarly prepared, as she summoned as best she could the cold, crushing weight of the deep.

Before either could strike, more feet pounded up the gang plank, bearing the growing uproar closer. Cami's gaze darted to the door.

Foolish, but she couldn't help it.

Zia struck. A tsunami of power slammed Camirel into the hull. She lay in the far corner of the cabin, stunned, barely holding on to consciousness, and could do nothing as the earthfire slid from her grip. There was the faint sound of shattering glass and Cami felt the ocean breeze, moist and cool upon her skin. Her eyes fought to focus. She found herself alone, feeling more than hearing the thud of heavy footsteps approaching the cabin.

She's gone, m'lady! Morrow said. *You have to get up, you have to get away!*

Cami shushed him, her hand lightly patting his runestone, which she again found herself clutching.

So, Malizia had fled, empty handed, leaving Camirel to the...mercy...of the authorities. Let the witch enjoy her reprieve. They would meet again; for now, content with the weight of the emberlings warming her chilled and aching body, Camirel drew enough earthfire to hide her from all senses, scaled skin reflecting wood tones. *It is well,* she said to Morrow. *Hush, my friend, and stop calling me m'lady. My name is Camirel.* He fell silent and she could feel a subtle change in him, a quiet joy. She lay there, undetected by the authorities, waiting with him in comfortable silence for the uproar to die down.

A Final Battle

BY STUART JAFFE

George Worthington groaned as he clambered back to his feet, his ears ringing with the echoes of cannon fire. Remnants of the battle covered the ocean in a milky fog and the familiar tang of gunpowder filled the air. A blood splotch near the staysails marked where Captain Taggart fell—his body had been removed to his cabin. Straightening his red waistcoat, the short, stout Worthington headed toward the foredeck.

Butler rushed up beside him and said, "Sir, sir, they've run. They're gone."

"Of course they're gone, Mr. Butler. They're lucky if they don't sink by sundown."

"Aye, sir," Butler said, moving back and forth on his feet like a child that had to pee. "Um, a question, sir."

Worthington ignored the man and stared at the fog. Their enemy, His Majesty's frigate *Osprey,* had not suffered serious damage and would not be sinking anytime soon—it just left. Why? They had killed Captain Taggart. They had blasted an enormous hole in the *Annabelle*'s side—a little lower and the brigantine would have sunk. Why leave with victory so close?

"Sir?"

"What?" Worthington said, controlling his anger with military precision. *Careful,* he thought. He had to hold back on the old ways—the crew mustn't know that before joining as a pirate, he had once belonged to His Majesty's naval forces. They wouldn't care that he hated the life, had been court-marshaled and discharged for assaulting a superior, and embraced the freedom of piracy whole-heartedly. They would see a navy man.

"Cap'n's dead, sir."

"I'm quite well aware of that," he said, praying his face did not betray the sorrow at losing a good friend or the anger at Taggart's insistence on dancing with evil.

"Don't that, um, make you Cap'n?"

"I suppose it does," he said, continuing to scan the smoke-covered sea.

Butler let out a derisive snort and said, "Fine by me, sir. You got any orders?"

It didn't make any sense—why would the *Osprey* just leave? No other ship had appeared. No significant damage had been inflicted. Why run?

"Sir?" Butler said again.

Waving his hand but not facing the man, Worthington said in a casual manner, "Get the carpenters working on the starboard hole and the seamsters on the maintopsail."

"Ain't that for the boatswain?"

"Mr. Pips is dead, and we lack the time to sort all that mess out."

"Then don't ya think ya should say something to the crew? Y'know, what with your being Cap'n now."

Worthington didn't answer. What could he say? Taggart had been a big brother to them all. His loss was like cannon fire through the heart—worse still because he'd be alive if he had just listened. But the captain had wanted that evil beast and he got her, no matter how much Worthington had protested.

"Sir?"

They could mourn later. Worthington sensed the battle had not ended yet. He stared at the sea, going over his naval training, wondering what protocol required a ship to disengage on the verge of victory. Perhaps they wanted to toy with the *Annabelle*. That didn't seem likely, though—too ungentlemanly. Unless toy was the wrong word. Perhaps the word was test. The *Annabelle* couldn't maneuver well until they fixed the damage, but she wouldn't sink either. If the *Osprey* had some new weapon they wished to test, crippling the *Annabelle* would give them a simple, easy target.

"We have to get out of here," Worthington whispered, his heart quickening at the sound of his voice. He spun around, ready to bark orders, only to find the whole crew standing on deck with an uncomfortable Butler at the front.

"Um," Butler said, taking a hesitant step forward. "Little bit of a problem, sir."

"So I see."

"Not that we don't like you, Worthy, and we all know Cap'n was fond of you, but we just don't think you got the right spirit for leading is all." Some of the crew grunted their agreement. "You is a bit proper."

Someone in the middle shouted, "Bring Cap'n Taggart back."

Worthington tried to hide his surprise even as darkness clouded his heart. Butler cleared his throat, and said, "Yeah, well, the boys wants the witch to bring back Cap'n Taggart."

"No," Worthington spat out, his face reddening as his body tensed. "Never. You don't want me for captain, so be it, but don't be fools. Raising the dead is the blackest of magics, and I cannot permit it on this ship." Worthington glanced into the fog—he had to get his men ready for battle. "Hell, even if it worked, what would come from the cabin would not be Captain Taggart, but a monster."

"Not true," Silverson said. His thick, tattooed arms crossed his broad chest. "My mum done did it for my dad and he was right fine."

"Your dad's dead," Billy Demott pointed out, his pencil-thin mustache just another line of dirt on his face.

"Spell didn't take for long, but while it did, he was right fine."

A shadow. Worthington saw a shadow in the fog—big like that of a ship. "Leave the witch below where she belongs," he said, wishing Captain Taggart had never brought her onboard in the first place.

"All's we're saying is give it a try," Butler said. "There's enough of us to put down the Cap'n if he don't come back all right."

"The answer is no. Now, there's work to be done."

Silverson shoved Butler forward and said, "Butler here said we ain't following your orders, and that we ain't."

Before Worthington could speak, a shriek like a herd of lambs being slaughtered pierced the air. The crew's eyes widened as they froze. A cackling laugh came from the port side smoke, and the horrid shriek echoed on the starboard.

"To arms!" Worthington said as he drew his sword. The men did not move.

A breeze picked up, shifting the smoke, confusing the eyes. The men held their breath. All around them, they heard a twisted, sing-song voice to an aimless tune.

"To arms, I say!" The men remained. Fear had them—Worthington could taste it like cold brass.

A witch burst from the smoke, flying through the air like an owl seeking prey, her mad eyes glinting, her pale face peeling, her jagged teeth rotting—her laughter shook the marrow in Worthington's bones. Two more witches followed. They swooped and shrieked and howled as the men scattered across the deck like frightened mice. One witch with stark, white hair grabbed hold of two men and tossed them into the sea.

She flew back to the ship and attacked Silverson. He fought with his cutlass, the sharp blade clanging against the witch's claws—long, filthy things like knives themselves. Sweat poured from his brow as he struggled to keep up with her attacks. Worthington watched as the witch dodged a blow and dug her hand into Silverson's neck. A fountain of blood spewed into the air, and she reveled in his quivering, lifeless body.

The third witch hovered over the battle like a general watching from hillside. Her back faced Worthington. He snarled at the beast. *For the captain*, he thought.

With his heart pounding and his hands shaking, he climbed the railing and struggled to keep his balance. He raised his sword. His face tightened; his breathing shortened. Yelling like a cavalry commander, he leapt from the rail and slashed the witch's back.

When he hit the deck, he felt a rib snap (though he couldn't be certain), jolting pain clear through to his teeth. He screamed but could not be heard, for the witch cried louder. She gazed down upon him, the gash in her back streaming blood to the deck. The hatred and madness in her eyes hot enough to burn him -- he hoped she could not spell fire. Letting out a vicious cackle, she shot toward him, her razor claws posed for attack.

Worthington tried to get to his feet, but he never had the chance. She moved too fast. Her claws sliced into his arm, sending chunks of flesh into the air and searing heat up to his shoulder.

As she pulled back to ready another assault, Billy Demott slammed against her, sending her into the throngs of other fights. Worthington had no chance to thank the young pirate, though. The white-haired witch grabbed Demott by the legs and flung him to sea.

As Worthington muttered a fast prayer for Demott,

he spied Butler slinking below deck. Their witch! Worthington raced to the nearest ladder.

He rushed down, his arm burning, his ribs screaming. Butler caught sight of him. "Fire with fire, sir," he said.

Worthington jumped the last rungs, the shock of landing making him cry out. After a few seconds breathing the stale air, he hurried to the next set of rungs as Butler's head disappeared to the bottom deck. Already the carnage above sounded dull and muted but still harsh enough to chill Worthington's skin. "Magic belongs to the devils and demons," he yelled.

"Then why'd Cap'n Taggart bring her aboard, if'n she's so evil? He brought her so we'd use her."

When Worthington reached the bottom he dashed toward the center. Sweat soaked his breeches making his movements more difficult. He saw Butler reaching for the chains that kept the witch strapped to the thick mast—and, of course, he saw the witch.

Draped in rags and smelling worse than the stagnant puddles surrounding her, the witch writhed against the mast in both pain and pleasure. Her stark white skin and ragged hair only added to the insanity gleaming from her pale, gray eyes. She watched Butler as if she had lusted for him all her life. Worthington fought the nausea creeping up his throat.

"It's the only way," Butler said, picking up the bulky padlock linked in the chains. "She can either raise Cap'n Taggart or fight off her friends, but ya saw what was happening up there. We won't last."

Worthington lifted his sword and said, "Drop it now, Mr. Butler, or I'll run you through."

"Can't do that, sir."

"I swear I'll do it."

The witch darted her head from one man to the other, her harsh breathing an unwelcome background. Butler spun fast and flashed a small blade, deflecting

Worthington's sword with a sharp clang. He slid forward and slashed at Worthington's bleeding arm.

"Sorry 'bout that," Butler said. "Can't let the men die up there without trying."

Worthington swung his sword but his injuries slowed him. Butler dodged the attack with ease and punched Worthington's side, breaking the rib for certain. With a shake of his head, Butler turned back to the witch.

"I ain't wanting to cause you trouble, see. Ya just don't ken to what I'm doin'. I'm fine with what it is I'm up to."

"We can save the crew without the witch."

"I ain't sure of that."

Worthington stepped toward Butler. "You aren't sure of anything. That's the problem. Let me tell you something before you finish those chains. She'll want something."

Butler laughed. "Course she's gonna want something. But if I don't let her free, there'll be nobody left alive to worry about paying for witch magic."

"She's a curse upon us. I warned Captain Taggart, he refused to listen, and now he's dead."

"I'll chance it."

"You'll curse us all. Magic is like cheating at things you can't do yourself."

"Cheating? I'm a pirate."

Worthington edged closer, the point of his blade just pressing against Butler. "I can't let you do this."

Butler raised his hands. "Fine, if that's how ya want it," he said, facing Worthington. His eyes widened and he nodded. "But ya ought to know Big Tim is behind you, and he'll pummel you if you don't drop that blade."

Worthington shook his head. "I'm no fool," he said. Then Big Tim struck and all went black.

When he woke, his head throbbed as if he had drunk too much rum. He glanced up—Butler, Big Tim, and the witch were all gone. Grabbing the chains, he pulled himself to his feet and waited for the spinning to subside.

The climb up did little to appease his aching head; however, when the sun hit his face and he inhaled the salt air, his senses awoke and his mind cleared.

Scanning the deck, Worthington saw three things of great importance. First, Butler and the crew were gathered aft—all on their knees, some with their heads bowed. Second, the three witch's heads dangled from a port rope ladder—their bodies were nowhere in sight. And third, Captain Taggart stood before the group, his witch at his side, the fatal hole in his head wide open.

He stood at six feet even but seemed larger now. The witch clung to him like a lustful, well-paid whore. Worse, Worthington noticed a faint, greenish hue covered the captain's skin like night-algae. Yet he still managed an authority in his presence—his wide-buckled boots, his blue doublet, his tri-cornered hat, his numerous swords and daggers all vested him as a genuine pirate captain.

"You boys've done well," the captain said, his voice wet and dense. He swaggered across the deck with the witch in tow—no longer the crew's big brother, but now their master. "That bastard ship that sent these vile beasts our way is still out there. Not far. They're hoping to get their witches back. And they think I'm dead."

"We got a surprise for them, right," Butler said, his voice more nervous than boastful.

"Indeed, we do. I want carpenters repairing the hull first, then the other woodwork as needed. I want those sails seamed up and ready."

"Aye, sir," Big Tim said, followed by a shaky chorus of others.

The witch pointed toward Butler with a demented grimace that chilled Worthington. The captain smiled. "Yes, love. Butler, come with us. Got a special duty for you."

"Me, sir?" Butler said, taking a slight step backward.

"Something wrong?"

"N-No, sir. Just, well, why me?"

The captain launched into a tirade and Butler shrank at the verbal assault. Worthington cursed his luck. Defending Butler left an unpleasant sensation in his gut, but he couldn't just drop below deck and forget everything. Even if he let Captain Taggart slaughter every crew member, eventually, Taggart and his witch would come looking.

"Sorry, sir," Butler said, dashing back his tears and dropping to his knees. "I beg you, please, don't do whatever you is planning on doing."

"Always pegged you for a stronger man than this."

"Not me, sir. I just keep my head down and follow orders."

"Then follow mine. Get in my cabin."

"I'm thinking Big Tim might join us. Y'know, maybe what ya got in mind might be too big for just little me."

Taggart pulled out his sword. "If you ain't in my cabin by the count of three, your head can join those witches." The crew gasped— the old Taggart would never undermine his strength and their morale with death threats. "One... two..."

"Enough!" Worthington said, stepping forward with his own sword out and ready—its weight a comfort in a tenuous moment.

The crew pulled back from Worthington, forming a large half-circle. Taggart grinned and pushed his witch behind him. "Well," he said, "I thought maybe you'd been thrown overboard by the men."

"Move back, Butler," Worthington said, and the whimpering man scrambled out of the way. "Captain, you don't belong here."

"Really now? And you do?"

"I'm still living."

"Not for much longer. Hell, even if I don't kill you, the crew will, once I tell them—"

Worthington lunged forward with a sloppy attack, his broken rib stabbing him with every awkward motion. Taggart deflected the blade and sniggered as he struck back. While the crew watched, the two men traded attacks and parries with stunning vigor.

Taggart always had been strong with a sword, but Worthington found the blows more difficult to absorb than he had expected. Perhaps the witch had spelled the dead man extra strength. Each strike reverberated straight into his bones. The sweet taste of blood filled his mouth.

"I always thought high of you," Taggart said as they fought toward the bow, each step pulling them further from the crew. The witch, always nearby, watched and giggled. "So, you give up and I'll let you live."

Worthington had no energy for banter. He struggled just to keep pace with Taggart's onslaught. *This won't work,* he thought. *I'll tire, and he'll kill me.*

Mustering all his strength, Worthington let loose a garbled yell and lashed out. He moved fast with fierce power, enough to startle the undead captain and push him back a few steps. Thrust upon thrust, slash upon slash, Worthington kept the pressure on, burning his energy with furious abandon. Taggart regained his stance but had to focus in order to defend the constant attacks. Worthington could feel his strength waning. His brutal offensive slackened. Victory lit Taggart's eyes. With a final burst, Worthington motioned left but spun right and skewered Taggart, turning his blade so as to slip between the ribs and puncture the lung.

Taggart froze for a moment, then looked down at the sword sticking from his chest. "Desperate?" Taggart said.

Worthington stumbled backward, pulling the sword with him, and fell to the deck. Sweat drenched his body as his lungs grappled for air.

Taggart stepped forward. "You can gut me all day,

but I'm already dead." The witch cackled, and the entire crew took one large step away, making a loud thrum. The witch took no notice.

That bothered Worthington. The crew's movement was loud and full of fright, yet the witch did not even flinch. She kept her focus on Taggart the entire time.

"Let this stand in your minds forever," Taggart said, standing over Worthington, waving his sword in the air, his greenish glow brighter and stronger with every passing minute. "Nobody challenges me and lives. Nobody."

Still, the witch's eyes never left Taggart. She never once checked for the crew's reaction. A thought leaped into Worthington's mind, and with his death imminent, he figured he had nothing to lose.

Taggart pointed his sword at Worthington and said, "Well, this ends you, military man, navy boy, better than a keel hauling, aye?"

He lifted the sword and sliced downward. Worthington rolled to the side, leaving Taggart's sword buried deep into the wood. Worthington sprang to his feet, wincing at the fire in his side, and raced toward the witch. Her eyes were on Taggart. If she saw Worthington coming, she made no sign of it.

"Get back here, swine!" Taggart said.

His feet slowed, but Worthington pushed on, moving more like a drunkard attempting to run than a man trying to save a ship. He heard Taggart stomping toward him but forced his mind to focus on running to that witch. A few more feet. He pulled back his sword, ready to strike, when his legs went out from under him and his cheek smashed into the deck.

"Got to be careful," Taggart said, his chuckling like a tiger's growl. "You tripped on my foot."

Looking up at the captain, the hot sun breaking through the last of the battle smoke like a spotlight on his failure, Worthington shook his head. He had no more in him. The witch had won. Still, he refused to let this undead thing kill him—better to kill himself. He reached toward his belt and pulled out a small dagger.

Taggart saw and nodded. "Very well," he said and sheathed his sword. "Butler, I ordered you into my cabin. Get there." He looked at the crew. "Where's Butler?"

"Right here, sir," Butler said from behind. Worthington watched a rusty sword slice into Taggart's waist. Taggart turned to face the shaking Butler.

"You'll die for that," he said.

"But I won't come back a monster," Butler said.

A few seconds passed before Worthington realized nobody watched him. He rolled to his knees, struggled to his feet, and saw that, as he expected, the witch held her gaze on Taggart. She had no choice.

He walked up to her, her fecal stench threatening to knock him out, and with no energy for a yell, simply swung his blade. The witch gave a startled yip. Her head batted to the deck, blood pooling around her decapitated body.

"No, no, no," Taggart said, his voice strained as if he couldn't find the lung power to speak. He clawed at his throat—a terrible chittering the only sound he produced. He crashed to his knees, and his color faded until becoming a solid gray. "I'm your captain," he whined. With a deflated sigh, he collapsed at Butler's feet, once more becoming a corpse.

Butler rushed to Worthington, supporting the battered man before he could fall. "Come on," he yelled to the crew. "Help Cap'n Worthington. He's hurt."

After several hours rest, a little bit of sewing up and little bit of rum, Worthington walked the deck. He moved slow and unsteady, but he knew he needed to make an appearance. The men were repairing the ship, washing the last of the blood off the wood, and dumping the dead into the sea. They needed to know they could trust him, that he wouldn't die and try to come back.

"Enemy! Portside!" a voice said from above.

All eyes looked port. The *Osprey*, the naval frigate that had caused all their damage, drifted with no sign of activity onboard.

"Butler," Worthington said.

"Sir?"

"Take us in slow, and send someone for my spyglass."

"Aye, Cap'n."

Twenty minutes passed. Hardly anybody spoke. The only steady sound was the repetitive slap of the ocean against the ship, like the clicking of a metronome.

Worthington caught a few odd glances—his men trying to decipher Taggart's reference to the military. No matter. Though they'd figure it out over time, they were his crew now. What once would have sent them into a blood rage would now be their unique badge. Captain Worthington—their captain—once sailed for His Majesty. They'd brag to the whores and drunkards about him—and they'd never ask for a witch aboard again.

Nearing the *Osprey*, Worthington peered through his spyglass. "All dead," he whispered.

Soon they were close enough for the entire crew to see for themselves. Barrels had been smashed, sails torn, glass shattered. Smoke poured from several portholes. The smell of Death hung like a storm cloud. "What happened?" Butler asked.

"Magic."

"But the witches attacked our ship."

"Something had to be controlling them. The navy men wouldn't just let the witches loose."

"What do ya use to control witches?"

Worthington now saw blood. Bodies, too. Not the carnage of man against man but as if an animal had ravaged its way through the entire ship.

"I think that secret's best buried here," he said, as they sailed passed the dead ship. "Sink her, Mr. Butler."

"Aye, sir," Butler said, and for several minutes the echoes of cannon fire rang in Captain Worthington's ears.

At Map's End

BY MISTY MASSEY

"How much farther, Captain?"

They'd been trekking through thick overgrowth for nearly an hour. Kestrel knew she'd lose the pirates' interest if she didn't lead them to something soon. She stopped, wiped the sweat from her face with her sleeve, and pulled out the map. She studied it carefully and pointed west. "Should be that way. Just over yonder ridge, I'd think."

Shadd, her quartermaster, was leading the way, chopping at vines and branches to clear a path. "Over yonder ridge, into a valley full of gold!" he started singing as he marched. Kestrel walked behind him, followed by Red Tom and Jaques. The rest of her men were waiting aboard the Thanos, probably rubbing their hands together in anticipation. Treasure the king didn't know about didn't have to be reported.

When Red Tom had first brought her the map, she'd laughed. Her helmsman was a rare pirate, the kind that loved books almost more than coin. He'd found the little painting tucked in the binding of an old book of poetry and brought it straight to her. Everyone in the Nine Islands knew treasure maps were nonsense. No one with any sort of smarts at all would hide her hoarded riches somewhere out of her sight. Even if she did, she'd never create a map that might fall into someone else's hands. Wealth was too hard to come by to let it vanish so easily. The old tale of pirates burying chests of gold and gems was nothing more than a children's story. Treasure maps were either pranks or party games for noble children needing diversions. If it had been the usual silly toy, she'd have rolled it up and used it to swat insects.

This map was different. "It's writ in that scribble you been studying," he said. Danisoban script, impossible to read unless one was trained to understand it, or had the ability to whistle the words into submission. Since the day she'd been named the King's Privateer, she'd been slaving at learning to read the seemingly incomprehensible symbols. All the royal accounts were kept in the script, since no one but the king and his magus could read it. Kestrel understood the need for security, but she detested the effort she'd spent studying it. Sometimes it was easier to whistle a quiet tune and bring up her own magic to force the words into a more understandable form. She could only do that when she was alone. The less her men knew about her magical abilities, the better she liked it. She'd thanked Tom and taken the map to her cabin. It was written in Danisoban script, which meant it might lead to some Danisoban treasure.

The Danisoban Brotherhood was the real power in the Nine Islands. Men and woman of great magic power, they served the King of the Nine Islands. Promises, children who displayed any sort of ability themselves, were claimed at an early age by the Brethren, taken to their school on Eldraga to be trained in the mysteries, and never allowed out into the world until they were thoroughly indoctrinated. Kestrel herself had almost been taken, until her parents had sacrificed their own lives to let her escape. She'd grown up on the streets but had always hoped to go to sea. The Danisobans' single known weakness was a reaction to sea water. A splash could make a magus nauseous; complete immersion could kill. Kestrel, as a Promise, should have suffered from the same trouble...except that she didn't. Being at sea made her stronger. The king's Danisoban, Menja Lig, couldn't touch her on the water, but he made sure she knew he was watching, always watching. Waiting for her to make a mistake and put herself in his hands. If this map led to an actual Danisoban artifact, she might be able to use it against them. Getting her hands on something valuable to the Brethren could go a long way toward keeping them at arm's length. Even better, she could hold it for ransom against them if she ever chose to leave the royal service.

The map was painted on a flat square of ancient paper, thick enough to hold up over years but old enough to be crumbly around the edges. The map drawing on one side had shown what appeared to be an uninhabited atoll, steep hills protecting a lagoon, with thick jungle filling in the space between. It was an excellent place to hide something. On the opposite side of the painting were the words. The writing was cramped and tiny, barely legible:

The Brethren's shining treasure waits in the garden of time's gate, until the day we send for it to enrich us once more.

It had been those words that changed everything. She'd pulled out all the old charts, comparing the tiny map with all the unnamed places in the Nine Islands until at last she was sure of the one they were looking for. They'd set course right away. A tickle of doubt teased at the back of her mind—what if someone else had already found the treasure long ago? Her men deserved a mighty haul, so she determined not to listen to the doubt.

"Captain!" Shadd said, over his shoulder. "Can you come up here and see what I'm seein'?" She pressed past his massive body and peered through the opening he'd made in the vines. They were standing at the top of the ridge, looking down into a valley. Soft grass carpeted the ground, and at the very bottom stood a shining crystal arch. The sun glistened from its faceted surface, and all around it lay brightly colored stones in a carefully placed ring. Shadd's voice dropped to a whisper. "Don't it look like a nice little garden to ye?"

She didn't want to get his hopes up, but her own heart was thumping. She'd hoped to get her hands on something to hold against the Brotherhood, but the arch was far too big to carry out. If the stones were what they seemed to be, though, they'd found a trove indeed. Bloodstones and markats big enough to be seen from up here, they had to be worth a fortune. She let a smile creep over her face. She'd let her men collect the jewels while she took a closer look at the arch. Maybe she couldn't take it away with her, but she might still find some use for it. "On we go, men."

They picked their way carefully down the hillside and soon found themselves standing at the edge of the ring. The precious stones surrounding the arch were each as big as a child's noggin. Kestrel peered left and right, and seeing no one, stepped past the ring and approached the arch. It was tall enough for Shadd to step through without bumping his head, and cut from a light pink crystal. Carved symbols danced from one side up and over to the other. Kestrel stepped closer to inspect them.

Behind her, Shadd was exclaiming over the jewels. "Fine cut, as fine as anythin' His Majesty's jewelers themselves might see," he said. "And at fifteen times the size!" He wasn't exaggerating. Even the quick glance she'd spared them told her that one of these stones could be worth enough to buy her whole ship, and leave change for a month of excellent dinners afterward. She caught a glimpse of her own reflection in the arch's facets, her eyes filled with awe. The arch seemed to glow with its own light. She ran her fingertips gently over the smooth stone, as if she could read the words with her hands instead of her eyes.

"Wonder how many of these I can carry with me?" Shadd said. "Help me here, Tom. I want to see how much it weighs."

They weren't paying her any attention. Kestrel drew a deep breath and began to whistle softly. The familiar tingle of magic began in her feet, tickling up her body until she felt suffused in power. She concentrated on the words before her, willing them to arrange themselves into a pattern she could read easily. The designs began to slither together and apart like tiny water creatures, rearranging themselves until they became words she could understand. "Hesh ferren fa, hesh mordea mea," she read in the Danisoban language, her voice almost a whisper. The line moved under the arch's curve, and she stepped into the opening to keep reading. Light exploded around her, and she felt herself being yanked off her feet and flung through the air. An instant later, she landed in cold water. Waves crashed over Kestrel's head, forcing water into her mouth and nose and grinding her body against the harsh sand. Pushing against the gritty bottom, she broke the surface and dragged air into her tortured lungs. Another wave curled behind her and struck, slamming into her back and knocking her face first into the wet sand. She hauled her feet under her and half-crawled to get above the break line, where she let herself collapse and rolled onto her back. The sky was dark and dotted with stars. How had she gotten here? And where was this place?

A wave licked at her bare feet, reminding her that she was still close to the edge. She struggled up the beach to a spot where the sand was dry and still warm from the day's sunlight, and dropped down again. It had to have been that bloody arch. She picked up a shell and flung it toward the water. She knew the blasted arch was Danisoban, and yet she'd stood there like a fool, reading magical words out loud. *Cack me for an idiot*, she thought. Having the magic was no good without knowing how to use it. Trouble was that she had no one to teach her. The Danisobans would have been delighted to assist her, but their price, lifelong servitude, was too high for her to pay. She'd become Privateer to the King of the Nine Islands precisely so that she could keep the Magi at arm's length. For a while, it had seemed enough for her to play with her skills in the privacy of her cabin, where no one could see her mistakes. Except that every day on a pirate ship was hard work, and so many nights she was too tired to bother. She'd survived all those years without magic, so it just didn't seem important enough to worry about. Until now.

The half-moon was near the horizon, providing enough light for her to see the beach around her, not enough to see far out to sea but enough to know that no ship floated at the horizon. She could imagine the men she'd left behind, suddenly noticing that she was nowhere to be found. Shadd would search for a while, bless his faithful heart, but even he'd give up eventually. He'd have to, or risk the crew turning on him as well. The Thanos couldn't continue without a captain. She had to figure out how to get back. But where was she now? She lay back in the sand, staring straight up at the familiar stars. There was the Traveller, his arm pointing out and away, and near him the Cudgel. Judging by their positions, she guessed she was about two days west of Eldraga, her childhood home and the main trade island. The atoll she'd come from was another three days east of here. With a small boat, she could put herself into the Thanos' planned path. If she missed them, she could always head for Eldraga, arriving in a few days. Maybe a week. Not that the thought was much comfort, marooned as she seemed to be. *How hard could it be to build a raft?* she thought, then laughed at herself. *Without tools? I wonder if I could whistle a tree to fall.*

Climbing to her feet, she turned away from the water, peering into the darkness of the tree line. The forest was swallowed in shadow. She risked injuring herself walking without her boots in the darkness; the last thing she needed was a foot punctured by a shard of wood. She was about to give up and find somewhere to sleep when she saw a glimmer of light in the distance. It was warm light, flickering like a fire. Where there was fire, there was usually someone tending it. Her heart thumped excitedly. If she was very lucky, that someone had a boat. A real boat, that could be driven along by a bit of magical breeze. Thinking of magic brought the question back to Kestrel's mind. How had she come here in the first place? What if the light led to some small Danisoban enclave? She sighed. She wouldn't know until she investigated. Kestrel stepped into the tree line, setting one bare foot gingerly down on the thick carpet of leaves.

Slowly, she made her way through the darkness. The ground was soft and springy under her feet, oddly clear of sharp stones and thorny twigs. As she drew closer to the light, she realized it looked less like a fire's flicker, and more like moonlight reflecting off of water. Another step, and she was standing in a clearing. Short velvety grass was cool against her skin, and a gentle breeze caressed her face. The light was neither fire nor moonlight, and Kestrel nearly shouted for joy. The light was shimmering from a crystal arch, identical to the one she'd stepped through, but without the ring of precious gemstones. This time she didn't care at all about the treasure, but ran for the arch.

"Hello!" A woman stepped out of the shadows of the trees. Kestrel stopped, turning to face her, one hand dropping to the hilt of her sword. She was dressed in ordinary skirts and a long-sleeved chemise of some lightweight linen, and her dark hair was tightly braided. Her eyes were strangely light-colored, although in the gloom Kestrel couldn't make out what color for certain. She didn't appear to be armed beyond the basketful of dark objects in the crook of her elbow. "Who are you?"

"Kestrel, late of the Thanos. And with any luck, back aboard again soon."

"That's a ship?" the woman asked, frowning.

"Aye, the finest on the water."

Her expression changed instantly, sharp wariness replaced by warm hope. "Oh, thank the gods! No one ever comes here. You're the first ship in...I don't even know how long I've been here. Please take me with you when you leave!" She clasped her hands together, knocking her basket against her body and spilling the contents. "My family will pay any amount for my safe return! At least, I think they will—I've been here so long..." She looked stricken. "Surely they haven't forgotten me?"

Kestrel nearly groaned out loud. She wasn't in the mind to deal with a little lost lamb. "I doubt they've forgot you. How did you come to be here?"

The woman edged backward, as if afraid Kestrel might throw something at her next. "I was on a ship. And then I was in the water."

"You fell over the side?"

The woman shook her head. She'd threaded her fingers into a knot, her knuckles white with tension. "I was in my cabin, preparing for bed. I'd just removed my shoes when I felt myself pulled into the air. I landed in the water and managed to swim ashore here. Where I've been ever since."

Kestrel rubbed her eyes. "Bloody Grace, but I hate magic."

"You think this was magic?"

Kestrel waved a hand toward the glowing stone arch. "I stepped through one of those, somewhere that the sun was shining only minutes ago. Do you have a better explanation?"

The woman shook her head. "I don't look at the arch. It's not safe." She untwisted her fingers, let herself sink to the soft grass, and started to refill her basket. "It's papacar fruit, if you're hungry." Kestrel shook her head. The woman began to peel the skin away from one of the fruits. "You said you're a sailor?" She tossed the peels away and looked up, hope shining on her face. "We could build a raft!"

"No tools." Kestrel tilted her head toward the trees surrounding them. "Knocking a tree down takes more than wishing." The arch's light was teasing at the edges of her vision. The woman had called it dangerous, but she didn't have any understanding of magic, so she was probably just afraid. Most people were, especially if they'd ever seen a Danisoban in action. "We can step through the arch again, let it take us back to where my men are waiting."

"Please!" The woman was on her knees, reaching out with one hand toward Kestrel. "You mustn't touch it!"

"Lady, I'm happy to take you back to Eldraga or Pecheta or wherever you want to go, but my ship is on the other side of this Gods-cacked arch." Kestrel took another step, and the woman threw herself on the ground at her feet, wrapping her arms around Kestrel's legs and shaking the pirate's balance. She fell over the woman, landing face first in the soft grass. She kicked herself free, but the woman kept grabbing at her.

"You'll die. They all died and so will you."

Kestrel stopped fighting, and scooted herself out of the woman's reach. Rising to her feet, she drew her sword and held it between herself and the woman. "Who died?"

"The men..." she gulped, and took a deep breath before continuing. "I was in the water with my brother and the two groomsmen my husband-to-be had sent to fetch me. We were looking for food, and we found the arch. Randell said he knew how to activate the arch, that it was a magical gateway the Danisobans used to travel without touching the water. He insisted you only needed to read the words, and said he'd learned from his cousin, who's in the order. He stepped under it and spoke some words I didn't know." She closed her eyes. "Fire sprang out of the stone, and he started screaming." She balled her hands into fists, pressing them against her eyes as if to push the memory out. "We were afraid to go near him, for all the screaming. It went on forever." Opening her hands, she placed both palms over her cheeks, staring off into the distance. "As the days went on, first Artur, then Finn tried. They said the words as best they could remember Randell doing it. It was the same way every time. They left me here alone."

Kestrel frowned. Danisoban magic was well-protected. Just admitting knowledge of certain Danisoban rites and practices could get a common person executed. And even though she knew far too little about them herself, she felt certain she'd have heard if the Danisobans had found a way to travel without getting near the water. The woman seemed like a dainty little houseflower, but something about what she said sounded suspicious. "Dangerous it may be, but my ship is waiting. And magic isn't entirely a stranger to me. Are you coming?"

"You can make magic?" The woman backed away, picking up her skirts as if to run. "You're one of them?"

Kestrel sighed. She should have kept her mouth closed, marched up to the arch and walked through without a backward glance. "No," she said, her jaw tightening against the tirade she wanted to unleash on the woman. "I am not one of them. But I can get through this arch without dying. At least, I think I can. As long as I read the words properly."

"As if a sailor can read." The woman marched to the edge of the grass, dropped to a sitting position and crossed her arms. "Go ahead, then. I won't cry over you. I hardly know you."

"Suits me, lady." Kestrel approached the arch, squinting against the glow to make out the symbols. They were the same as on the other side, except written in the opposite order. *As long as I don't say the words out loud, I should be safe enough*, Kestrel thought. As before, she began to whistle a low tune, waiting for the symbols to change themselves.

"When you're on fire, I won't even be listening."

Kestrel rolled her eyes, trying to focus on the magic instead of the annoying woman's words. The symbols swayed, wiggled and moved into the more familiar shapes just as they had before. Soon the whole arch was filled with glowing text, and Kestrel took a deep breath. "If you're coming," she said over her shoulder, "you might want to get close."

"And burn to death? No thank you."

Kestrel snorted, and turned back to the arch. "Hesh ferren fa, hesh mordea mea," she began, running her fingers over the carved words to keep her place. As she read, the glow increased, and she thought she could hear a humming. Her heart was pounding, but she kept reading. It was the only way out. "Hesh ferren fa, hesh lepparus mea." The light and humming increased, almost too much for her to bear. Kestrel squeezed her eyes tight, and lifted her foot to step forward. Something hit her from behind, knocking her through the arch and onto her face. She slid on the grass, bumping her head against one of the huge jewels that glittered in the sunlight. Sunlight?

"Captain!" Hands grabbed her, dragging her to her feet. "By the gods, where'd ye go off to?"

She'd never been so happy to hear Shadd's voice. It had worked. She'd never have believed she could use the Danisobans' own magic, and now that she knew she could, she wondered if she'd ever be able to use it against them. The sun was blinding after being in the dark, and an ache was beginning in her head. She hadn't realized she'd hit it so hard. She leaned forward, resting her hands on her knees, to get her balance back.

"Who's this then?" Shadd asked. Kestrel turned her head, opening her eyes a crack.

The woman was standing in the arch, smiling. Something was different. The vacant, spoiled attitude was gone, replaced by an air of superiority. She wasn't sure what had happened, but she knew she didn't want to have her back to the woman.

"Thank you, captain," she said, her voice low and throaty. "I've had such trouble getting through that door."

"Who are you?" Tom and Jaques had closed in next to Kestrel, and Shadd was looming behind her.

The woman widened her eyes and pouted her lips. "A poor lost soul, like you." She laughed, and the sound sent a chill down Kestrel's spine. "I'm ever so grateful for the rescue." She sashayed toward the pirates, muttered a few words and waved her hand in the air. The men thudded to the ground behind Kestrel, unconscious. She dropped to Shadd's side, feeling his neck for a heartbeat, but he was breathing peacefully. The woman had her hand high, and was saying more words. Light sparkled from her palm, extending out until it began to resemble a sword. She swung it twice, and fell into position. "I haven't done this in a while. I might leave one of you alive."

Kestrel drew her weapon and faced her, watching every movement. "You could have killed me on the other side."

"And risk you being the one who could decipher those runes and release me? You're the first person to come along who could actually read them." She sprang forward, jabbing at Kestrel's midsection. The pirate jumped back, the light weapon missing her by a fraction. She imagined she could feel heat from it.

"You're Danisoban."

The woman spat at the ground. "They made me. Trained me to be an assassin. Called me their treasure." She spun, then dropped, her sword singing through the air. Kestrel leaped, pulling both feet high. She landed and attacked, but the woman moved out of the way in an instant. They both took a step backward.

"Who were you meant to kill?"

"Whoever. I liked killing. Cutting the skin, watching the blood stream out of the wound like a babbling brook, seeing the light in the eyes fade to dullness. There's nothing like it." She frowned, and swung at Kestrel again. "When I took my instructor's life, they decided I was too dangerous to keep in the Enclave. They trapped me in that place. Told me they'd come back when they had a need, but they never taught me how to read the runes."

"So the stories about your brother and the men...lies?" Kestrel skipped to her left, and aimed for the woman's face, the tip of her sword catching her soft cheek enough to raise a thin line of blood.

The woman pressed a hand to the cut, then smiled and licked her bloodied palm. "Not entirely. They died." She brought her sword up and over in a vicious chop, narrowly missing Kestrel.

"You told them the words to say, but you didn't know them all. You were guessing from what little you'd heard before." Kestrel swung the flat of her blade at the woman's exposed back, knocking her to the grass. She moved to take the killing blow, but the woman rolled out of the way and back to her feet.

"Wouldn't you? You were only trapped there a little while, and you couldn't wait to leave. I'd been there for years. And now I'm free." She tossed her sword of light from one hand to the other. "This has been fun, stretching my muscles and all, but you can't win against magic, little sailor." She raised her sword and ran at Kestrel.

She was right. It took magic to best magic. Kestrel pressed her lips together and whistled, a loud, sharp blast. Once, long ago, it had been enough to bring a whole crew's weapons flying at her. She stared at the light sword emanating from the woman's hand, sending her own power to force it away. The light sword faded, shortened, and blinked out of existence just as the woman reached Kestrel's range. The pirate lunged, sinking her sword's tip into the woman's unprotected belly and driving forward until they were nearly face to face. For an instant, they stood, staring at each other, until the woman's legs lost their strength, and she collapsed to the ground.

"They said...I was their...treasure," she whispered. Her eyes darkened, and her head lolled to the side.

Kestrel stared at her slack face. In another time, this might have been her own fate. She should have guessed the Danisobans would never leave a map to ordinary gold. Or jewels. Costly as they looked to be, she was inclined to leave the jewels where they lay. Who knew what danger they might attract her way? She bent and wiped her blade clean on the grass, then hunkered down at Tom's shoulder. "Tom? Wake up, man." She shook the others, and after a short time, they began to rouse.

"We missed the fight, did we?" Shadd sounded disappointed. "Was she a worthy opponent?"

"Never mind that. We've been anchored long enough. This was a fool's errand."

"What about the jewels, Kes?" Shadd asked.

Before she could say anything, Tom and Jaques bent to lift one of the gems, but let go with a cry. "It's hot!"

As they stared, the jewels began pulsating with a light that grew brighter and brighter with every second. The pirates scrambled away, just as the first gem gave a loud pop and a cloud of steam. When the steam cleared, where the gem had laid was now a man. In quick order the other jewels did the same thing. Soon the arch was surrounded by a half-dozen men, all asking where the poor stranded woman had gone and waiting for answers from the bemused pirates.

Kestrel gathered them together and tried to explain, but soon gave up and directed them to start walking down the trail Shadd had made coming in.

"Ye're takin' 'em on?" Shadd asked. Kestrel shook her head.

"Just giving them a ride to Eldraga. Maybe one or two have families who'll pay a reward for their safe return."

"Aye, that's a thought," Shadd said. He rubbed his chin, staring over at the crystal arch standing along in the grass. "What if we crack yonder arch into pieces? Surely that stone's worth a bit, ye think?"

As if responding to his suggestion, the arch brightened, until it too gave a loud pop and disappeared. The pirates watched the twinkling dust shimmer down to the grass, leaving no trace of what had seemed to be a life's fortune only a short time before. "It's gone," Shadd said. "A treasure I could have retired on, and it's all gone in the wind."

Kestrel slapped her quartermaster on the shoulder. "You know what they say, boyo. A faithful friend is the truest treasure."

He cut his eyes at her. "Does that faithful friend plan to buy me all the ale I can drink?'

She laughed. "Get along with you. There's a ship full of men waiting for an explanation, and the sun's setting." They moved away up the path, their shadows laying a velvet darkness on the glittering grass.

Author Biographies

MJ Blehart

MJ Blehart is working on an epic series called *The Source Chronicles*, as well as any number of other projects. Be on the lookout for an upcoming podcast of *Seeker*, the first book in the series. MJ is extremely active in the Society for Creative Anachronism, fencing and recreating a great many aspects of Europe before 1600AD. More information about the author, and examples of his work can be found on www.mjblehart.com.

Stuart Jaffe

Stuart Jaffe is the author of numerous short stories found in magazines, on-line, and in many anthologies. He is also the co-host of *The Eclectic Review podcast* (http://eclectic.libsyn.com) and blogs at Magicalwords.net. He lives in North Carolina with his wife, son, five cats, three aquatic turtles, one bunny, one tortoise, one albino corn snake, one Brazilian tarantula, numerous fish, and a horse. Thankfully, the horse does not stay in the house.

Misty Massey

Misty Massey is the author of *Mad Kestrel*, a rollicking adventure of magic on the high seas. She in employed as a middle school librarian (at least for now!), and when she's not writing, she studies Middle Eastern dance and is a member of the Beledi Beat dance troupe. Misty is presently finishing the second volume of Kestrel's exploits.

Bryan Prindiville

Bryan Prindiville has worked as a Sr. Graphic Designer & Illustrator for the Catholic Relief Services (CRS) since late 2000. In his free time he has created or partnered in the creation of a number of webcomics including *Bassetville* and *Hello with Cheese*. Traditionally published work can be found in *Bad-Ass Faeries 2: Just Plain Bad* and Tee Morris' *All a Twitter*. More information and work are available at his sketch blog, bryanprindiville.com.

Laurel Anne Hill

Author and Former Underground Storage Tank Operator, Laurel grew up in San Francisco, with more dreams of adventure than good sense or money. Her close brushes with death, love of family, respect for honor and belief in a higher power continue to influence her writing and life. In 2007, KOMENAR Publishing released Laurel's award-winning novel, *Heroes Arise*. Laurel's short stories and narrative nonfiction have appeared in a variety of publications during the past 15 years. She lives in California with her husband, David, and their affectionate 100-pound werewolf. Visit Laurel's website at http://www.laurelannehill.com.

Gail Z. Martin

Gail Z. Martin is the author of *The Summoner, The Blood King, Dark Haven* and *Dark Lady's Chosen (The Chronicles of The Necromancer series)*. A new series set in her world of the Winter Kingdoms, *The Fallen Kings Cycle*, debuts from Orbit Books in 2011 with *Book One: The Sworn*. For book updates, tour information and contact details, visit www.ChroniclesOfTheNecromancer. com Gail is the host of the *Ghost in the Machine Fantasy Podcast* , and you can find her on MySpace, Facebook, GoodReads, BookTour, BookMarketing.ning, Shelfari and Twitter. She is also the author of a series on book marketing. *The Thrifty Author's Guide to Launching Your Book* comes out in early 2010.

Danny Birt

Danny Birt has played the roles of author and editor in science fiction, fantasy, and professional publications such as *The Raintown Review, Strange Worlds of Lunacy, Flashing Swords Magazine,* and *Musica Ficta.* He is also an editor for Cyberwizard Productions. His fantasy series *The Laurian Pentology* is being published through Ancient Tomes Press, with the books *Ending an Ending* and *Beginning* already in print. When the literary world is not claiming him for its own, Danny is a music therapist at a hospital in Winston-Salem, NC. Visit his website www.DannyBirt.com for more information.

BA Collins

BA Collins lives in a cottage on the shores of Lake Champlain, listening to the bikers ride by all summer long and dreaming up adventures for them, sometimes on motorcycles and sometimes somewhere in history going back and forth between powerboats and sailing ships.

Michael A. Ventrella

Michael A. Ventrella's fantasy novels *Arch Enemies* and *The Axes of Evil* are available wherever you find a good bookstore (which means hardly anywhere) and through online sources like Amazon (which means almost everywhere). His web page is www. MichaelAVentrella.com and he can be easily found on Facebook and other social networking sites. Mike lives in the beautiful Pocono Mountains of Pennsylvania with a tolerant wife and four obnoxious cats. In his spare time, he is a lawyer.

Danielle Ackley-McPhail

Award-winning author Danielle Ackley-McPhail has worked both sides of the publishing industry for over fifteen years. Her works include the urban fantasies, *Yesterday's Dreams, Tomorrow's Memories*, and *The Halfling's Court: A Bad-Ass Faerie Tale*. She has edited the *Bad-Ass Faeries* anthology series, and *No Longer Dreams*, and has contributed to numerous other anthologies and collections, including *Dark Furies, Breach the Hull, So It Begins, Space Pirates, Barbarians at the Jumpgate*, and *New Blood*. She can be found on LiveJournal (damcphail), Facebook (Danielle Ackley-McPhail), and Twitter (DMcPhail). To learn more about her work, visit www.sidhenadaire.com.

Davey Beauchamp

Davey Beauchamp is the author of the *Agency 32* series, *Amazing Pulp Adventures*, and the *Writers for Relief* charity anthology series. He is also the creator of the award-nominated podcast, *Amazing Pulp Adventures Radio Show*. And he is currently atteneding UNCG working on his MLIS.

Tera Fulbright

Tera Fulbright has been a fan of the speculative fiction genre since first reading C. S. Lewis's *The Chronicles of Narnia* in the 4th grade. Her experiences and interests range from costuming and stage combat to working and running conventions to writing. When not doing one of those, she works as Substitute Teacher while attending Grad School for her Master's in Education. In her, admittedly limited, spare time, she enjoys miniature painting, playing *D&D*, reading and spending time with her husband and daughter at their home in Greensboro, NC. This is her first published short story.